U0127330

IELTS

雅思口說
里茲螞蟻
英文說話術

作者／IELTS 口說女王 **May Lin**
IELTS 國際資深名師 **Amy Lovestrand**

眾文圖書股份有限公司

前言

Time flies.，雅思一教就十幾年了。身為第一線的老師，每天持續在接觸雅思考生，每天都有新的想法與教法在我腦中產生。這幾年，我的教學開始轉向批判性思考的強化，在寫作跟口說的課程中，都加入許多讓學生開口回答的機會，然後我再引導學生說出更多支持論述。一來一往間，可以漸漸看到許多學生從說話空洞、沒有提出具體例子支持論點，到有能力選擇適切的內容，並完整組織出有層次的答案，更重要的是，成為一個有信心的考生。我的內心著實獲得很大的成就感。

把話說好，「邏輯」很重要！

台灣的教育方式讓學生長期缺乏獨立思考的機會，導致考生只要碰到需要稍微深度思考的問題，答案就經常缺乏邏輯與連貫性。面對雅思口說，考生最常做的事就是背範本或是粗淺地回答考官的問題，所以答案經常不是毫無說服力，就是沒辦法達到一個深度。我認為邏輯養成的重要性刻不容緩。一年前我開始構思如何把邏輯的發展呈現在紙本上，幫助考生解決說話空洞的問題。現在，這個願望終於透過這本書達成了！

里茲媽蟻的高分說話術

本書的編排是根據雅思口說的 Part 1～Part 3 三部分，分別設計高分答題策略。

「Part 1 一般性問題」的暖身問答準備上相對容易，本書提供的高分策略是 **1+1 答題法（快答＋支持句）**，只要在每個快答之後多加 2～3 句話來延伸，就可以讓考官留下美好的第一印象。

「Part 2 小演說」需要的是一個有組織的兩分鐘演講，而從 Part 2 開始就是台灣學生的弱點。雖然能夠講到兩分鐘的考生不算少，但要把這兩分鐘講得生動、引人入勝，讓考官身體都往前傾聽得意猶未盡，則是高手才有的武功。針對 Part 2，本書提供的高分

策略是**心智圖 (mind map) 答題法**，藉由流動的思路動線來幫考生準備一個有凝聚力的小演說。

「Part 3 雙向討論」的答辯題需要具備快速的思辨技巧。考生必須回答一個可能很抽象的問題，並且能夠深入說明以支持或捍衛自己的想法。在這個部分，考官經常會提問比較尖銳性的問題，考生需要配備一套答題 SOP，本書提供的高分策略是 **AEC 三步驟答題法**。考生確實熟練後便可兵來將擋，水來土掩。

孫子說：「知已知彼，百戰百勝」。考場如戰場，準備上場之前，考生一定要知道考試的評分標準是哪些，平時準備時才能朝成功的方向前進。所以本書的一開始，就收錄了雅思四項評分標準的重點解說，並提供如何因應的高分祕訣。

最後，本書附上了八回雅思口說模擬試題，加進新鮮活潑的問題。而在書末的附錄，則詳細整理出考生在「準備期」與「考試當天」應注意的事項，考生一定要善用。

本書使用方式

本書最好的使用方式是先熟悉雅思四項評分標準，接著詳讀各部分的應答技巧攻略，並參考書中回答範例的組成邏輯，再以模仿的方式更換地點、人物、時間等，改成自己專屬的答案。有些題目的點子在 Part 1～Part 3 三部分都可以共用，考生要試著靈活運用。希望這些練習與技巧可以讓考生在口說上大躍進，得到理想的分數。

May Lin

Contents 目錄

認識 IELTS 口說

Part 1 General Questions 一般性問題

Part 2 A Short Talk 小演說

Part 3 Two-way Discussion 雙向討論

IELTS 口說評分標準

評分標準 1 語言的流利度和連貫性

評分標準 2 詞彙變換

評分標準 3 句式豐富性和文法準確性

評分標準 4 發音

認識 IELTS 口說

Part 1：General Questions　一般性問題

流程介紹　IELTS 口說 Part 1 是一個 4～5 分鐘的暖身賽。考生應該放輕鬆，表現出願意多說話的友善態度，跟考官有眼神接觸（當然也不需要一直盯著人家眼睛看），像跟朋友說話一樣。基本上考官手上有題目卷，會一題一題往下問，不會因為考生的答案而改變提問的方向。

Part 1 通常都會包含三個相當生活化的主題，常見的主題為考生的故鄉、教育、家庭、嗜好、習慣、個人物品或職業等。每個主題會問 3～4 個問題。轉換主題的過程中，考官會用 Now let's talk about...（現在我們來談談……）或 Now let's move on to...（現在我們繼續談談……）的句子來引導考生。

Part 1 的回答力求簡單、流暢，避免犯錯。想到什麼就講什麼，簡短回答後再延伸補充兩三句支持句，等到 Part 2 或 Part 3 再用比較長、比較難的句子來展現自己的英文程度。

題目範例　Part 1 通常都會包含三個相當生活化的主題，每個主題會問 3～4 個問題。以下範例是針對一個主題可能發展出來的問題：

問題

How much time do you spend at home?
你待在家裡的時間多長？

Do you prefer to spend your free time at home or outside the house?

你有空的時候喜歡待在家還是外出？

What do you do when you have some free time and you're at home?

你待在家時若有空會做些什麼？

Would you like to spend more time at home in the future?

你未來想多花一點時間待在家裡嗎？

Part 2：A Short Talk 小演說

流程介紹　IELTS 口說 Part 2 是一個小演說。考官會給考生一張題卡，上面有一個問題。考官也會同時給考生一枝鉛筆及一小張白紙，並跟考生說明接下來要做些什麼。考生有一分鐘的時間準備，可用紙筆稍微規畫一下自己想說的內容，做一點筆記。一分鐘後便必須做一個 1～2 分鐘的小演說。講超過兩分鐘會被考官打斷，但不會被扣分。

演說過程可以看著自己剛才做的筆記，但禮貌上還是偶爾要跟考官有眼神上的接觸。講完以後，考官會再問一兩個跟主題有關的衍生問題。接下來就會進入口試 Part 3。

題目範例　以下為 Part 2 題卡的範例，題目要考生描述 a gift you've received（你收過的禮物），下方有四個提示問題。

Describe a gift you've received.

You should say:

what the gift was

who gave it to you

when you received it

and explain how you felt when you received it.

Part 3：Two-way Discussion 雙向討論

流程介紹　IELTS 口說 Part 3 長度約 4～5 分鐘，考官會問 3～6 個問題。雖
然被定義為 'two-way' discussion（雙向討論），但其實絕大部分
時間說話的人仍是考生，考官只是負責提問而已。Part 3 討論的
主題比較抽象，長度也比較長，有些問題甚至長達十秒以上。注
意聽考官的問題，若真的聽不懂，可以請考官再問一次問題。

考官會依考生的程度調整問題難度，程度較差的考生被問的問題
會比較簡單（題目難度是指概念的抽象程度、問題的複雜度，以
及答題所需具備的語言能力）。在這最後的一哩路一定要使出渾
身解數，因為負責評分的考官在聽完 Part 3 之後便會打分數，這
個部分若是回答得好，可以讓考官留下好印象，增加高分的機
率。

題目範例　Part 3 的問題會跟 Part 2 的卡片題有些微關連，但問題通常會比
較有深度，也會比較抽象，不過都是一些常見的主題，像是健
康、娛樂、教育、科技、環境議題等。例如：

快問快答類

Is pollution a big problem in your country?
汙染在你的國家是個很嚴重的問題嗎？

看法類

Is it better to buy clothes in small shops?

在小店買衣服比較好嗎？

比較類

How do you think school life differs from university life?

你認為中學生活和大學生活有什麼不同？

因果關係類

What effects can watching television have on children?

看電視對兒童有什麼影響？

假設類

What would happen if there were no Internet?

如果沒有網路，會出現什麼情況？

Tip

針對 Part 1 與 Part 3 這兩個部分，考生不要惜字如金，但也不必口若懸河。Part 1 的作答長度大約是每個問題1～4 句，Part 3 則大約 3～6 句。Part 2 的部分則大概需要15～30 句，或者至少要講到一分半鐘。不過每個考生的程度不同，思維也不同，建議的句數只能當作參考，如何組織句子才是高分的重點。考生看過本書的應答技巧後，應該就能找到適合自己的句數和節奏。

IELTS 口說 評分標準 ❶
語言的流利度和連貫性
Fluency and Coherence

IELTS 口說並不是一個要求使用正式語言或學術用語的考試。反之，在口試現場，語言愈自然愈好。若是為求表現刻意使用艱深詞彙，或是在心裡先組織高難度的句型再說出口，就會造成停頓，降低流利度。

評分重點

1. 作答時是否流利順暢？

「說話流利」指的是語速不能過慢，要能不急不徐地表達自己的觀點，像 TED 演講的速度就是不錯的參考指標。

Tip

口試參考語速
TED 演講

口試中若發現有些地方講錯，嘗試修正無妨，但最好的方式還是繼續講下去，不要一直中斷。自我糾正的次數太多，流利度就會下降，這個項目就會失分。

2. 作答內容是否條理清楚？

回答的邏輯必須清晰易懂，像枝枒生長般看得出脈絡，下一句要比上一句提出更進一步的資訊，不要只是同一件事不斷地換句話說，或突然天外飛來一筆，讓考官搞不清楚到底在講哪一件事。

3. 是否運用指標詞製造連貫性？

考生的回答聽起來要流暢連貫，就要善用各種指標詞，如表達語意順序的 First/Next/Finally，或表達語氣轉折的 But 或 Although等。Part 2 跟 Part 3 的回答較長，尤其更需要使用各種指標詞，例如講完某件事的優點，接著用了 however 一字，考官就理所當然地認為接下來是要講該件事的缺點。

善用指標詞也意味著不過度使用，避免讓連接詞、連接副詞、轉折語變成無意義的口頭禪。另外，指標詞的選擇變化要多，使用時機也要恰當。

<h2>高分祕訣</h2>

1. 注意題目的關鍵字、回答要切題

考生常常因為粗心沒仔細看題目，導致回答時文不對題。漏聽或漏看關鍵字是口試的大忌，因為遺漏了資訊，答案就無法切題，便無法取得高分。儘管「回答要切題」未列在上述評分重點當中，卻是 IELTS 口說裡最需要注意的一點。

舉例來說，在 Part 1 或 Part 3，如果被問到：

問題

How can technology benefit elderly people?
科技對年長者有何助益？

很多考生只聽到 technology 就急著回答，但這個問題還提到了 elderly people，答案就必須針對年長者，不能只講科技有哪些好處。

那針對 elderly people 回答的話，以下哪個回答最切題呢？

回答1

Well, my grandmother isn't very computer literate, but she's benefitted from the laptop we gave her. She uses it mainly for texting and listening to songs, so it helps her stay in touch with friends and family and enjoy herself.
我奶奶不太會使用電腦，但我們送她的筆記型電腦讓她獲益不少。她主要用電腦傳訊息和聽歌，所以電腦幫助她和親友保持聯絡、自得其樂。

回答 2

Technology has helped the entire human race. I guess the most obvious examples are in medicine. X-ray machines and other such technological advances have saved countless lives.

科技幫助了全人類。我想最顯著的例子在於醫療領域，X 光機等先進科技拯救了無數生命。

回答 3

I think technology has the potential to enhance our quality of life in our later years. Electronic wheelchairs help older people who can't walk well. There are also apps to help elderly people track their blood pressure and blood sugar levels.

我想科技有辦法提升人類晚年的生活品質。電動輪椅幫助不良於行的年長者，還有應用程式能幫助年長者追蹤血壓和血糖。

回答 1 只提到自己的奶奶，而非針對老人族群。**回答 2** 根本沒有提到老年人。**回答 3** 是三個回答裡最理想的。這個題目有很多類似的變化型，例如只要把題目中的 elderly people 換成 children 或 people living in remote areas（住在偏遠地區的人）就變成完全不一樣的口試題。

至於 Part 2 的卡片題，雖然說考生可以「看」到題目，卻常發生沒看到重點或誤解問題的情況。到底題目是要你描述一個**情況**，還是一個**人**？是要你描述一個**經驗**，還是一個**地點**？

我們來實際練習一下 Part 2 卡片題的一個題目。看題目時請試著畫出關鍵字。

Describe a country that you enjoyed visiting.

You should say:

where it is

when you visited it

why you visited it

and explain why you enjoyed going to this country.

Tip

若沒有出國的經驗，可以在開頭第一句就表明自己還沒有機會出國，所以接下來只能講一下自己最想去的國家。因為已經告知考官還沒有出國的經驗，考官就知道考生並非答非所問。

這個問題是要你描述一個你**想去**的國家，還是你**曾去過**的國家？

題卡上問的是 a country that you enjoyed visiting，顯然是問「你去過的」，並且「喜愛」的國家，所以你回答的內容一定會有一部分必須以**過去式**作答才能切題。若從頭到尾只描述一個你沒去過的國家，根本沒有提到自己的親身經驗，就沒辦法得到高分。

2. 回答的內容要有 層次感及連貫性

Fluency and Coherence 這個項目的評分標準中，很注重 coherence（連貫性）。回答時除了要善用指標詞創造連貫性，考生還要注意作答的內容前後要有層次感，以創造出前後語意的連貫性。我們以實際的例子來講解會比較清楚，例如若被問到：

What sorts of films do you enjoy most? Why?
你最喜歡哪種影片？為什麼？

回答這類型的問題時，答案盡量朝有深度的方向，而不是朝廣度的方向來思考。也就是不要丟出一大堆電影的類別（例如romantic、horror、comedy 等），因為這樣的回答只是列舉出一大串名詞，聽起來很混亂，也很難接著延伸回答 Why。要創造出有 coherence 的答案，回答時可以先提出一種電影類型當開頭的主題句，然後再深入說明自己為何喜歡這類型的電影。

針對上面的問題，若考生想回答喜歡 action films（動作片），你
覺得以下 A、B、C 三句話應該如何排列，才能創造具 coherence
的答案？

A

I watch action films all the time.
我經常看動作片。

B

I think action films are really cool.
我覺得動作片真的很酷。

C

I've watched many action films.
我看過很多動作片。

你可能會發現 A、B、C 三句話好像怎麼排都可以，好像誰當第
一句都無所謂。像這樣的答案，就是連貫性不佳的例子。事實上
這三句話根本只要其中兩句就講完了，不需要講到三句。

 連貫性較佳的句子要如同下面這樣的範例，每一句話都比前一句
提供了更多的訊息。

A I think action films are really cool.
我覺得動作片真的很酷。

B I've watched many of **them**.
我看了很多動作片。

C I just love **the explosions, the fights and the loud sounds**!
我喜歡爆炸場面、打鬥和巨大的聲響！

再來看一個比較長的例子。若被問到自己喜歡的一座城市，你覺
得下面這個答案要如何調整成一個比較有連貫性的回答呢？

Tokyo is my favourite city because it has so many shops and restaurants. It's very convenient. I like shopping and eating, and there are many things to buy and eat. For example, I love buying cosmetics and eating ramen. There are many kinds of ramen that I like to eat.

東京是我很喜歡的城市，因為那裡有很多商店和餐廳，非常方便。我喜歡購物和美食，那裡有很多東西可買可吃。舉例來說，我喜歡買美妝品和吃拉麵，那裡有很多種我想吃的拉麵。

這個回答把購物與美食混在一起講，一會兒講吃東西，一會兒又提到化妝品，訊息顯得有點雜亂。只要好好組織一下，就可以大大減少凌亂的感覺。下面是修正過後的版本：

Tokyo is my favourite city. I love shopping, and Tokyo <u>has a lot to offer</u>. There are lots of different shops that sell clothes, cosmetics, and electronic products. I always come back to Taiwan <u>with my luggage overloaded</u>. The food is **also** amazing in Tokyo, which is another reason I keep going back.

東京是我很喜歡的城市。我喜歡購物，而東京<u>應有盡有</u>，那裡有很多販賣衣服、美妝和電器的各種商店。我回台灣時行李總是超重。東京的食物也很令人驚艷，那是我一再造訪東京的另一個原因。

改過的版本只是把兩件事分開講，一件事講完了再講另一件，中間用 also 連結前後兩件事，就可以讓回答顯得有組織、有層次。

3. 善用代名詞

善用代名詞來取代前面講過的名詞，除了可以讓回答聽起來具有連貫性，也可以大大降低重複用字。例如下面的範例：

My brother and I love watching action films at the IMAX cinema near our house. <u>My brother and I</u> saw a great <u>film</u> at the cinema recently. <u>The movie</u> is one of the Marvel series, and <u>the movie</u> is called 'Avengers: Infinity War'.

這樣的回答聽起來相當冗長不自然，回答時可以善用代名詞替代前面出現過的名詞，例如上面例子的畫線處，若善用代名詞或地方副詞取代，便可讓回答精簡許多：

My brother and I love watching action films at the IMAX cinema near our house. **We** saw a great **one there** recently. **It**'s one of the Marvel series, and **it**'s called 'Avengers: Infinity War'.
我哥哥和我喜歡在我家附近的 IMAX 戲院看動作片。我們最近在那裡看了一部很棒的電影，片名叫《復仇者聯盟：無限之戰》，是漫威漫畫系列的其中一部。

4. 善用連結詞、轉折語等指標詞

指標詞可能是單字、短語或句子，主要作用在使句子間的連結更流暢。有些是連接詞 (conjunctions)，有些是副詞 (adverbs)，雖然性質不一，但功能都是一樣的，就是創造連貫性。

另外像填補詞 (fillers)，或稱串場用字，像是 Well, it's hard to say, but I guess... 等句型若用得恰當，可以用來填補思考時的空白，讓回答不會出現停頓，創造出流利感。不過這些沒有實質意義的字只能讓你聽起來好像有在講話，若過度使用反而會凸顯內容空洞，必須審慎運用。

下面來看一些指標詞被誤用或濫用的例子：

for example
Many foreign tourists visit Taroko Gorge when they come to Taiwan. For example, Japanese, Korean and so on.

For example（例如）之後舉例哪些國家的觀光客會造訪太魯閣，讓人搞不懂考生的重點是要講太魯閣還是觀光客了。重點如果是太魯閣，那要進一步延伸說明的內容應該是太魯閣有哪些景點，而非哪一國觀光客。

however

however（然而）是很多考生的愛用字，有些考生會在無意間大量使用，但如果仔細聽，會發現就算拿掉 however，也不會影響內容的連貫性，那也就不需要使用了。更何況 however 其實比較像是寫作用字，英語母語人士較少用在日常口語中。

first of all/firstly

有些考生會習慣性地使用 first of all 或 firstly（首先），但從頭到尾講得卻只有一件事，根本沒有提到 next 或 secondly 的內容。所以如果一定要用 first of all，就要努力另外想一個梗套用到 next，才能讓回答具有連貫性和整體感。

in other words

用了 in other words（換句話說），最怕接著提到的內容跟前面毫不相干，導致連貫性盡失。這個用法只能用在接下來的話是要做進一步解釋時。

to be honest with you

To be honest with you, I'm a sales representative.

To be honest with you, I live in the suburbs.

To be honest with you, it's a very challenging job.

以上幾句都用了 To be honest with you（老實說）開頭，但仔細看，其實有或沒有 To be honest with you，句子根本沒有任何差別，所以用了就顯累贅。

最後以 Part 2 的小演說為例，示範如何運用指標詞（加粗部分）創造連貫性與流暢度。

Describe an activity you do to keep fit.
描述一個你用來維持健康的方式。

In terms of my diet, the main thing I do to stay healthy is to eat lots of fruit and vegetables. **Well**, some days I eat more than on other days, but I try! I eat meat, but not with every meal. I drink wine sometimes, but I don't drink beer because I'm scared of getting a 'beer belly'! **Let's see, what else** ... oh, I also avoid sugary things like fizzy drinks, **and** I almost never eat at fast food restaurants. Their food is terrible for you.

All in all, I'd say the most important thing is to make healthy choices every day. You don't have to completely stop eating the things you like, **and** you don't have to train for a marathon. Just use common sense.

說到我的飲食,我最主要的保健之道就是吃很多蔬果。某些日子我會吃的比平時多些,但我會盡量控制!我吃肉,但不是每餐都吃。有時會喝葡萄酒,但我不喝啤酒,因為我怕會有「啤酒肚」!我想想還有什麼……喔,我也會避免含糖的東西,例如汽水,還有我幾乎不吃速食餐廳的東西,那些食物對身體很不好。

總而言之,我認為最重要的是每天都要做出健康的選擇。你不必完全不吃你喜歡的食物,也不用接受馬拉松訓練。只要善用常識即可。

IELTS 口說 評分標準 ❷
詞彙變換
Lexical Resource

雖然說單字用得愈多樣化、愈精確，分數就會愈高，但若是使用簡單的單字，卻用得自然無誤，仍然可以得到一個理想的分數。考生在詞彙這個項目的準備可以不必壓力太大。程度較好的考生運用進階字彙的成功率較高，一般程度的考生對此評分項目的應考策略最好是以「不要誤用單字」為主。

評分重點

1. 是否能正確使用大量字彙？

考生除了要具備足夠的單字量，才有辦法兵來將擋，水來土掩，不費力地應付各種話題，還必須能夠以精確的單字來表達出自己的意思。

2. 是否具備換句話說的能力？

考生除了要能用精確的單字正確傳達意思，還要訓練換句話說的能力，能用不同的詞彙與說法去詮釋自己前面說過的內容。

3. 是否運用合適的口語用字及搭配詞？

英文用字會因不同的場合使用不同的 style（文體），例如有 written/spoken（寫作／口語）、formal/informal（正式／非正式）、technical（科技）或 slang（俚俗語）等。口語使用的英文詞彙跟寫作不同，一般來說，口語用字比寫作用字來得親切常見。口試時，考生應使用適合口語的英文詞彙，而非搬出文謅謅的罕見用字。

另外，搭配詞 (collocation) 使用要恰當。很多英文用字都有固定的搭配方式，不能自己胡亂搭配，例如 global warming（全球暖化）不能說成 global heating、greenhouse gases（溫室氣體）也不能說成 warmhouse gases。

4. 是否使用進階字 彙或慣用語？

考生是否能正確無誤地使用進階字彙或慣用語，這個評分項目有相當的難度，比較適合程度中上，要追求八分以上的考生。進階字彙或慣用語，對一般程度的考生挑戰很大，出錯的機率很高。若沒有徹底了解字彙或慣用語的意思，或沒有依照上下文的語意邏輯運用，反而會讓考官聽得一頭霧水。所以對英文程度中等的考生，不建議使用難字或慣用語。

高分祕訣

1. 不要複誦考官的 問題

在口試中，如果考官問你 Do you like singing?，不要回答 Yes, I like singing.；被問到 What's your favourite food?，不要回答 My favourite food is desserts.；被問到 Do you like swimming?，不要回答 No, I don't like swimming.。因為這樣你只是在複誦考官的問題，無法展現你的字彙能力，便無法在字彙與文法的評分項目上得到高分。

雖然考生可能會繼續用其他句子延伸說明，但如果一開始就使用不同的表達方式，然後再讓答案順勢往下延伸，會讓考官更印象深刻。例如被問到 What's your favourite food?，便可回答 I love desserts. I eat a lot of sweets. Sometimes, I even eat them every day. （我喜歡甜點，我吃很多甜食，有時候甚至會天天吃。）

要改變這樣的回答方式對有些考生來說可能不太容易，因為有很多人從小時候學兒童美語時就已經養成這樣的習慣了。一般英語母語人士其實是不會這樣回答的。我們可以用中文來試試看，如果有人問你「你最喜歡的食物是什麼？」我們可能會直接回答「火鍋」、「牛排」或「沒有特別喜歡哪一樣耶」，而不是像小學生照樣造句般回答「我最喜歡的食物是火鍋」。要創造自然流暢的說話方式，考生要時時提醒自己不要複誦考官的問題。

2. 不要亂用艱澀的 罕見單字　有很多考生誤以為使用愈難的英文字，就會讓考官印象愈深刻，也會因此得到比較高的分數。舉例來說，English is **opaque**. 這句話就讓人聽了摸不著頭腦，其實考生想表達的是「英文很難」，但又覺得 English is **hard/difficult**. 用字太簡單，所以才用了 English is **opaque**. 這個令人莫名其妙的說法。在這個情況下，其實講 English is **hard/difficult**. 反而是比較適當的。

3. 避免使用 寫作用字　有些單字雖然看起來「很高級」，但用在口語中卻會顯得古怪。例如：

✗ I can't buy a car because I still need to **obtain** a driver's license.
○ I can't buy a car because I still need to **get** a driver's license.
我不能買車，因為我還得取得駕駛執照。

✗ My family and I **reside** in a residential area.
○ My family and I **live** in a residential area.
我家人和我居住在住宅區。

✗ **It is said that** my friend Jenny has a hundred pairs of shoes in her closet.
○ **My friends say that** Jenny has a hundred pairs of shoes in her closet.
我朋友說珍妮的衣櫃裡有一百雙鞋。
○ **I think** my friend Jenny has a hundred pairs of shoes in her closet.
我想我朋友珍妮的衣櫃裡有一百雙鞋。

查字典的時候，也可以注意一下，有些字典會標示該字是 formal 或 informal，若看到 formal 就要避免在口語中使用。

想要在詞彙上得到高分，很多時候不只是要換個單字，還要會換句話說。以上面提到的「英文很難」為例，除了 English is **hard/ difficult**.（英文很難 / 很困難。）這樣的說法，還可以換個說法講成 English is really **hard to master**.（英文真的很難掌握。）然後再用其他句子進一步說明：

English is really **hard to master**. I've been learning it for a long time, but I still **get confused** with **the usage of many words**.
英文真的很難掌握。我已經學了很久，但對許多字的用法還是感到困惑。

以下是幾個換句話說的例子，程度中上的考生可以試著把這些用法學下來。

I **like** Katy Perry. 我喜歡凱蒂·佩芮。
→ I'm **a big fan of** Katy Perry. 我是凱蒂·佩芮的超級粉絲。

There are **too many cars** in the city. 城市裡的車子太多。
→ **Traffic congestion** is a big problem in the city.
城市裡的交通擁擠是個大問題。

I don't **enjoy** reading about history. 我不喜歡讀歷史。
→ I'm not very **keen on** history. 我對歷史不是非常熱衷。

He **doesn't talk much**. 他不多話。
→ He's **a man of few words**. 他很寡言。

Ken was so **happy** about the news. 肯恩聽到這個新聞很高興。
→ Ken was **overwhelmed** when he heard the news.
肯恩聽到新聞時樂不可支。

5. 描述細節時要清楚具體

很多考生只要被問到食物，就會用到 delicious，被問到居住地點，就會用到 convenient，說到出國留學，就會用到 broaden my horizons。這些用字不只太常見，意思也不夠清楚具體。以「城市」這個常考的主題來說，若被問到 describe where you live（描述你居住的城市），最常見的回答大概就是：

I live in a big city. It's very convenient. It has everything I need. I can do whatever I want anytime.
我住在大城市裡，那裡非常方便，我所需的一切應有盡有，我隨時都能做任何想做的事。

大城市方便，是哪裡方便？你所需的又是什麼？是東西還是服務？你隨時能做的任何事又是指什麼？「方便」有很多面向，可以針對交通，也可以針對生活機能，若能把 convenient 的涵義具體表達清楚，答案就會顯得更明確清楚。

修正過後比較具體的版本：

I live in a big city. **Public transport** is easily **accessible** in the form of buses and MRT trains, so it's fairly **easy** and **efficient** for me to **commute to work** or **get to any other destination**.
我住在大城市裡，公車或捷運等公共運輸都很方便使用。所以對我來說，不管是通勤上下班或是要去哪裡都很容易又有效率。

再來舉一個也很常見的例子。當考官要你 describe the kind of house you want to live in（描述一種你想居住的房子類型），除了考生最常回答的 I want to live in a big house，還可以怎麼講才能讓答案更顯具體又令人耳目一新呢？

I want to live in a **spacious** and **bright** house. It needs to have **high ceilings** and **no barriers** such as walls and doors between the kitchen, sitting room, and dining room.
我想住在寬敞明亮的房子裡，要有挑高的天花板，而且廚房、客廳和飯廳之間不能有牆和門那些間隔物隔開。

針對這類型的問題，考生可以練習描述自己身邊的人、事、時、地、物。喜歡一位藝人、一個朋友、一件衣服、一樣食物、一門課程，是為什麼喜歡呢？試著用更具體的詞彙來描述。

6. 正確使用搭配詞

換句話說雖然重要，但也不能隨意亂換。例如，智慧型手機就是 smart phone，不能說成 intelligent phone。講到小孩的話題時，有時可以將 children 換成 kids，但有些用法是固定搭配，不能隨意替換，例如 child support（子女撫養費）或 child abuse（虐待兒童）就不能說成 kid support 或 kid abuse。這些英文中常見的搭配用法，到底應該怎麼搭很多時候並沒有規則可循，不確定時就多多善用 Google 大神吧！

動詞跟名詞的搭配是考生很容易出錯的地方，例如名詞 effort 常見的搭配有 put effort into 或 make an effort，就是沒有 take an effort。而常見的 pay attention to，也不可以改成 pay attention on，講錯就會失分，要特別留意。

常見搭配詞

Adj. + N.	V. + N.	N. + V-ing
global warming 全球暖化	do the shopping 採購（日用品等）	bungee jumping 高空彈跳
greenhouse effect 溫室效應	break the rules 打破規則	problem solving 解決問題
teething problem 初期困難	make a difference 造成影響	face painting 臉部彩繪
senior citizen 老年人	make an effort 作出努力	people watching 觀察行人
military service 兵役	make room 挪出空間	sleep walking 夢遊
young learner 兒少學習者	make a profit 賺錢	day dreaming 白日夢
minimum wage 最低薪資	go extinct 絕種	island hopping 跳島（旅行）
on-site training 現場培訓	take medicine 服藥	
lifelong learning 終生學習	draw a conclusion 做出結論	
	launch a project 展開計畫	

7. 多背實用的慣用語　考生平時可多背一些各種情境下皆通用的慣用語，例如 it's no big deal（沒什麼大不了的）、once in a blue moon（偶爾）、put yourself in someone's shoes（設身處地為他人著想）或 lose one's temper（發脾氣）等。避免一些只能用在特定情況下的用語，例如 better to be a live dog than a dead lion（活狗勝過死獅），這種片語跟中文的「三個臭皮匠勝過一個諸葛亮」一樣，在口語中使用的情況不多，用不好又顯得格格不入，投資報酬率太低。

不過要注意，慣用語的使用一定要 100% 正確。Desserts are not **my cup of tea**（我不喜歡吃甜點）不能掉字變成 Dessert is **not my tea**；My new laptop **cost me an arm and a leg**（我的新筆電花了我一大筆錢）不能變成 My new laptop cost me **a finger and a leg**；I was **as sick as a dog**（我病得很嚴重）不能變成 I was as sick as a **cat**，考生一定要特別注意。

最後，慣用語的使用也不能讓人覺得太突兀。It was **raining cats and dogs**（外面傾盆大雨）這樣的用語突然出現在一個平淡無奇的故事中，或是從一個英文程度中下的考生口中突然蹦出一句 **I shit my pants**（我嚇壞了），都會顯得格格不入。考生要盡量選擇概括層面較廣的、用法較多元的慣用語，較能避免使用不當的問題。

IELTS 口說 評分標準 ❸
句式豐富性和文法準確性
Grammatical Range and Accuracy

文法跟句型在 IELTS 口試中，並不是最重要的評分項目，當考生太在乎文法正確性以及句型複雜度時，流利度就會降低，出錯的機率也會提高。所以應試時，盡量使用相對簡單，自己可以掌握的文法句型。文法跟句型與單字一樣，先求有，再求好。如果一定想用比較複雜的句型，也切記千萬不要把寫作中會用到的複雜文法句構搬進口說裡。

評分重點

1. 是否使用文法正確清楚易懂的句子？

在文法準確性的評分項目中，考官在意的是考生有沒有能力持續使用沒有文法錯誤或是稍有錯誤但不影響理解的句子。所以即便考生使用的大多是簡單句，只要沒有錯誤，仍然有機會在文法項目得到高分。

2. 是否有能力混搭各種句型？

口試不是從頭到尾都用一些艱澀的文法句型就能得到高分。考生需要有能力混用各種文法句型，要學會將簡單句、複合句及複雜句交錯使用。有些句子有連接詞，有些句子有子句，善用祈使句、條件句、被動語態等，時態上也能依內容使用現在、過去、未來式，有沒有能力 mix and match（混搭）這些基本的文法概念，才是評分重點。

高分祕訣

1. 避免基礎文法錯誤　簡單來說，基礎文法錯誤就是主動詞不一致、時態搞混、名詞單複數誤用、形容詞跟副詞混淆等。本書「**附錄 1**」(p. 270) 列出的例子都是一些大家耳熟能詳，說話時卻容易疏忽的文法概念，考生務必在考前花時間徹底學會正確運用這些基礎文法概念。

2. 混搭簡單句與「高級句」　簡單句是指一個句子裡只有一個主詞、一個動詞的句子結構。例如：

I haven't got a favourite colour.
我沒有喜歡的顏色。

My boyfriend and I work for the same computer company.
我男朋友和我在同一家電腦公司工作。

Children in this country are only expected to study and get good scores.
這個國家的孩子只被期待要好好念書，拿到好成績。

「高級句」是指複合句及複雜句，也就是由多個子句組成的句子，簡單說就是用連接詞或連接副詞，把兩句以上的話串在一起，形成比較長的句子。在寫作中因為會牽涉到標點符號的使用，需要注意的地方比較多，但在口試中並不需要在意標點符號，可以少擔一點心。以下是一些高級句的示範：

My colleague had a car accident last month, **so** he took a month off.（複合句）
我同事上個月發生車禍，所以他休假一個月。

When I was a child, I lived with my grandparents in Yilan.（複雜句）
我小時候和爺爺奶奶住在宜蘭。

Drinking wine is good for your health **as long as** you don't drink too much.（複雜句）
只要你別喝太多酒，飲酒有益健康。

一開始的幾句話先用簡單句，較能講到重點。接下來想表現英文程度，再使用高級句。例如提到自己喜歡的食物，可以這麼說：

I love rice and noodles.（← 簡單句）I eat one of them with almost every meal **because** if I don't have anything solid, I'll feel hungry straight after.（← 複雜句）
我喜歡飯和麵。我幾乎每餐都會吃其中一種，因為如果沒吃點固體食物，馬上就會覺得餓了。

又如提到自己的名字時：

One of my first names means 'wisdom'.（← 簡單句）My brothers and sisters all have this name.（← 簡單句）It's just something my family has done with our generation.（← 複雜句）I'll probably do something similar **if** I have kids.（← 複雜句）
我名字其中一個字的意思是「智慧」。我兄弟姐妹的名字裡都有這個字，我的家族用這個方式為我們這一代命名。如果我有小孩，或許也會這麼做。

常見的連接詞及連接副詞

以下是一些口說常用的連接詞及連接副詞。很多寫作比較常用的連接詞與連接副詞，例如 nevertheless、furthermore、yet，在口說中若沒有搭配程度相當的內容與用字，會給人格格不入的感覺，應避免使用。

and	when/while	either ... or/neither ... nor
or	because	on the one hand/on the other hand
but	although/though	consequently
so	since	however
then	otherwise	besides
if	as well as	not only ... but also（避免濫用）

3. 混用主動語態與被動語態

舉個例子來說，如果想表達「台灣製造很多電子產品」，可以先用主動語態的句子：

Taiwan **makes** a lot of electronic products.
台灣製造很多電子產品。

接下來的延伸句再用被動語態的句子：

They'**re** usually **manufactured** in the Hsinchu Science Park.
這些產品通常是在新竹科學園區製造的。

使用被動語態的句子可以給人英文很好的感覺。下面列出一些很實用的常見用法：

The world population **is expected to** reach 8.5 billion by 2030.
全世界人口預計二〇三〇年到達 85 億。

Children should **be encouraged to** eat healthy food and do physical exercise.
兒童應受鼓勵吃健康食物和運動。

When a large proportion of a country's citizens are old, its power and workforce can **be** seriously **affected**.
如果一個國家的人口大部分是老年人，國家力量和勞動力可能受到嚴重影響。

Many Taiwanese children **are brought up** by their grandparents.
許多台灣小孩是由祖父母帶大的。

4. 多背實用句型

英文有很多句型是一種約定俗成的概念，若沒有使用慣用的英文句型，聽起來就是中式英文。例如「小朋友學英文很重要」這句話若直接依字面中翻英，會變成：

✕ Children learn English is important.

若沒有英文老師幫忙修正，自修者可能不會知道慣用的英文說法是：

○ It's important for children to learn English.
對兒童來說，學英文是重要的。

或是：

○ Learning English is important for children.
學英文對兒童來說是重要的。

同樣地，「城市裡有很多車」的英文，很多考生也會說成：

✕ There have many cars in the city.

但正確的英文說法必須是：

○ There are many cars in the city.
城市裡的車子很多。

這些基本句型因為看似簡單，台灣學生通常不會特別留意，但其實考生要確實學會運用這些基本句型，才有能力運用更難的句型。

下面示範用三種不算難的英文句型來回答問題：

1. There is/are...
2. Ving + is/are not as + Adj. + as...
3. It's + Adj. + for people to + V.

Where do people in your country buy food?

在你們國家，大家都去哪裡購買食物？

回答

In Taiwan **there are** many cheap restaurants and eateries. **Eating out** here **is not as expensive as** it is in Europe or America. **It's** also very **common for people to eat** takeout now.

eatery

台灣有許多便宜的餐廳和小飯館。在這裡外食不如歐洲或美國那麼昂貴，現在外帶食物也非常普遍。

以上這些句子都不難，但混用了好幾種不同的句型，已經達到口說文法項目的高分要求了。

5. 使用縮略型式

英文口說跟寫作除了用字不同，另一項差異是口說通常使用縮略形式，否則不只不接近英語母語人士的說話方式，聽起來也會很不自然。想得高分的考生一定要習慣多多使用縮略形式。

常見縮略形式

I will = I'll	is not = isn't	should have = should've
you will = you'll	are not = aren't	should not have = shouldn't've
he will = he'll	does not = doesn't	could have = could've
she will = she'll	did not = didn't	could not have = couldn't've
it will = it'll	will not = won't	would have = would've
we will = we'll	has not = hasn't	would not have = wouldn't've
they will = they'll	should not = shouldn't	
	could not = couldn't	

IELTS口說 評分標準 ❹
發音
Pronunciation

發音這個評分項目除了要求考生的單字發音必須正確之外，也必須具備英語母語人士的一些發音特色。另外，考生的音量要夠大，講起話來不能含糊不清。平常練習時就要讓自己聽起來是一個講話有自信，語調自然，表現落落大方的人。

台灣考生受到中文母語的影響，講英文時一般都會有台灣人的口音，這不是大問題，不過要注意口音不能嚴重到干擾考官的理解。另外，不管考生是英國腔、美國腔、澳洲腔都不是問題，只要在口試時固定使用一種口音說話即可。

評分重點

1. 是否使用所有發音特色？
考生必須注意英文的所有發音特色 (pronunciation features)，發音特色主要包括子音及母音的發音，例如長短母音、雙母音等；另外，連音、弱音、重音、語調等這些能讓英文聽起來更像英語母語人士的發音特色也是評分一大重點，這些發音特色都要做到才能得到高分。

2. 是否持續使用發音特色？
考生在口試過程中必須要持續使用英語的發音特色，不能這一句記得連音、下一句就忘記，或同一個單字的發音前後不一致。

3. 發音是否清楚易懂？
考生的發音及口音必須讓考官不費力地聽懂，若因為發音問題而造成考官理解困難，這個項目的分數就會節節下降。

高分祕訣

1. 勤查發音 很多英文單字的發音是沒有規則的，要怎麼發音只有靠查字典才能確定。例如 many, can't, father, angel, breakfast 這幾個單字，字母 a 的發音都不一樣。若有心想學好發音，就有必要把音標學好，以便增加音準。另外，不確定發音時一定要查字典看清楚每個字怎麼發音，而不是胡亂靠自己的感覺瞎掰。

001

常見的發音錯誤

母音有短母音、長母音跟雙母音，子音分有聲子音跟無聲子音。台灣學生最容易搞混的是母音 /e/ 跟 /æ/，以及雙母音 /eɪ/ 常發成 /e/*。（以下發音示範，MP3 先唸錯誤發音，再唸正確發音）

母音發音錯誤

Mek → 應為 Mac
averyday → 應為 everyday
abble → 應為 able
code → 應為 called
conform → 應為 confirm
becose → 應為 because

短音發成長音

I leave in Taipei. → 應為 I live in Taipei.
I'm really fool. → 應為 I'm really full.

長音發成短音

I need some slip. → 應為 I need some sleep.

雙母音發成短音

What did she sed? → 應為 What did she say?
It tests gret. → 應為 It tastes great.
Don't west food. → 應為 Don't waste food.

短音發成雙母音

It's spacial. → 應為 It's special.

子音尾音太強調

I lie ka i ta. → 應為 I like it.

子音發音錯誤

war → 應為 wall
penso → 應為 pencil

子音無發出

I went out with my frien.
→ 應為 I went out with my friends.

無故發出子音

I'm from Taiwant. → 應為 I'm from Taiwan.
Its depends. → 應為 It depends.

*本書的音標標示為 IPA 音標，非 KK 音標。

單字的音標查好了，發音也都對了，考生仍然需要將字跟字流暢地組合成一句語調自然、讓人容易聽懂的句子。而這時候，弱音、連音、重音、語調等發音特色就可以派上用場了。

弱音
(002)

英語母語人士說話時常把有些單字的母音唸成輕音 /ə/，不會用力唸出來，這樣才能說得比較快、比較流暢。例如下面句子中畫線的部分，會唸得比較小聲、比較短。

What are you doing?
你在做什麼？

Have you been to Oxford yet?
你去過牛津嗎？

Are you buying a present for him?
你正在買給他的禮物嗎？

連音
(003)

當單字的尾音是子音，後面的單字是母音開頭時，英語母語人士會很自然地把兩個音連起來唸，有時甚至會將一些子音削弱再連音。

not at all

pick it up

I need him to finish it.
我需要他完成它。

Let them meet you.
讓他們見見你。

而母音接母音時也必須連音，中間不能斷開。

Let me in!
讓我進去！

She'll tell you all about it.
她會告訴你那件事所有細節。

Ben wants to be alone.
班想要獨處。

I actually studied Ancient Egyptian literature at uni.
其實我大學念的是古埃及文學。

省略音

為了讓英文講起來順暢，字尾的 t 跟 d 經常不發音（尤其是英式英語）。

next day
it depends
most popular
father and son

有些字更像是變魔術一樣變短了，例如 definitely 跟 absolutely，若說話速度快，中間 -te 那個音節幾乎都聽不見了。

單字的重音

英文幾乎每個多音節的字都會有重音。重音是指有重音的音節要：

- 大聲一點
- 長一點
- 高音一點

拿 English 這個字來說，Eng- 這個音節是重音節，所以它要大聲一點、長一點，音調也會高一點；反之，-lish 的部分就要小聲一點、短一點，音調也會低一點。

單字的重音放錯位置，除了可能讓別人聽不懂你在說什麼，還可能讓人誤解意思，因為有些單字重音位置改變，除了改變了詞性，意思也可能大不相同。例如 produce 當動詞時，重音在後面 -duce 這個音節，但當名詞時，重音則在前面 pro- 的音節，重音擺錯就會造成聽者的混淆。以下是幾組重音很容易混淆的單字：

produce (n.) 農產品 / pro**d**uce (v.) 製造
record (n.) 紀錄；唱片 / re**c**ord (v.) 記錄
desert (n.) 沙漠 / de**s**ert (v.) 遺棄
present (n.) 禮物 / pre**s**ent (v.) 出席

句子的重音

考生除了要注意單字的重音，也要注意句子的重音。一般情況下，句子的重音會落在名詞、動詞、形容詞或副詞上；冠詞跟介系詞的發音則會輕輕帶過，所以聽起來就像被前後的字給「吃掉」的感覺。說話者也可以根據自己想強調的內容或重點，改變句子裡的重音位置。請聽 MP3 示範以下句子的重音：

Lisa saw a `**man** in the garden. （強調「看到一名男子」）
Lisa saw a man in the `**garden**. （強調「地點是在花園」）
麗莎看到花園裡有一名男子。

I went to the `**supermarket** last night. （強調「超市這個地點」）
I went to the supermarket `**last** night. （強調「時間是昨晚」）
我昨晚去了超市。

I was the first person `there!（強調「地點」）

I was the `first person there!（強調「第一個」）
我是第一個到那裡的人！

朗讀練習

朗讀下面三個句子，盡量從句子中找出一兩個字來強調，音量要比較大、比較長，音調也要比較
高。（務必自己練習之後再聽 MP3 示範）

I'm running seriously late!
This book will help you become a more fluent speaker.
If you want to read more about it, please visit our website at bbclearningenglish.com.

示範 （下面只是其中一種可能性）

I'm running `seriously `late!

This book will `help you become a `more `fluent speaker.

If you want to read `more about it, `please visit our `website at `bbc`learningenglish `dotcom.

節奏感

英文是一種有節奏感的語言，一個句子需要有快慢及停頓，除了
有逗點處我們知道語氣需要停頓，有時一個沒有逗點的句子也必
須依語意區塊 (chunks) 稍微停頓。例如下面畫線的字通常會連在
一起講，中間不可停頓：

Jazz is not my cup of tea.
爵士樂不合我的胃口。

It depends on what you want to do.
這要視你想做什麼而定。

Do you know where the restaurant is?
你知道餐廳在哪裡嗎？

沒有節奏感，或是在應該連在一起講的地方停頓，會像中文亂用逗點一樣，造成聽者理解上的混淆。

語調

英語母語人士通常會在某些情況下將一句話的音調上揚或下降。例如，提問或表示有疑問時，句尾的音調就會往上揚。表達命令或陳述事實時，句尾的音調就會往下降。若講一串同樣詞性的單字時（例如：I need to get eggs, flour, milk and cheese.）前面幾個項目的音調會上揚，最後一個項目會往下降。

語調單調無高低音的英文（若又加上沒有節奏感），聽起來就像手機轉接語音信箱時的機器人：「您已經進入零。玖。伍。捌。陸。肆。貳。玖。柒。零。的信箱」一樣古怪。

試著唸以下這幾個句子，你覺得它們的語調會往上揚還是往下降呢？請先試著自己唸，再聽 MP3 示範。

I was the first person there!
Were you the first person there?
The conference call was at 10.
Was the conference call at 10?

語調中的抑揚頓挫是用來表現說話者的語氣。想表示情緒的高低、提出疑問或傳達諷刺的態度等，都需要靠說話者掌握整句話的語調，而語調跟重音更必須是相輔相成的。口試中想在發音上得到高分，單字重音、句子重音以及整句話的高低起伏都各自扮演重要的角色。

朗讀練習

以下摘錄一小段 Part 2 的小演說，試著自己先唸一遍，然後再聽 MP3 的示範：

I work in the sales department of a medium-sized company, and we have a sales department meeting every month in the conference room. The most recent one was last Monday. The sales manager leads the meetings and all seven of us sales staff attend them.

In the meetings, the manager reminds us of the monthly sales targets. It's nothing new—we already know our targets, and they don't change. Then, she reviews our results from last month and asks each of us to report on how we're doing this month. But we're already required to keep a record of our sales on a document, and we all have access to this document. Then, the sales manager talks for a while about working hard and making more sales. It's really boring. Sometimes, I see people texting or checking Facebook on their phones under the table while she's talking. We take turns taking the meeting minutes, and we all have to sign the minutes to prove that we were there and we know what happened during the meeting.

I remember these meetings because they happen every month, and we just had one recently. I wish we could stop having them! They're really a waste of time.

Part 1 考試技巧大揭密

應答技巧　一個快答＋支持句

口說高分練習題

Part 2 考試技巧大揭密

應答技巧　用心智圖規畫小演說

口說高分練習題

Part 3 考試技巧大揭密

應答技巧　AEC三步驟答題法

口說高分練習題

Part 1
考試技巧大揭密

應答技巧攻略

雖然 Part 1 的問題算簡單，真的可以用一個字來回答，但除非是 Yes/No 的問題，否則回答時還是盡量用完整的句子比較好。例如被問到：

Q   **Where are you from?**
你來自哪裡？

很多考生會反射性地回答：
Taiwan.

不然就是：
Kaohsiung.

建議考生回答時可以先反射性地快答（盡量用完整的句子），再將這個快答用支持句 (supporting sentences) 進一步延伸說明。

例如：

快答   I'm from Kaohsiung.
我來自高雄。

支持句   ... in southern Taiwan. I was born and raised there. But I moved to Taipei two years ago.
……位於台灣南部，我在那裡出生長大，但兩年前搬到台北了。

再換個例子，若被問到：

問題

Do you like shopping for shoes?
你喜歡買鞋嗎？

快答

I hate shopping for shoes.
我討厭買鞋。

支持句

... because it's difficult to find my size and embarrassing to ask if they
have a size that big.
⋯⋯因為很難找到我的尺寸，而且問他們有沒有那麼大的尺碼讓人覺得尷尬。

話多的人甚至可以講更多：

 It's hard to find shoes that fit comfortably, look nice, and don't break
the bank. But on those rare occasions I'm successful, I guess I like it!
很難找到舒適、好看又不傷荷包的鞋。但難得幾次可以成功找到時，我想我也
挺開心的。

延伸支持句的 6 種方法

Part 1 的問題有兩種。一種是 Yes/No 問題，一種是 Wh- 問題。

Yes/No 問題

Do you like music? Why/Why not?
你喜歡音樂嗎？為什麼喜歡？為什麼不喜歡？

Do you think older and younger people like different types of music?
你覺得老--輩的人和年輕世代喜歡不同種類的音樂嗎？

Has the type of music that you listen to changed since you were
young?
你聽的音樂類型和年輕時聽的有不同嗎？

What kind of music do you listen to?
你聽哪種音樂？

When do you listen to music?
你什麼時候聽音樂？

Why is pop music popular?
為什麼流行音樂受歡迎？

不管是哪一種問題，都可以用前面提過的「快答＋支持句」的方式作答。而要如何將點子用支持句延伸，以下介紹六種延伸支持句的方法：

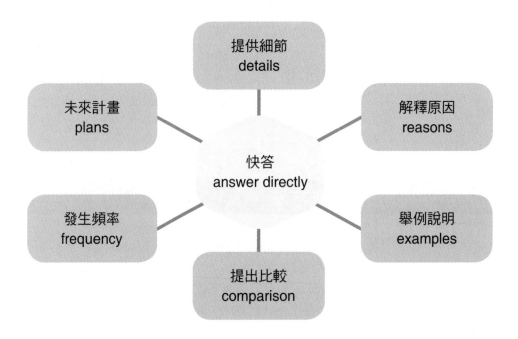

1. 提供細節　　例如被問到 Where's your hometown?（你的家鄉在哪裡？），除了回答家鄉在哪裡之外，可以接著提到自己在那裡住了多久或已離開多久，現在又住在哪裡。

2. 解釋原因　例如被問到 Do you like flowers?（你喜歡花嗎？），除了回答喜不喜歡之外，可以進一步提供喜不喜歡的理由。為什麼喜歡花？因為「看到花心情就很好」；為什麼不喜歡花？因為「一下子就枯了，蠻浪費錢的」。

3. 舉例說明　例如被問到 What games are popular in your country?（你的國家有哪些遊戲受歡迎？），可以先提出一個涵蓋性廣的類別，例如 phone games（手機遊戲）或 board games（桌上遊戲），然後再從大類別中舉例。例如提到了 phone games，接著便可舉例 Pokémon Go 或 Candy Crush 等遊戲。

4. 提出比較　例如被問到 How popular are bicycles in your hometown?（在你的家鄉，腳踏車有多受歡迎？），若想講很受歡迎，可以「跟過去比較」，說說「現在是否有較多人騎腳踏車」，或者「跟其他城市比較」，例如「台北市有 Ubike 所以比較多人騎腳踏車」。

5. 發生頻率　例如被問到 Do you prefer travelling in a group or alone?（你喜歡團體旅遊還是一個人旅遊？），除了回答「喜歡自己一人自助旅行」以外，還可以加上「我已經自己出國旅遊三次了」，再接「希望可以每年自己出國旅遊一次」。

6. 未來計畫　例如被問到 How did your parents choose your name?（你父母是怎麼幫你取名字的？），除了回答「是算命師取的」以外，你也可以加上「我以後若生小孩，絕對不會找算命師取名字」來延長答案。

以下提供四個問題讓考生腦力激盪，請試著用「快答＋支持句」的方式回答問題。

Tip

Part 1 回答的支持句可以是這六種方式六選一或六選二，但不要過多，因為時間緊迫，後面還有 Part 2 跟 Part 3，考官不會讓考生的每次回答講太多句話。

How much time do you spend at home?
你待在家裡的時間多長？

快答
_____

支持句
_____

_____

_____

_____

參考答案：

Not much. I go out with friends a lot. Some of us play music together in a band. We spend a lot of time practising, and I can't do that at home. It's too noisy!

不多，我經常和朋友出去。我和其中幾個朋友有一起玩樂團，我們花很多時間團練，我不可能在家練習，太吵了！

問題

Do you prefer to spend your free time at home or outside the house?
你有空的時候喜歡待在家還是外出？

快答
_____

支持句
_____

_____

_____

_____

參考答案：

I like to go out. There aren't many things to do at home. I like to sit in a coffee shop, surf the Internet or read magazines. It just feels different.

我喜歡外出。家裡沒什麼事可做，我喜歡坐在咖啡廳裡上網或看雜誌，感覺很不一樣。

問題

What do you do when you have some free time and you're at home?

你待在家時若有空會做些什麼？

快答

支持句

參考答案：

I watch a lot of American television series. There's always something I'm following. It was 'The Walking Dead', then it was 'Game of Thrones'. I don't get bored.

我常看美國電視影集，我總是有正在追蹤的影集，之前是《陰屍路》，後來是《冰與火之歌：權力遊戲》。一點都不會無聊。

問題 Would you like to spend more time at home in the future?

你未來想多花一點時間待在家裡嗎？

快答

支持句

參考答案：

Sure. I'd like to stay at home more because it saves money! I guess I should go home right after work or stay home on the weekend.

當然，我想更常待在家，因為可以省錢！我想我下班後應該馬上回家，或是週末待在家裡。

Part 1 應試小提醒

1. 不要一直說 because...

雖然說 because 很適合用來當作支持句的開頭，但也不需要每個句子都用 I ... because I... 的句型。很多時候喜不喜歡一樣東西是不需要給原因的，例如一個喜歡吃辣的人，若被問到為什麼喜歡吃辣，可以說：

I love spicy food. I put chili sauce or chili powder on almost everything I eat. It's just so boring without it!

我喜歡辣的食物，我幾乎吃什麼都會加辣醬或辣椒粉，不加辣真是淡而無味！

每個句子都用 because 回答，聽起來會像是個小學生在說話！

2. 不是每個問題都要回答 Yes

回答 No 並不會被扣分,只要答案有延伸就可以了。事實上,回答 No 常常可以為自己帶來更多話題。例如,被問到:

Do you like animals?
你喜歡動物嗎?

比起回答:

Yes, I do. They're so cute.
是,我喜歡,動物很可愛。

若回答 No.,則可以帶出:

I'm allergic to animal hair.
我對動物毛髮過敏。

這樣的回答顯得更有深度,較容易在字彙的評分項目上得到高分。

Part 1 口說高分練習題

以下兩個主題是 IELTS 的歷屆考題，提供考生參考，考生如果時間充裕，可以作為額外的口試訓練。

練習方法   接下來，我們要實際運用前面學過的技巧，每一個問題都會提供兩種不同的答題方向。建議考生先不要看答案，想想看你會用哪一種延伸支持句的方式來回答問題，並試著作答，最後再參考答案範例。切記，不要用單字來答題，盡量用完整的句子。

答案分為兩層：

第一層是「反射」，是考生在聽到問題時可能馬上想到的點子。建議先忍耐一下，不要馬上說出來，想一想如何運用前面學過的六種延伸支持句的方式「包裝」一下這個點子再講出來，讓你的答案更周全。

第二層是「快答＋支持句」，也就是考官真正聽到的回答。

常考主題 1：Hometown

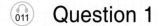 **Question 1**

問題

Where are you from?
你是哪裡人？

反射

Jilong.
基隆。

Kaohsiung.
高雄。

回答

I was born and raised in Jilong, but I've lived in Taipei for the past few years.
我在基隆出生長大，但過去幾年都住在台北。

▶▶▶ 提供細節

I'm from Kaohsiung, in southern Taiwan. I was born and raised there. **But** I moved to Taipei two years ago.
我來自南台灣的高雄。我在那裡出生長大，但兩年前搬到台北。

▶▶▶ 提供細節

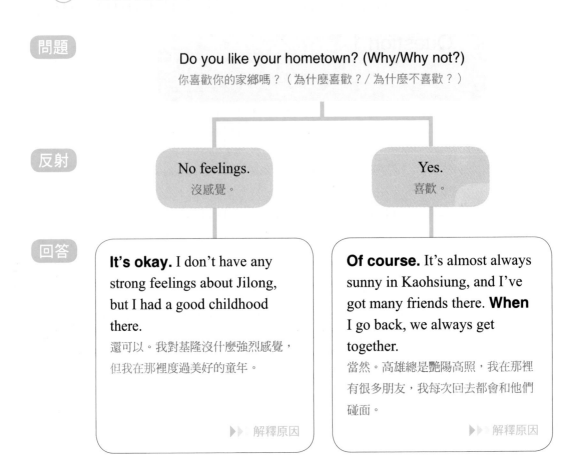

Question 2

問題

Do you like your hometown? (Why/Why not?)
你喜歡你的家鄉嗎？（為什麼喜歡？／為什麼不喜歡？）

反射

No feelings.
沒感覺。

Yes.
喜歡。

回答

It's okay. I don't have any strong feelings about Jilong, but I had a good childhood there.
還可以。我對基隆沒什麼強烈感覺，但我在那裡度過美好的童年。

▶▶ 解釋原因

Of course. It's almost always sunny in Kaohsiung, and I've got many friends there. **When** I go back, we always get together.
當然。高雄總是艷陽高照，我在那裡有很多朋友，我每次回去都會和他們碰面。

▶▶ 解釋原因

048

(013) # Question 3

問題

Do you think your hometown is a good place for young people?

你認為你的家鄉對年輕人來說是個好地方嗎？

反射

Yes.
是。

No.
不是。

回答

Yeah. It's a great place for young people. There's so much to do. We have a lot of parks, museums, nightclubs ... **that kind of thing**.

是，對年輕人來說，那是個很棒的地方，生活多采多姿，那裡有很多公園、博物館、夜店之類的地方。

▶▶▶ 解釋原因．舉例說明

Hmm. I would say no **because** there aren't many job opportunities. Most people find their work here in Taipei.

嗯，我覺得不是，因為那裡的工作機會不多。大多數人都來台北找工作。

▶▶▶ 解釋原因

(014) # Question 4

Would you prefer to live somewhere else? (Why?)

你想住到別的地方嗎？（為什麼？）

反射

| Maybe England. | No. Stay here. |
| 或許英國吧。 | 不，留在這裡。 |

回答

At the moment I'm planning to study in England, **so** I'm looking forward to living there and experiencing a different culture. I'll know what I like after I've lived in a few different places.

目前我計畫到英國念書，所以我很期待住在那裡，體驗不同的文化。住過幾個不同的地方後，我會知道自己喜歡什麼。

▶▶▶ 未來計畫

No. **Now that** my life is here in Taipei, I don't see myself leaving. The older you get, the harder it is to relocate.

不會。現在我的生活都在台北，沒想過要離開。人的年紀愈大，就愈難搬到另一個地方。

▶▶▶ 解釋原因

常考主題 2：Photographs

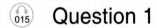

015 **Question 1**

問題

> **What do you do with photos you take?**
> 你怎麼處理所拍的照片？

反射

> **Post them.**
> 張貼發表。

> **Nothing.**
> 不處理。

回答

Well, if they're good, I post them on Instagram or Facebook. What's the point of taking photos if you don't share them?

這個嘛，如果是好照片，我會上傳到 IG 或臉書。如果不分享，幹嘛拍照？

▶▶▶ 提供細節‧解釋原因

Not much. I just upload them to my computer and keep them. **Once in a blue moon**, I look at old photos and remember the places I've been.

不會特別處理。我只會上傳到電腦保存。偶爾我會看看舊照片，回憶一下曾經去過的地方。

▶▶▶ 提供細節‧發生頻率

(016) # Question 2

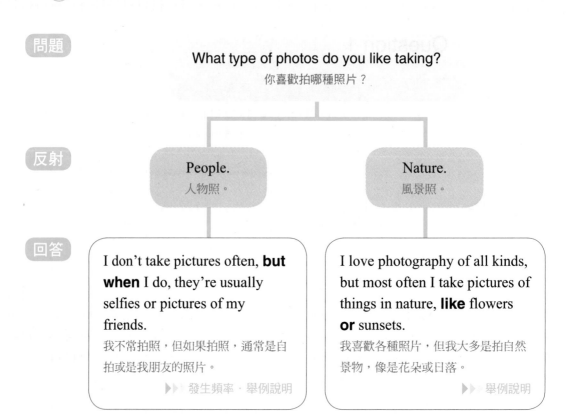

問題

What type of photos do you like taking?

你喜歡拍哪種照片？

反射

People.
人物照。

Nature.
風景照。

回答

I don't take pictures often, **but when** I do, they're usually selfies or pictures of my friends.

我不常拍照，但如果拍照，通常是自拍或是我朋友的照片。

▶▶ 發生頻率・舉例說明

I love photography of all kinds, but most often I take pictures of things in nature, **like** flowers **or** sunsets.

我喜歡各種照片，但我大多是拍自然景物，像是花朵或日落。

▶▶ 舉例說明

(017) # Question 3

When you visit other places,
do you take photos or buy postcards? (Why?)
當你到外地旅遊，你會拍照還是買明信片？（為什麼？）

反射

Both.
都會。

Take photos.
拍照。

回答

Hmm ... I try to take photos, but I'm not a very good photographer, **so** I usually get a couple of postcards **as well**.

嗯……我會試著拍照，但我的技術不太好，所以經常也會買幾張明信片。

▶▶ 解釋原因

I always take my own photos. It's my chance to practise my photography skills and record my memories. I wouldn't want someone else's picture of a place I went to—that was their experience, not mine.

我都會自己拍照，這是練習攝影技術和記錄回憶的機會。我也不想要別人拍攝那個地點的照片，那是他們的見聞，不是我的。

▶▶ 解釋原因

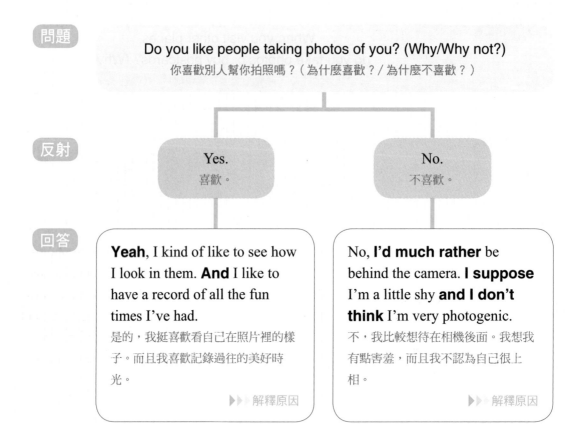

018 **Question 4**

問題

Do you like people taking photos of you? (Why/Why not?)
你喜歡別人幫你拍照嗎？（為什麼喜歡？／為什麼不喜歡？）

反射

Yes.	No.
喜歡。	不喜歡。

回答

Yeah, I kind of like to see how I look in them. **And** I like to have a record of all the fun times I've had.

是的，我挺喜歡看自己在照片裡的樣子。而且我喜歡記錄過往的美好時光。

▶▶▶ 解釋原因

No, **I'd much rather** be behind the camera. **I suppose** I'm a little shy **and I don't think** I'm very photogenic.

不，我比較想待在相機後面。我想我有點害羞，而且我不認為自己很上相。

▶▶▶ 解釋原因

常考主題3：Names

(019) Question 1

問題

> Does your name have any special meaning?
> 你的名字有任何特殊意義嗎？

反射

> No idea.
> 不知道。

> Yes.
> 有。

回答

I don't really know—it's just a name! It was given to me by a fortune teller, **and as far as I know**, there's no hidden meaning.

我不太清楚，那就只是個名字！是一個算命的人取的，就我所知，沒有什麼含意。

▶▶▶ 提供細節

I think so. One of my first names means 'wisdom'. My brothers and sisters all have this name. It's just something my family has done with our generation. I'll probably do something similar if I have kids.

我想應該有。我名字其中一個字的意思是「智慧」。我兄弟姐妹的名字裡都有這個字，我的家族用這個方式為我們這一代命名。如果我有小孩，或許也會這麼做。

▶▶▶ 解釋原因・未來計畫

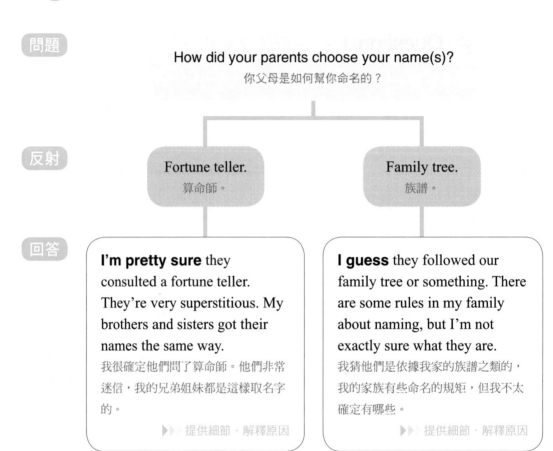

Question 2

問題

How did your parents choose your name(s)?

你父母是如何幫你命名的？

反射

Fortune teller.
算命師。

Family tree.
族譜。

回答

I'm pretty sure they consulted a fortune teller. They're very superstitious. My brothers and sisters got their names the same way.

我很確定他們問了算命師。他們非常迷信，我的兄弟姐妹都是這樣取名字的。

▶▶ 提供細節 · 解釋原因

I guess they followed our family tree or something. There are some rules in my family about naming, but I'm not exactly sure what they are.

我猜他們是依據我家的族譜之類的，我的家族有些命名的規矩，但我不太確定有哪些。

▶▶ 提供細節 · 解釋原因

(021) # Question 3

問題

If you could change your name, would you? (Why/Why not?)
如果可以改名，你會改嗎？（為什麼會？／為什麼不會？）

反射

| Yes. 會。 | No. 不會。 |

回答

Well, I never really liked my Chinese name **because** it's so common. **But** I haven't thought of a new name I'd rather have.
這個嘛，我一直不太喜歡我的中文名字，因為太普通了。但我沒想過要換什麼新名字。

▶▶ 解釋原因

I've never thought about changing my name. **I mean**, why? I can't think of any reason to do that.
我從未想過要改名。我是說，為什麼要改？我想不出為何要這麼做。

▶▶ 解釋原因

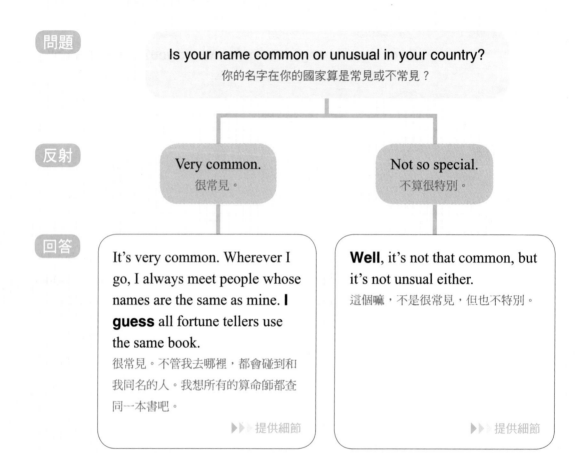

Question 4

022

問題

Is your name common or unusual in your country?
你的名字在你的國家算是常見或不常見？

反射

Very common.
很常見。

Not so special.
不算很特別。

回答

It's very common. Wherever I go, I always meet people whose names are the same as mine. **I guess** all fortune tellers use the same book.

很常見。不管我去哪裡，都會碰到和我同名的人。我想所有的算命師都查同一本書吧。

▶▶▶ 提供細節

Well, it's not that common, but it's not unusual either.

這個嘛，不是很常見，但也不特別。

▶▶▶ 提供細節

常考主題4：Friends

 Question 1

問題

> Tell me about your best friend at school.
> 聊聊你在學校最要好的朋友。

反射

| Sandy. | I didn't really have one. |
| 珊蒂。 | 沒有最要好的朋友。 |

回答

I had a very close friend in high school called Sandy and we would go to each other's homes just to hang out. **But** now, we're not that close anymore.

我在高中有一位非常親密的朋友叫珊蒂，我們會去彼此家玩。但我們現在沒那麼親了。

▶▶▶ 提供細節

It's hard to pick one friend **because** there were a group of them. I'm still in touch with almost all of them and still see them sometimes.

很難選出一個朋友，因為我有一群朋友。我和其中多數人都還有聯絡，有時候也會見面。

▶▶▶ 解釋原因・發生頻率

(024) Question 2

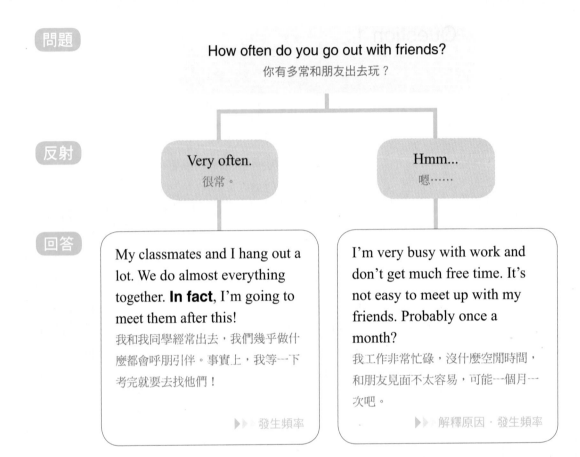

問題

How often do you go out with friends?
你有多常和朋友出去玩？

反射

Very often.
很常。

Hmm...
嗯……

回答

My classmates and I hang out a lot. We do almost everything together. **In fact**, I'm going to meet them after this!
我和我同學經常出去，我們幾乎做什麼都會呼朋引伴。事實上，我等一下考完就要去找他們！

▶▶ 發生頻率

I'm very busy with work and don't get much free time. It's not easy to meet up with my friends. Probably once a month?
我工作非常忙碌，沒什麼空閒時間，和朋友見面不太容易，可能一個月一次吧。

▶▶ 解釋原因‧發生頻率

(025) # Question 3

問題

Which is more important to you, friends or family?
朋友或家庭，哪一個對你比較重要？

反射

Both.	Friends.
都重要。	朋友。

回答

I can't tell you which is more important **because** they are both important. **I mean**, I love my friends, but I'm **also** very close to my family.

我沒辦法告訴你哪個比較重要，因為兩個都很重要。我是說，我愛我的朋友，但和家人也非常親近。

▶▶▶ 解釋原因

I love my family but my parents don't always understand me. **When** I have an important decision to make, I usually get advice from my friends first.

我愛我的家人，但我的父母不一定了解我。當我要做重要決定時，通常會先聽取朋友的建議。

▶▶▶ 解釋原因

Question 4

問題

What kind of activities do you do with your friends?
你和朋友在一起時都做些什麼？

反射

> **Many things.**
> 很多事。

> **Drinking!**
> 喝酒！

回答

As students, we do a lot of things together. We practise dancing, go to the cinema and just hang out really.

我們都是學生，會一起做很多事。像是練舞、看電影，總之就是一起玩樂。

▶▶▶ 舉例說明

My friends and I all love eating and drinking. **When** we meet up, we usually find a decent Japanese restaurant and have a beer or sake.

我的朋友和我都喜歡吃吃喝喝。當我們聚會時，通常會找個不錯的日式餐廳，喝杯啤酒或清酒。

▶▶▶ 舉例說明

(027) # Question 1

問題

> Who normally does the cooking in your home? (Why?)
>
> 你家通常是誰煮飯？（為什麼？）

反射

My mum.	No one.
我媽。	沒人。

回答

My mum is the one who usually does the cooking. If she doesn't feel like cooking, we just each grab something on the way home.

煮飯的人經常是我媽。如果她不想煮飯，我們會各自在回家的路上買東西吃。

▶▶▶ 發生頻率・提供細節

No one. I live alone **so** I usually eat out. Sometimes I cook something simple, but I'm not good at cooking at all.

沒人煮。我一個人住，所以我經常外食。有時候我會煮點簡單的東西，但我的廚藝不好。

▶▶▶ 解釋原因

Question 2

What sorts of food do you like eating most? (Why?)
你最喜歡吃哪種食物？（為什麼？）

> Taiwanese food.
> 台灣食物。

> Rice.
> 米飯。

I like food from all different cultures, **but most of the time**, I have my mum's food or eat out in Taiwanese restaurants.

我喜歡各種文化的食物，但多數時間，我吃媽媽煮的菜，或是到台式餐廳吃飯。

▶▶ 舉例說明・發生頻率

I would say rice and noodles. I eat one of them with almost every meal **because** if I don't have anything solid, I feel hungry straight after.

我會說是米飯和麵食。我幾乎每餐都會吃其中一種，因為如果沒吃點固體食物，很快就餓了。

▶▶ 舉例說明・解釋原因

(029) # Question 3

問題

> In general, do you prefer eating out or eating at home? (Why?)
> 一般來說，你喜歡外食或在家吃？（為什麼？）

反射

Eating at home.
在家吃。

Eating out.
外食。

回答

I usually eat at home. Food safety has been a big issue in Taiwan and you can't trust people in the catering industry. I'd rather cook myself.

我通常在家吃。食物安全在台灣一直是個很大的問題，你不能相信餐飲業的人，我寧願自己煮。

▶▶▶ 解釋原因

My friends and I love going to different restaurants. It's not that expensive to eat out, and there's always something new to try.

我朋友和我喜歡去不同的餐廳。外食並不貴，而且總是能不斷嘗鮮。

▶▶▶ 解釋原因

Question 4

問題

Do you watch cookery programmes on TV? (Why/Why not?)

你會看電視上的烹飪節目嗎？（為什麼會？/ 為什麼不會？）

反射

Yes.	No.
看。	不看。

回答

I watch them all the time! I can even name a few famous chefs from different countries. They're my favourite programmes.

我常看！我甚至可以舉出幾個不同國家的名廚，那是我最喜歡的節目類型。

▶▶ 發生頻率．提供細節

Hmm ... I watch them sometimes, but only when there's nothing else on. **To me**, those programmes are just background noise.

嗯……我有時候會看，但只有在沒其他節目可看時。對我來說，那些節目只是背景雜音。

▶▶ 解釋原因

歷屆主題 1：Mirrors

🎧031 Question 1

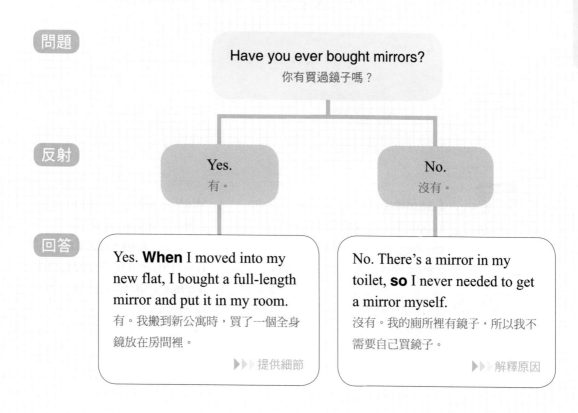

問題

Have you ever bought mirrors?
你有買過鏡子嗎？

反射

Yes.
有。

No.
沒有。

回答

Yes. **When** I moved into my new flat, I bought a full-length mirror and put it in my room.
有。我搬到新公寓時，買了一個全身鏡放在房間裡。

▶▶▶ 提供細節

No. There's a mirror in my toilet, **so** I never needed to get a mirror myself.
沒有。我的廁所裡有鏡子，所以我不需要自己買鏡子。

▶▶▶ 解釋原因

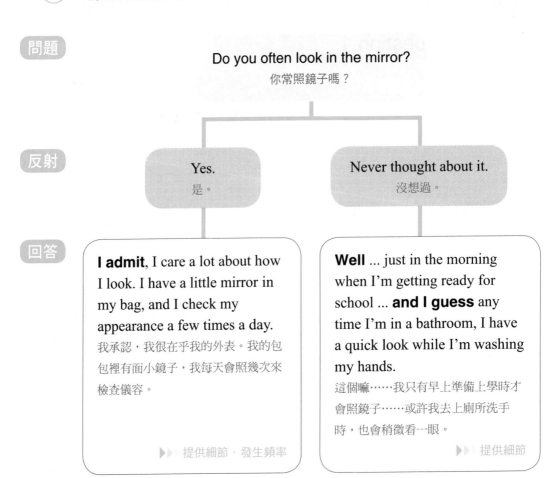

Question 2 (032)

問題

Do you often look in the mirror?
你常照鏡子嗎？

反射

Yes.
是。

Never thought about it.
沒想過。

回答

I admit, I care a lot about how I look. I have a little mirror in my bag, and I check my appearance a few times a day.

我承認，我很在乎我的外表。我的包包裡有面小鏡子，我每天會照幾次來檢查儀容。

▶▶ 提供細節‧發生頻率

Well ... just in the morning when I'm getting ready for school ... **and I guess** any time I'm in a bathroom, I have a quick look while I'm washing my hands.

這個嘛……我只有早上準備上學時才會照鏡子……或許我去上廁所洗手時，也會稍微看一眼。

▶▶ 提供細節

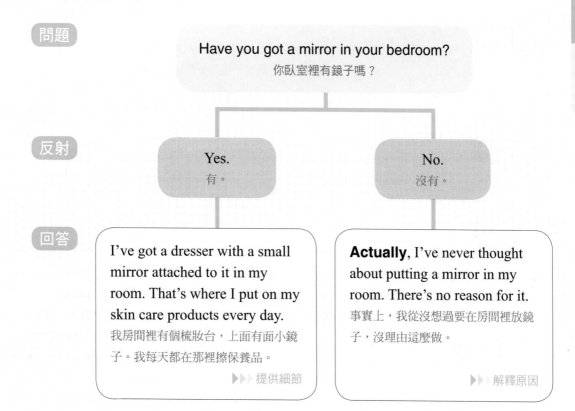

(033) **Question 3**

問題

Have you got a mirror in your bedroom?
你臥室裡有鏡子嗎？

反射

Yes.
有。

No.
沒有。

回答

I've got a dresser with a small mirror attached to it in my room. That's where I put on my skin care products every day.

我房間裡有個梳妝台，上面有面小鏡子。我每天都在那裡擦保養品。

▶▶▶ 提供細節

Actually, I've never thought about putting a mirror in my room. There's no reason for it.

事實上，我從沒想過要在房間裡放鏡子，沒理由這麼做。

▶▶▶ 解釋原因

069

Question 4

Do you think mirrors are a necessary decoration in the house?

你覺得鏡子是屋子裡的必要裝飾品嗎？

反射

| Sure. Why not? | I don't really care. |
| 當然，為什麼不是？ | 我不太在乎。 |

回答

Sure. It would be strange not to have any mirrors **because** they're useful. They can **also** make your place look bigger and brighter.

當然是。完全沒有鏡子會很奇怪，因為鏡子很有用。鏡子也可以讓家裡看起來更大更亮。

▶▶▶ 解釋原因

I don't even think of mirrors as decorations. They're more functional, **like** a sink **or** a microwave. **Anyway**, I don't give the decor much thought. Anything is fine, **as long as** my flat looks tidy.

我甚至沒想過鏡子是裝飾品。鏡子比較像功能性產品，像是水槽或微波爐。不管如何，我不太在意裝飾，什麼樣的裝飾我都無所謂，只要我的公寓看起來整齊即可。

▶▶▶ 解釋原因

歷屆主題2：Dreams

 Question 1

問題

> ### Have you ever had a nightmare?
> 你做過惡夢嗎？

反射

Sometimes.
有時候。

Not really.
算不上。

回答

Once in a while, I might have an unpleasant dream or a nightmare, but it doesn't happen very often.

我偶爾會做些討厭的惡夢，但不是經常發生。

▶▶▶ 發生頻率

I don't remember the last time I had a nightmare. It must've been a long time ago, when I was little.

我不記得上次做惡夢是什麼時候了。一定是很久以前，當我還小的時候。

▶▶▶ 提供細節

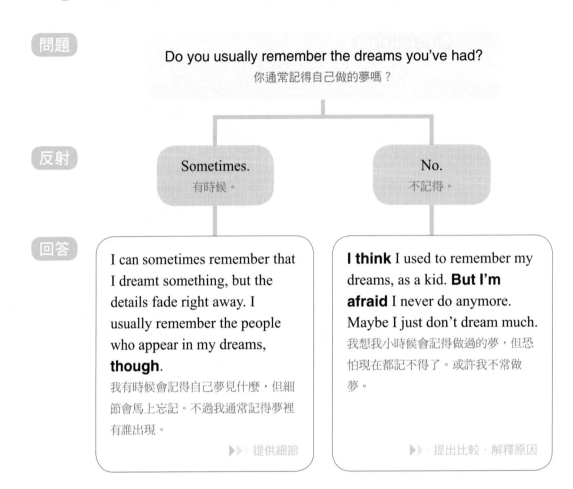

Question 2

問題

Do you usually remember the dreams you've had?

你通常記得自己做的夢嗎？

反射

> Sometimes.
> 有時候。

> No.
> 不記得。

回答

I can sometimes remember that I dreamt something, but the details fade right away. I usually remember the people who appear in my dreams, **though**.

我有時候會記得自己夢見什麼，但細節會馬上忘記。不過我通常記得夢裡有誰出現。

▶▶ 提供細節

I think I used to remember my dreams, as a kid. **But I'm afraid** I never do anymore. Maybe I just don't dream much.

我想我小時候會記得做過的夢，但恐怕現在都記不得了。或許我不常做夢。

▶▶ 提出比較 · 解釋原因

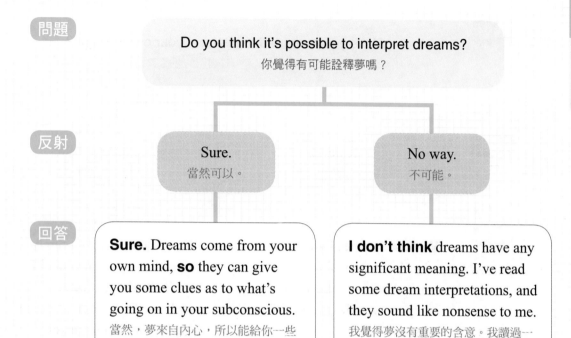

Question 3

問題

Do you think it's possible to interpret dreams?
你覺得有可能詮釋夢嗎？

反射

Sure.
當然可以。

No way.
不可能。

回答

Sure. Dreams come from your own mind, **so** they can give you some clues as to what's going on in your subconscious.
當然，夢來自內心，所以能給你一些線索，了解你的潛意識。

▶▶▶ 解釋原因

I don't think dreams have any significant meaning. I've read some dream interpretations, and they sound like nonsense to me.
我覺得夢沒有重要的含意。我讀過一些夢的詮釋，在我看來都很無稽。

▶▶▶ 解釋原因

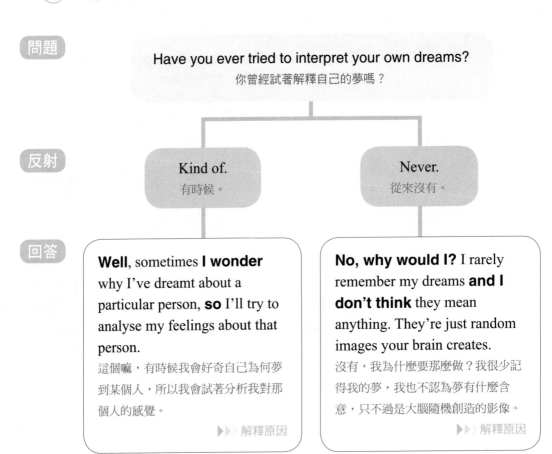

Question 4

問題

Have you ever tried to interpret your own dreams?
你曾經試著解釋自己的夢嗎？

反射

Kind of.
有時候。

Never.
從來沒有。

回答

Well, sometimes **I wonder** why I've dreamt about a particular person, **so** I'll try to analyse my feelings about that person.
這個嘛，有時候我會好奇自己為何夢到某個人，所以我會試著分析我對那個人的感覺。

▶▶▶ 解釋原因

No, why would I? I rarely remember my dreams **and I don't think** they mean anything. They're just random images your brain creates.
沒有，我為什麼要那麼做？我很少記得我的夢，我也不認為夢有什麼含意，只不過是大腦隨機創造的影像。

▶▶▶ 解釋原因

Part 2
考試技巧大揭密

小演說的結構

雖然是口試，但其實 Part 2 小演說的結構跟寫作文一樣，必須有開場白 (introduction)、本文 (body) 跟結尾 (conclusion) 才算完整。

√ **1. 開場白** 約 2～5 句。開頭第一句一定要提到主題，或解釋為何選擇描述某個人 / 某件事。這點非常重要，考生必須讓考官清楚知道你有看懂題目。若你覺得這個主題很難，也可以藉此給考官打預防針，讓他知道你會盡力描述。

√ **2. 本文** 約 10～20 句。需要有層次、有組織地回答題目問到的人、事、物，但不一定要按照題卡上提示問題的順序，也不一定要回答所有提示問題。考生可以把提示問題當成構思的參考，只要整體內容組織完整、凝聚力佳，少回答一個提示問題是不會被扣分的。

√ **3. 結尾** 約 2～5 句。簡單做出結語，讓考官知道你的小演說即將結束。

應答技巧攻略

用心智圖規畫小演說

只要一張紙跟一枝筆,把腦中的想法寫下來,演說時就能知道哪裡是起點,要往哪個方向走。如果沒有把想講的東西寫下來,腦袋裡的想法就會像吹出的泡泡一樣四處飄,不容易安排順序,最終更可能隨時煙消雲散。

在畫心智圖的過程中,你會發現宛如不小心打開記憶的盒子,挖出某些對你來說很特別的人事物。例如想起一張很久沒看到的照片,或想起一個小時候的朋友,當下回憶就會湧上心頭,因此讓小演說的內容更個人化、更吸引人。

我們以下面的題卡來示範如何畫心智圖。

問題

> Describe a gift you've received.
>
> You should say:
> > what the gift was
> > who gave it to you
> > when you received it
> and explain how you felt when you received it.

描述一個你收過的禮物。
你要提到:
> 是什麼禮物
> 誰送你的
> 你什麼時候收到的
並說明你收到禮物時的感受。

1. 第一圈泡泡　看到 gift 這個字，腦袋可能會閃過很多東西——手機、皮夾、巧克力、機票，什麼都可以。我們以「手錶」為例，來為「手錶」編出一個故事，故事可以是真實的，也可以是虛構的，或是真假參半，重點是你選擇講的物品必須要讓你有很多話可以描述。

先在白紙中央畫個泡泡寫下 **a watch**，然後以這個泡泡為中心，往四周畫出數個泡泡，這時就可以參考題卡上的提示問題，寫下跟這支手錶有關的關鍵詞彙：**birthday present**、**my best friends**、**a Seiko watch** 跟 **wear every day**（這些心智圖中的詞彙不用在意文法或拼字錯誤）。

所以 **a watch** 外面現在有了第一圈泡泡。

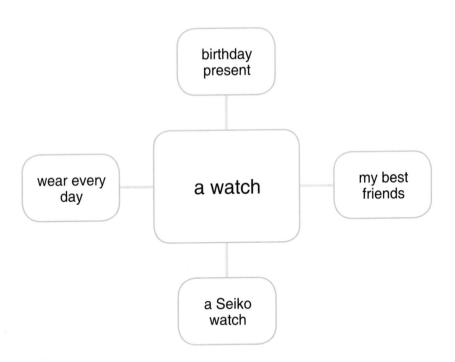

2. 第二圈泡泡　第一圈泡泡完成後，接著便可繼續往外延伸，在第一圈泡泡的四組詞彙，分別往外延伸出更多泡泡，寫入更多細節。每個泡泡只講一件事，盡量不要寫超過三個字，這些事可以是真實的，也可以是虛構的。不過要特別注意，細節不能過於偏離主題，例如有幾個朋友來幫你慶生、他們叫什麼名字、在哪間餐廳慶生等都不是重點，重點是手錶這個禮物，可以多講一些手錶的外表跟功能等。

第二圈泡泡完成後便是長這樣。

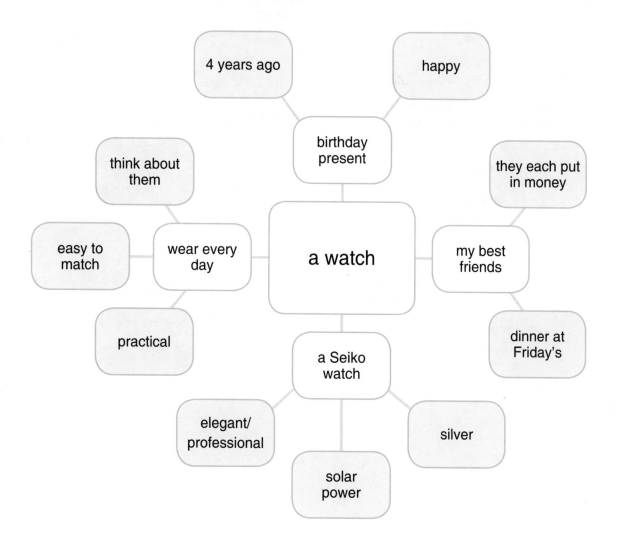

3. 標上號碼　接著將心智圖標上號碼。這個步驟是為了要確保演說時連貫順暢。不需要在每個泡泡上都標上號碼，只要在第一圈泡泡上標上號碼即可。練習時可以多嘗試幾種不同的編號順序。

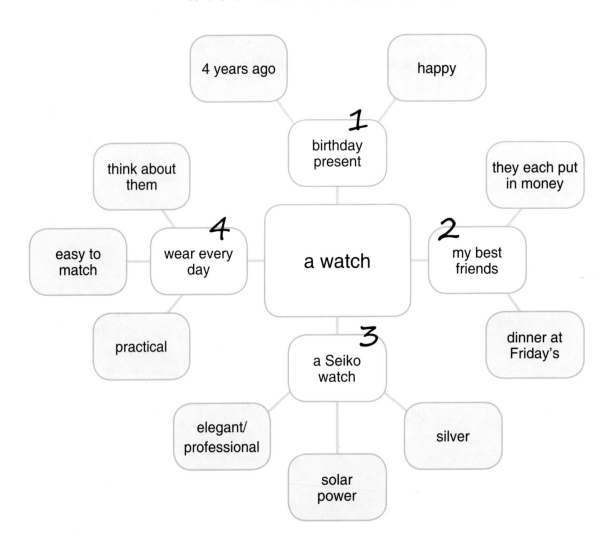

4. 開始演說　標上編號後，便可開始準備演說。在開始演說之前，可以快速在腦中排練一下你的指標詞（開場白 I'm going to talk about...、各個泡泡之間的連接詞 because/so 等）。指標詞等固定說法務必在考試前就已經熟練，考生可參考本書「**附錄 2**」(p. 275) 整理的各種指標詞。

要把心智圖中的單字、詞組變成句子，一開始並不容易。考生可以從本書提供的範例中看到很多實用的句子，挑出自己喜歡也背得起來的句子，試著換成自己想講的內容，這會是最好的起步作法。

小叮嚀

下面的範例是一個比較簡短的答案示範。本節後半收錄的答題範例，每個題目都會提供一短、一長的例答。短的答案難度較低，長的答案難度較高。

根據標示的號碼依序往下講，你可以將筆尖或手指放在正講到的泡泡上，該泡泡的主題講完時，才知道下一步要往哪一個泡泡進行。

以下提供上一頁心智圖的回答範例，其中標示的數字便是心智圖上的編號。小演說的架構也會融入前面介紹過的開場白 (introduction) ＋本文 (body) ＋結尾 (conclusion) 的概念。

Introduction

I'm going to talk about a gift I received. 1 2 About four years ago on my birthday, my best friends and I celebrated at Friday's. **After** we ate dinner and some birthday cake, one of them took a box out of her bag.

我要談談我收到的一份禮物。大約四年前的生日，我最好的幾個朋友和我在星期五餐廳慶祝。我們吃完晚餐和蛋糕後，其中一個朋友從袋子裡拿出一個盒子。

Body

3 It was a beautiful black gift box with 'Seiko' written on it! I knew it was a watch right away, and I was so happy! It wasn't a cheap watch, so my friends had each put in some money to get it for me. It's silver and looks very elegant and professional. It's solar powered so I never need to worry about changing the battery, **as long as** I wear it often. 4 I've been wearing it almost every day because it's easy to match with my clothing.

那是個漂亮的黑色禮物盒，上面寫著「SEIKO」！我馬上知道那是支手錶，我好高興！那不是便宜的錶，所以我的朋友合資出錢才能買給我。那是支銀色的錶，看來非常高雅專業，它是太陽能手錶，所以只要常戴，就不用擔心換電池的問題。我幾乎每天都戴，因為它很好搭衣服。

Conclusion 4 I think my watch is one of the best presents I've ever got because it's practical and whenever I wear it, I think about my friends. Some of them have since moved to different cities, so it's nice to look at my watch and think of them.

我想這支錶是我收過最好的禮物，因為它很實用，而且我只要戴著它就會想到我的朋友。他們有些後來搬到別的城市，所以看著我的錶想念他們，是很美好的事。

Part 2 應試小提醒

1. 練習計時

在練習時可以先不計時，但隨著考試時間接近，畫心智圖的步驟一定要在一分鐘內完成。多多練習，畫心智圖的速度一定可以加快，甚至可以將一張紙畫滿泡泡。

演說時間也要控制在一分半到兩分鐘之間。因為考官不見得會讓你看手錶，所以平時就要熟悉不看手錶也大概知道一分半到兩分鐘是多久。

2. 練習畫泡泡

心智圖要畫到什麼程度可能每個人會有所差異，以一分鐘的準備時間來說，考生也不太可能畫太多泡泡，但也不能少到只有兩三個泡泡。

第一圈可以畫出3～4個泡泡當主要的話題，每個泡泡可以再各自延伸出2～3個泡泡，一個小演說可能需要15～20個泡泡左右。

畫出來的泡泡如果太多會顯得雜亂，也沒辦法在時間內講完，但如果泡泡太少，也很難撐到兩分鐘。考生平時要多多練習畫泡泡的節奏及數量，練習一段時間後，應該就可以找到一個畫心智圖的節奏感。

3. 練習練習再練習！

要把泡泡內的單字或詞組變成一個完整的英文句子，有些考生可能會覺得很困難，所以剛開始練習時，可以先將句子寫下來，但照稿子唸會讓演說聽起來僵硬死板，只能當成過渡時期的作法。考前一定要練習到只看心智圖的詞彙，就能講出一句完整英文句子的熟練度。

練習時，可以幻想自己是 TED 的講者，拿著一張小紙片，站起來走來走去，邊走邊講，順便用手勢來輔助整體的流暢度。

4. 一梗多用之變化形

有些「梗」可以「借」給其他題目使用，以豐富演說內容。例如，若題目為 Describe someone who is special or means a lot to you（描述一個對你很特別或很重要的人），上述手錶那題的點子，就可以融入這題作為答案的一部分——除了描述這個人的個性和外表、你們認識的經過、為何他／她對你很特別，最後還可提到對方曾送你一支手錶。

同理，若題目為 Describe your favourite city（描述你最喜愛的城市），若你想講 Tokyo（東京），手錶的點子也可以融入。你可以說你喜歡 Tokyo 是因為有很多好東西可以買，你曾在那裡買到一支你非常喜愛的手錶。

考生在準備時，可多活用這種一梗多用的技巧，以節省準備不同主題的時間。

Part 2 口說高分練習題

五大常考主題　常考主題 1：Interests and Activities 興趣及活動

Question 1：電視節目

Question 2：特殊事件（例如：節日）

Question 3：想擁有的技能

Question 4：未來的目標

Question 5：保持健康的方法

常考主題 2：Objects 物件

Question 1：一件美勞作品

Question 2：一輛想購買的車

Question 3：一件買了卻鮮少使用的物品

Question 4：一件小時候的玩具

Question 5：一件經常穿戴的衣物

常考主題 3：Past Experiences 過去經歷

Question 1：一個工作經驗

Question 2：一場有趣的演講

Question 3：一場會議

Question 4：一件感到驕傲的事

Question 5：一場衝突

常考主題 4：People 人物

Question 1：一位你認識的長輩

Question 2：一位你想見的名人

Question 3：一種優秀的人格特質

Question 4：一位聰明人士

Question 5：一位歷史人物

Question 1：一個你最喜歡的地方

Question 2：一個歷史古蹟

Question 3：一間你想居住的房子

Question 4：一間你喜歡的餐廳

Question 5：一個你想造訪的國家

練習方法　考生平常就要利用這五大常考主題收集資料、擴充字彙，做造句練習（方法請見 p. 260「IELTS 雅思口說　準備期增分祕技：**筆記學習法**」），再開始下面的練習，以達到最好的效果。

接下來，我們要實際運用前面學過的技巧。建議考生讀完題卡之後，先不要看範例，練習運用前面介紹過的心智圖應答攻略，實際拿出紙筆並計時一分鐘，畫出心智圖，構想順序及開場白、各段連接方法，然後計時兩分鐘作答。最後再參考答案範例。

Part 2 的每一個口說練習題都提供了短、長兩種不同長度的答題範例，短答 (Short Answer) 難度較低，適合英文程度中下或說話語速較慢的考生，長答 (Long Answer) 難度較高，適合英文程度中上或說話語速較快的考生。考生可以觀察範例如何使用心智圖發展出一篇小演說，並參考範例中指標詞（粗體字部分）的使用方式，試著運用到自己的小演說中。

Question 1

Describe a television programme that you watch.

You should say:
>   what kind of television programme it is
>   what usually happens in the television programme
>   why you enjoy watching the television programme
> and explain whether or not you would recommend the
> television programme to others.

描述一個你有在收看的電視節目。

你要提到：

>   那是什麼樣的電視節目

>   該節目的內容主要是什麼

>   你為何喜歡收看這個節目

並說明你是否會推薦這個節目給其他人。

這算是最常考的主題之一了，平時最好就準備好一個電視節目備戰。若真的沒有喜歡的電視節目，可以先跟考官表明 I don't watch television much.（我不常看電視。）然後挑個 YouTube 頻道（有很多有名的 YouTuber）或其他 vlogger（影音部落客）來描述。

一些相關點子

- Discovery 探索頻道
- Nat Geo 國家地理頻道
- Food Network 美食頻道
- variety show 綜藝節目
- singing competition 歌唱比賽
- Korean/Japanese drama 韓劇／日劇

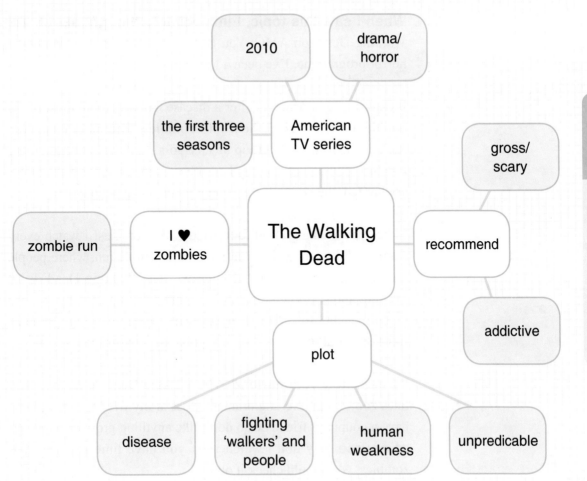

The Walking Dead

- 2010
- drama/horror
- American TV series
- the first three seasons
- I ♥ zombies
- zombie run
- recommend
  - gross/scary
  - addictive
- plot
  - disease
  - fighting 'walkers' and people
  - human weakness
  - unpredicable

When I saw this topic, I immediately thought about 'The Walking Dead' on AMC. You could say it's both a drama and a horror programme. I've been a loyal fan since 2010.

It takes place in America after a disease has wiped out most of the population and turned them into zombies. The main character, Rick, is the leader of a group of survivors. They have to fight some zombies and search for food or other supplies. **Since** resources are limited, they often have to fight other living people **too**.

I like 'The Walking Dead' **because** I like zombies! I watch every zombie film I can, and I even joined the zombie run, where people dressed like zombies and chased us! 'The Walking Dead' is an exciting show. Some episodes are more exciting than others, but that's like real life. **Another reason I like** this programme **is because** it **also** shows people's weaknesses in different situations.

I'd definitely recommend 'The Walking Dead' to anyone who likes zombies or exciting dramas. Most of my friends love it, but I have a couple of friends who don't like anything gross or scary, **so of course** they don't watch it. If you have time and you like zombies, you should check it out.

當我看到這個主題，我馬上想到 AMC 的《陰屍路》。它可說是劇情片兼恐怖片，自二〇一〇年開始，我就一直是忠實的粉絲。

故事發生在美國，一種疾病帶走多數人的性命，將他們變成殭屍。主角瑞克是一群倖存者的領袖，他們得對抗殭屍，尋找食物或其他補給品。因為資源有限，他們也常得和其他倖存者對抗。

我喜歡《陰屍路》，因為我喜歡殭屍！每部殭屍片我都會看，甚至參加殭屍路跑，活動中會有人打扮成殭屍來追你！《陰屍路》是很刺激的影集，有幾集會特別精彩刺激，就跟真實人生一樣。我喜歡這部影集的另一個理由，是因為它也呈現出人在不同情況下的種種弱點。

我絕對會向喜歡殭屍或刺激戲劇的人推薦《陰屍路》。我的朋友大都很喜歡，但有幾個朋友不喜歡噁心或嚇人的東西，所以他們當然不看。如果你有時間，也喜歡殭屍，你應該看看。

Vocabulary

loyal fan 忠實粉絲
wipe out 摧毀，消滅
zombie (n.) 僵屍
supplies (n.) 補給品
episode (n.) （影集）一集

When I saw this topic, I immediately thought about 'The Walking Dead' on AMC. It has zombies in it, **so I guess** it would be classified in the horror genre. **But** it's definitely **also** a drama. I've been a loyal fan since the show first debuted in 2010. The first three seasons were especially good. I've been binge-watching them again in my free time.

I like the show **because** I like anything zombie-related! I watch pretty much every zombie film I can, and I even joined the zombie run, where people dressed up like zombies and chased us! Watching zombie movies and shows makes me grateful to live in this relatively peaceful world where we don't have to deal with such things.

Anyway, in 'The Walking Dead', the main character, Rick, is the leader of a group of survivors after a new disease causes a zombie apocalypse. **Actually**, they're usually called 'walkers' instead of 'zombies', but it's the same idea. Each episode is different, but they usually have to search for food or other supplies and fight some walkers in the process. **Since** resources are scarce, they often have to fight other groups, **too**. A lot of the people who are left are really nasty and violent.

I find the show really interesting. Some episodes are more exciting than others, **but to me**, that's realistic, and it keeps it unpredictable. This programme really explores people's weaknesses in different situations. **I find it** fascinating to see how people's principles can change when their survival is at stake.

I'd definitely recommend 'The Walking Dead' to anyone who likes this type of thing. Most of my friends love it, but I have a couple of friends who don't like anything gross or scary, **so of course** they don't watch it. It's a bit addictive, but if you have the time, you should check it out.

Part 2

Interests and Activities

Vocabulary

genre (n.) 類型，風格
debut (v./n.) 首演
binge-watch (v.)
（影集）一集接著一集看
apocalypse (n.) 大災難
關 apocalyptic (adj.)
　預示大災難的
scarce (adj.) 稀少的
nasty (adj.) 卑鄙的
at stake 在危急關頭
addictive (adj.) 上癮的

當我看到這個主題，馬上想到 AMC 的《陰屍路》。劇裡有殭屍，所以我想會被分類為恐怖片，但它絕對也是部劇情片。從二〇一〇年影集首映後，我就一直是忠實粉絲。前三季尤其好看，我有空時就會一集接一集再看一次。

我喜歡這部影集，因為我喜歡所有和殭屍有關的東西！幾乎每部殭屍片我都會去看，甚至還參加過殭屍路跑，活動中會有打扮成殭屍的人追著你跑！看殭屍電影和影集讓我慶幸可以活在相對安寧的世界，不用去面對這些事。

《陰屍路》的主角叫瑞克，是一種新疾病引發殭屍災難後，一群倖存者的領袖。事實上，影集裡一般不稱他們為殭屍，而稱為「行屍」，不過是一樣的概念就是了。每集的劇情都不同，但他們通常都得尋找食物或其他補給品，同時對抗一些行屍。因為資源短缺，他們也常得對抗其他群體。倖存者當中有許多人都相當卑鄙且殘暴。

我覺得這部影集很有趣，其中有幾集特別刺激，但我覺得那是很實際的做法，如此才能保持懸疑。這部影集確實暴露出人在不同情況下的弱點，看到人會因為生存危急而改變自己的原則實在挺有趣的。

我絕對會向愛好此道的人推薦《陰屍路》。我大部分的朋友也都喜歡，但有幾個朋友不喜歡噁心或嚇人的東西，所以他們當然不看。這部片如果一開始看就有點難停下來，但如果有時間，你應該看看。

一梗多用之變化形

- a hobby of yours
- a novel you've read
- a sports event you've participated in
- a film you've watched and want to watch again

Question 2

Describe a special event (e.g. a festival, carnival or other celebration).

You should say:
   when the event takes place
   why it takes place
   what people do
and explain why the event is special.

描述一個特殊事件（例如：節日、嘉年華或其他慶祝活動）。

你要提到：
   這個活動舉辦的時間
   為什麼會舉辦這個活動
   人們會做些什麼事
並解釋為什麼這個活動很特別。

回答這類有關節慶的題目需要具備相關背景知識與單字，若沒有事先準備，臨時發想很難撐到兩分鐘。考生在考前一定要收集一兩個傳統節日或特殊慶祝活動的資料。

一些相關點子
- Moon Festival 中秋節
- Lantern Festival 元宵節
- Ghost Festival 中元節
- Dragon Boat Festival 端午節
- Taiwan LGBT Pride Parade 台灣同志遊行

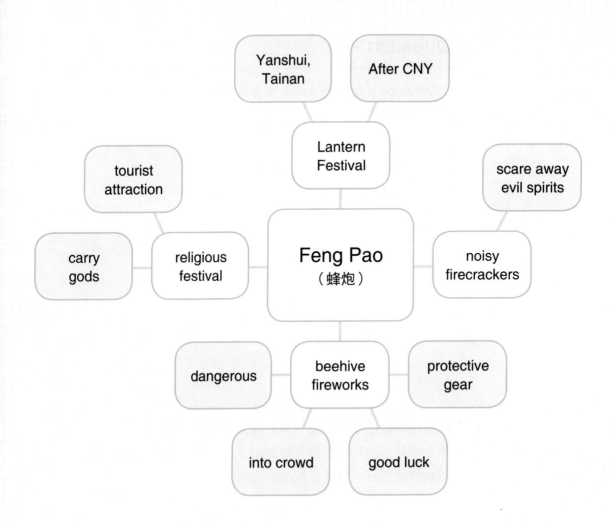

This is a great question for me because I just saw a programme about the Yanshui Feng Pao Festival. 'Feng Pao' means 'beehive fireworks' in English, and the festival takes place every year during Lantern Festival, which is right after Chinese New Year. It happens in Yanshui, a small town in the southern part of Taiwan.

Many of my friends have gone to Feng Pao, but I've only seen it on TV. I'm too scared to actually go! If you go, you'll see people walk through the streets carrying figures of different gods and beehives. They're not real beehives, **though**. They're made of little bottle rockets that go off in every direction all at once—**not just** into the sky, **but also** into the crowds! There are also big walls full of fireworks that they shoot into crowds. People believe getting hit with these fireworks is good luck. **Of course**, they have to wear thick clothes and helmets for protection. **Besides** being good luck, the noisy firecrackers are supposed to scare away evil spirits and call on the gods for help. **So**, it's a religious festival, or at least it started that way. **Now** it's become a big tourist attraction!

It's really crazy and dangerous. People get injured every year, but they still think it's fun and exciting! It's quite a popular festival.

這對我來說是個好問題，因為我剛看了有關鹽水蜂炮慶典的節目！蜂炮用英文說就是像蜂巢般的煙火，在每年的元宵節舉辦，就在中國新年之後沒多久。舉辦地點在鹽水，是位於台灣南部的一個小鎮。

我有很多朋友都去看過蜂炮，但我只在電視上看過。我太害怕了根本不敢真的去！如果去了，會看到人們扛著各種神像和蜂巢炮台穿過街道，那不是真的蜂巢，而是由爆破時會四處亂竄的小鞭炮組成，不只衝向天空，也會射向人群！還有許多面裝滿鞭炮的巨牆，會朝群眾發射。人們相信被這些鞭炮打中會帶來好運，當然，他們必須穿上厚厚的衣服、戴上安全帽做為保護。除了祈求好運外，吵鬧的鞭炮聲被認為能嚇走惡靈，還能祈求神祇前來幫助。所以這是個宗教節慶，至少最開始是那樣。現在則已成為盛大的觀光盛事。

這個活動真的很瘋狂又危險，每年都有人受傷，但大家仍認為這個活動有趣又刺激！這是個相當受歡迎的節慶。

Vocabulary

beehive (n.) 蜂巢
fireworks (n.) 煙火
go off 爆炸
firecracker (n.) 鞭炮
evil spirit 惡靈

Part 2

Interests and Activities

This is a great question for me because I just saw a programme about the Yanshui Feng Pao Festival. It's held every year during Lantern Festival, which is right after Chinese New Year, usually in February. It happens in the small town of Yanshui, in Tainan County, and it has made that town famous.

To be honest, I've never experienced Feng Pao first-hand, but I've seen it on TV and many of my friends have been there. Throughout the evening, people shoot off fireworks. **But** it's not like a New Year's fireworks display. There are strings of firecrackers along the road and walls of little rockets in various places that shoot into the crowd. People parade through the streets with figures of different gods and beehives of fireworks. The beehives are contraptions that shoot off rockets in every direction all at once. It's like a warzone! People don't mind getting hit with the fireworks—**in fact**, that's why they go. They believe it brings them good luck! **Of course**, they wear protective gear such as thick clothes and scooter helmets. You **also** have to put a towel around your neck to make sure no bottle rockets go up into your helmet.

Don't quote me on this, but I believe it started **because** there was a cholera outbreak in the south. To scare away the evil spirits that people believed caused the disease, they lit all the firecrackers they could find. **I guess** the cholera problem went away, **so** they keep doing it every year to make sure it doesn't come back.

Feng Pao is a unique religious event, **and now** it's a popular tourist attraction. **But I'm sure** most foreigners and even a lot of us Taiwanese people think it's bizarre. **I don't think** any other country has a festival where people actually expect and want to get hit with fireworks. **I'm sure** if you're an adrenaline junkie, it would be really fun and exciting, but it's not for me!

這對我來說是個好問題，因為我剛看了有關鹽水蜂炮慶典的節目！蜂炮每年在元宵節舉辦，就在中國新年之後不久，通常是在二月。舉辦地點在台南的一個小鎮——鹽水，蜂炮讓這裡聲名大噪。

老實說，我從未親身體驗過蜂炮，但我在電視上看過，也有很多朋友去過。一整晚大家都在放鞭炮，但不是像新年的煙火表演。馬路上沿路有成串的鞭炮，到處還有小鞭炮築成的牆，朝群眾發射。人們扛著各種神像和蜂巢炮台在街上遊行，那種蜂巢炮台是可以讓鞭炮同時向四面八方發射的奇妙裝置。現場就像戰區！人們不在乎是否被鞭炮打到，事實上，他們就是為此而來。他們相信這樣能帶來好運！當然，他們穿戴了保護裝備，例如厚厚的衣服和機車安全帽。除此之外，一定要在脖子圍上毛巾，避免有鞭炮鑽進安全帽裡。

我的話或許不足採信，但我相信這活動起源於南部的霍亂爆發，為了嚇走被認為是引發疾病的惡魔，人們點燃所有能找到的鞭炮。我想霍亂問題解決了，所以他們每年都繼續這麼做，確保疾病不會再發生。

蜂炮是獨特的宗教活動，現在也是個人氣觀光盛事。但我確信多數外國人，甚至很多台灣人認為它很匪夷所思。我認為其他國家不會有參與者期待被鞭炮擊中的節慶活動。如果你是個愛冒險的人，我確信這個活動對你來說一定是非常好玩且刺激，但我可不喜歡！

一梗多用之變化形

- an unforgettable trip
- a noisy place you've been to
- a tourist spot in your country
- an interesting tradition

Question 3

Describe a skill that you'd like to have.

You should say:
      what the skill is
      how you can get the skill
      what you can do with the skill
and explain why you'd like to have this skill.

描述一個你想擁有的技能。

你要提到：

      是什麼技能

      要如何習得這個技能

      有了這個技能你可以做什麼

並解釋你為什麼會想擁有這個技能。

一些相關點子

- public speaking 公開演講
- writing 寫作
- photography 攝影
- time management 時間管理
- critical thinking 批判性思考
- foreign language 外語
- playing a musical instrument 彈奏樂器
- cooking 作菜
- wine tasting 品酒
- coding/programming 編碼、寫程式
- social skills 社交

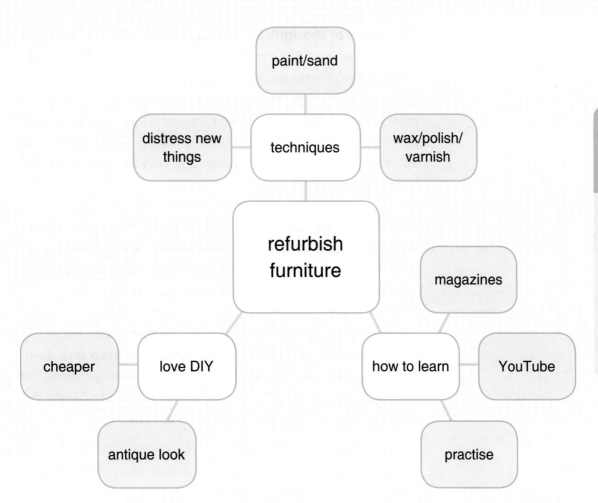

After a bit of thought, I'd say the skill I'd like to learn next is how to refurbish furniture. **Basically**, I want to be able to make cheap pieces of furniture look like antiques. If the furniture is new, you can make it look old by hitting and scratching it. **Then** you paint it, sand it and wax it. If the furniture is old, you can improve how it looks by sanding it and polishing it. There are lots of different techniques to learn depending on what sort of finished look you're going for.

I know a little bit about how to do these things **because** I recently watched a couple of YouTube videos about it. **But** I haven't really learnt the skill yet as I haven't tried it myself. I have a desk I might practise on, but I need to buy some tools and supplies first.

I want to learn how to refurbish furniture **because** I really like the antique look, but I can't afford antiques! I **also** love do-it-yourself projects of any kind. It's really satisfying to make or improve something with your own hands. I'd like to fill my flat with beautiful furniture that I worked on myself.

在簡短的思考後,我想我接下來想學習的技能是如何翻修家具。基本上,我想讓便宜的家具看起來像古董。如果家具是新的,能藉由敲打刮傷使其顯舊,然後上漆、磨光、上蠟。如果家具是舊的,你可以磨光擦亮以改善其外觀。根據你想要的成品外觀,有很多種不同的技術可以學習。

我知道其中一些技巧,因為我最近看了兩三個相關的 YouTube 影片。但我還沒真正學會這項技巧,因為我還沒親自嘗試。我有個可以用來練習的桌子,但我需要先買些工具和零件。

我想學習翻修家具的技巧,因為我真的很喜歡古色古香的風格,但我買不起古董!我也喜歡親自動手做各種東西,能用雙手製作或改善東西,真的很讓人滿足。我很想在公寓放滿自己做的美麗家具。

Vocabulary

refurbish (v.) 翻修,整修
antique (n.) 古董
sand (v.) 用沙紙磨
polish (v.) 磨亮

Long Answer

After a bit of thought, I'd say the skill I'd like to learn next is how to refurbish furniture. I already do a lot of DIY projects. I watch videos on YouTube and make things, like recently, I made a jewellery stand and a lantern. I'm a bit clumsy, but my stuff usually turns out okay if I find a good tutorial.

Recently, I've been watching videos about ways to give wooden furniture a vintage, antique look. If the furniture is new, there are various ways to distress it. **For example**, you could buy a cheap bookshelf from IKEA, **then** make dents and scratches and holes in the wood. **Then** you paint it a little, and sand off most of the paint. I know it sounds weird but that's what they do to make it look old! **Then** you finish it with varnish or wax. **Another option is** to get used wooden furniture at a second-hand shop and fix it up. Sometimes, you can find good-quality vintage items that just need to be sanded down, stained, and re-varnished.

I know how to do these things in theory **because** I recently watched a couple of videos about it. **Also**, I've read 'how to' articles in interior decorating magazines and on blogs. **But** the best way to learn a hands-on skill like this is to practise, and I haven't done that yet. I have a desk I could experiment on, **but first**, I'll need to find a good place to work, and I'll have to buy some supplies and tools.

I suppose the reason I want to learn about refurbishing furniture **is because** I love the idea of turning something ordinary or even discarded into something beautiful and special. I'm actually thinking about redecorating my flat, and I'd like to go for an elegant, old-fashioned style. Developing this skill would allow me to have furniture with that vintage look without having to break the bank on buying real antiques.

Vocabulary

clumsy (adj.) 笨拙的
tutorial (n.)（書籍、影片
等）教學教材
vintage (adj.) 古老的
distress (v.) 使看起來老舊
varnish (n.) 亮光漆
in theory 理論上
hands-on (adj.)
親自動手的
discard (v.) 丟棄
break the bank 傾家蕩產

在簡短的思考後，我想我接下來想學習的技能是如何翻修家具。我有許多 DIY 作品，我會看 YouTube 的影片，並製作一點東西，例如最近我做了珠寶架和一個提燈。我有點笨手笨腳，但如果找到好的教學材料，我做出來的東西通常都還不錯。

最近我看了些影片，內容是為木製家具增添古樸質感。如果家具是新的，有許多方式可以讓它變舊，例如你可以從 IKEA 買便宜的書架，然後在木頭上製造凹陷、刮痕和坑洞，再上點漆，再磨掉大部分的漆。我知道這聽來很怪，但要讓東西變舊就是要這麼做！最後再上亮光漆或打蠟。或者你也可以從二手店找用過的木製家具進行修繕。有時候你能找到高品質的古董，只需要打磨、著色和拋光即可。

我知道做這些事的理論，因為最近看了幾部相關的影片。同時，我也看了室內裝潢的雜誌以及部落格中「如何做」的文章。但學習這類手作技巧最棒的方式是透過練習，但我還沒開始做。我有一張可以試驗的桌子，但首先我得找到好的工作地點，也還得買些零件和工具。

我想要學習翻修家具技巧的理由，是因為我喜歡將平凡、甚至是被丟棄的物品變成美麗且特別的東西。事實上，我正想重新裝潢我的公寓，希望有高雅、老式的風格。習得這項技巧可以讓我擁有古色古香的家具，又不用傾家蕩產去購買真正的古董。

一梗多用之變化形

- an artist
- an old thing your family keeps
- something you did that was a success
- a project you did with someone

Question 4

> Describe a goal you would like to achieve in the future.
>
> You should say:
>   what the goal is
>   when you hope to achieve it
>   what you need to do to reach your goal
> and explain why this goal is important to you.

描述一個你希望在未來可以達到的目標。

你要提到：

　　　那是什麼樣的目標

　　　你希望在什麼時候達成

　　　要達成這個目標你需要做什麼

並解釋為什麼這個目標對你很重要。

目標可以是具體或抽象的（如下面的例子）。選定目標後，想想有哪些具體步驟可以增加執行力。

具體目標
- pass an exam　通過考試
- lose 5 kilograms　減重五公斤
- quit smoking　戒菸
- cut down on Facebooking　減少使用臉書
- find a rich husband/wife　找個有錢的老公 / 老婆

抽象目標
- to be more positive　更正面
- to be a nicer person　當個更好的人
- to step out of my comfort zone　走出舒適圈

Okay, this is not really a specific goal, but I have a strong desire to expand my mind and broaden my horizons. My friends seem happy shopping at the same shops, watching the same shows and talking about the same things all the time. **But** I want to know and experience so much more.

One way to do this is to learn as much as possible. I want to read more and watch more documentaries about different topics, especially social issues. I need to find people to discuss these things with. I'd **also** like to take some courses in my free time **like** public-speaking, wine-tasting **or** art appreciation. **Maybe** I'll go to museums more often.

But actually, I think the best way to expand my worldview is through adventure and experience. I want to travel and even live abroad. I want to meet lots of people and make new friends. I want to be brave and try new things, **even if** they scare me. That's how you grow!

This is a long-term goal. I'll probably be working on it my whole life. I just want to live my life to the fullest **so that** I don't have any regrets when I'm old.

好的,這其實不是個明確的目標,但我有強烈的欲望,想擴展我的心靈和視野。我的朋友似乎都滿足於一直在同一些商店購物、看同樣的節目、談同樣的話題。但我想了解、想體驗更多更多。

其中一個方式是盡量學習。我想多方閱讀、收看更多不同主題的紀錄片,特別是有關社會議題的。我需要找到可以談論這些主題的人。我也想在空閒時間去上一些課程,例如公開演講、品酒或藝術欣賞。或許我會更常去博物館。

但事實上,我認為擴展世界觀最好的方式,是透過冒險和體驗。我想要旅遊,甚至住在國外,我想要遇見很多人,交新朋友。我想要勇敢,嘗試新事物,即使很嚇人也要嘗試,因為這樣人才會成長!

這是個長期目標,或許我這輩子都會為此努力。我只想讓我的人生更充實,這樣我老了以後才不會有任何遺憾。

Vocabulary

documentary (n.) 紀錄片
course (n.) 課程
worldview (n.) 世界觀
regret (n./v.) 後悔

Long Answer **I'm going to try to describe** a goal of mine that's very important to me but a bit hard to explain. It's not really something specific I hope to achieve; it's more like a way I want to live. **I guess** you could say my goal is to expand my worldview. I want to be more cultured and broad-minded.

I've been feeling like my world is too small. My friends seem happy doing the same things all the time. They're content to spend their free time shopping or watching Korean dramas. There's nothing wrong with that, but it's not enough for me.

I want to learn more about the world. I want to be the type of person who can talk intelligently about important social issues. Sometimes, I do read about these things, but I've got no one to discuss them with. I want to watch more documentaries, but I've got no one to watch them with. **I think** I should visit museums and take some courses, **like** public-speaking, wine-tasting **or** maybe art appreciation.

But that's not enough. I really believe that the best way to learn and grow is to step out of your comfort zone and experience new things. I feel I need a new environment, and I want to meet new people from all different backgrounds. **Of course**, one way to do that is to travel abroad, but I'll have to save money first. **In the meantime**, I'll look for ways to challenge myself and make new friends where I am.

I don't have a time-limit for achieving this goal—**I think** it's going to be a lifelong journey. **I think** I just have to remember to be brave and take advantage of every interesting opportunity I can. If I'm still in the same place, doing the same things and having the same conversations when I'm sixty, I'm going to have some serious regrets. I don't want to feel as though I've wasted my life.

Vocabulary

cultured (adj.) 有知識的
broad-minded (adj.) 心胸開闊的
關 open-minded (adj.) 思想開放的
反 narrow-minded (adj.) 心胸狹窄的
closed-minded (adj.) 思想保守的
comfort zone 舒適圈
in the meantime 同時
關 meanwhile (adv.) 同時
lifelong (adj.) 終身的
take advantage of 利用

我要試著描述一個對我來說十分重要的目標，但有點難解釋。我想達成的並非是某種具體的目標，而比較像是一種我想要的生活方式。我想你可以說我的目標是擴展世界觀。我想要更有知識，心胸更開闊。

我一直覺得我的世界太小了。我的朋友似乎都很開心可以一直做一樣的事，也滿足於將空閒時間花在購物或看韓劇上。這沒什麼不對，但對我來說是不足夠的。

我想多了解這個世界，我想成為可以有智慧地談論重要社會議題的人。有時候我會讀這些東西，但沒有人可以談論。我想多看紀錄片，但找不到人一起看。我想我應該要去博物館，並且上一些課程，例如公開演講、品酒或藝術欣賞。

但那樣還不夠。我真心相信學習和成長最好的方式是走出舒適圈，體驗新事物。我覺得我需要一個新環境，也想認識來自各種背景的新朋友。當然，其中一種方式是到國外旅遊，但我得先存錢。同時，我會想辦法在我身處的環境中挑戰自我、結交新朋友。

我沒有為這個目標設下時限，我想這會是一輩子的旅程。我想我得要記得鼓起勇氣，把握每個有趣的機會。如果我六十歲時，還在同一個地方，做同樣的事，說同樣的對話，我會非常後悔。我不想要感覺浪費了自己的人生。

一梗多用之變化形

- a language you'd like to learn
- a course you'd like to take
- someone you admire
- a skill that you'd like to have
- an area of science that you're interested in (such as physics or biology)

Question 5

Describe an activity you do to keep fit.

You should say:
     what you do
     when you do it
     how often you do it
and explain why you like to do this activity.

描述你為了保持健康而做的一項活動。
你要提到：
     是什麼活動
     什麼時候做
     多久做一次
並解釋你為什麼喜歡做這個活動。

並非每個人都喜歡運動，或把健康當成第一優先事項。若是沒有運動健身的習慣，可以說說你會想開始做什麼來達到健康的目的。

一些相關點子

- go to the gym 去健身房
- play football/badminton 踢足球 / 打羽球
- do yoga 做瑜珈

這題也可以從「你不做的事」「有害健康的事」的角度來作答。例如：

- I avoid junk food. 我不吃垃圾食物。
- I don't stay up late. 我不熬夜。
- I don't smoke/drink. 我不抽菸 / 喝酒。
- I don't sit all day. 我不會整天坐著。

not much meat

no beer

fruit & veg

no fast food

no fizzy drinks

stay fit

a little is better than nothing

walk

be consistent

overall

stay active

ride my bike

use common sense

join a gym

watch exercise videos

If it's okay, I'll talk about more than one thing I do to keep fit **because** one thing isn't enough. You have to eat well and also do some exercise.

In terms of my diet, **the main thing I do** to stay healthy is to eat lots of fruit and vegetables. **Well**, some days I eat more than on other days, but I try! I eat meat, but not with every meal. I drink wine sometimes, but I don't drink beer **because** I'm scared of getting a 'beer belly'! **Let's see, what else ... oh,** I **also** avoid sugary things **like** fizzy drinks, and I almost never eat at fast food restaurants. Their food is terrible for you.

I'm not much of an athlete, but I try to stay active. I walk or ride my bike almost every day. **A couple of times a week**, I exercise at home, following an exercise video. I'd like to join a gym, but gym memberships are very expensive in Taiwan.

All in all, **I'd say the most important thing is** to make healthy choices every day. You don't have to completely stop eating the things you like, and you don't have to train for a marathon. Just use common sense.

如果可以，為保持健康所做的事，我會說的不只一件，因為一件事不夠，你必須有良好的飲食，同時也要做運動。

說到我的飲食，我最主要的保健之道就是吃很多蔬果。某些日子我會吃的比平時多些，但我會盡量控制！我吃肉，但不是每餐都吃。有時會喝葡萄酒，但我不喝啤酒，因為我怕會有「啤酒肚」！我想想還有什麼……喔，我也會避免含糖的東西，例如汽水，還有我幾乎不吃速食餐廳的東西，那些食物對身體很不好。

我算不上運動員，但我會努力維持運動。我幾乎每天都會走路或騎腳踏車，每週會在家跟著健身影片運動兩三次。我想加入健身房，但台灣的健身房會員非常昂貴。

總而言之，我認為最重要的是每天都要做出健康的選擇。你不必完全不吃你喜歡的食物，也不用接受馬拉松訓練。只要善用常識即可。

Vocabulary

fizzy drink (BrE) 汽水
（美式英語為 soda）
athlete (n.) 運動員
marathon (n.) 馬拉松賽跑
common sense 常識

048

I was glad to get this topic because it's something that's been on my mind more and more as I've got older. **But if it's okay, I'll talk about** more than one thing I do to keep fit and healthy, **because** one thing isn't enough. **Both** exercise and a healthy diet are important.

When it comes to my diet, I make sure to eat fruit or vegetables with every meal. I'm not a vegetarian, but I rarely eat red meat. **I think** fish and chicken are healthier than pork and beef. I often have a glass of wine in the evening, but I try not to drink too much, and I avoid beer **because** it has a lot of calories. Recently, I've been trying to cut down on sugar, **too.** I don't put it in my coffee anymore, and I never have fizzy drinks. **Oh,** and I almost never go to fast food restaurants **like** McDonald's. **But in general**, I'm not very strict with myself. I do indulge in unhealthy treats sometimes. I just try to keep it to a minimum.

I don't consider myself to be athletic, but I'm pretty active. I don't have a car or scooter, **so** any time I want to go somewhere, I **either** take public transportation, which includes some walking, **or** I ride my bike. I'd like to work out or take an exercise class at a gym, but the membership fees are outrageous. **So**, if I'm looking for something different to do, I'll find a fun exercise video online.

Overall, I'd say the most important thing is to be consistent and develop good habits. You don't have to completely stop eating the things you like, and you don't have to be a total exercise freak. Everything in moderation, **as they say**. Making small changes in your diet or exercising a little more will make a difference in the long run if you keep at it.

Part 2
Interests and Activities

Vocabulary

indulge in 放縱，享樂
keep it to a minimum
保持在最低限度
outrageous (adj.)
離譜的，令人吃驚的
consistent (adj.)
堅持的，始終如一的
freak (n., slang) 怪咖
everything in moderation
凡事當有度
in the long run
從長遠來看
keep at it 堅持下去

我很高興拿到這個主題，因為當我年紀愈大，關於這件事就想得愈多。但如果可以的話，為保持健康所做的事，我會說的不只一件，因為一件事不夠，運動和健康的飲食這兩件事都很重要。

關於我的飲食，我會確保每餐都吃蔬菜水果，我不是素食主義者，但我很少吃紅肉，我認為魚肉和雞肉比豬肉和牛肉健康。我晚上經常會喝一杯葡萄酒，但我盡量不喝太多，也避免喝啤酒，因為它的熱量很高。最近，我也試著減少糖份攝取，我的咖啡已經不再加糖，也都不喝汽水。喔，還有我幾乎不去麥當勞那種速食店。但整體來說，我對自己不是非常嚴格，我偶爾會縱容自己吃不健康的甜食，但有努力減到最少。

我算不上運動員，但我經常運動。我沒有汽車或機車，所以只要想去某個地方，我不是搭大眾運輸，順便走點路，就是騎腳踏車。我想去健身房運動或上健身課程，但會員費高得離譜。所以如果要找不同的健身運動，我會上網找有趣的健身影片。

總的來說，我會說最重要的事情，是堅持和培養好習慣。你不必完全不吃喜歡的東西，也不必發狂似地做運動，就像俗話說的，凡事要有度。在飲食做點小小的改變，或增加一些運動量，只要堅持下去，一段時間下來就會有所改變。

一梗多用之變化形

- a hobby
- an athlete
- a method that helps you save money
- a sport you enjoy doing
- an outdoor activity you like to do
- a long walk you enjoyed

Question 1

Describe a piece of art you made as a child.

You should say:
    what you made
    how you made it
    what you did with it
and explain how you felt about this artwork.

描述你小時候做過的一件美勞作品。

你要提到：
    它是什麼
    你怎麼做的
    你拿它來做什麼
並說明你對這件作品的感覺。

一些相關點子

- birthday card 生日卡
- paper carnation 紙康乃馨
- ice lolly stick house 冰棒屋
- mask 面具
- watercolour painting 水彩
- origami 摺紙

I've never been much of an artist. I just don't have the talent **or** the passion for it. **But** every Taiwanese child has made a lantern for Lantern Festival, **so** I'm going to describe one I remember making with my dad when I was about 11 years old.

You need a large tin can, **so** I got a baby formula tin from our neighbour. My grandfather lent me his hammer and nails. He found a piece of wire for me, **too. First**, I drew a dragon on the tin with a marker. **Next**, my dad helped me use a hammer and a nail to make holes along the lines of my design. **Then** he helped me set up the candle in the middle at the bottom. We used melted wax to make it stick. **Finally**, we attached a wire handle.

It may seem simple, but it was actually a lot of work. It hurt my fingers and gave me blisters. **But even though** it was hard, I really enjoyed the project. **In the end**, we went outside to light the candle in the dark. It didn't really look like a dragon—it was more like a snake. We all had a good laugh about it.

我從來都不是個藝術家，既沒有天份也沒有熱情。但每個台灣小孩在元宵節都會做燈籠，所以我要描述印象中十一歲時和我爸一起做燈籠的事。

你需要一個大錫罐，所以我從鄰居那裡拿了個嬰兒奶粉罐。我爺爺把他的鎚子和釘子借給我，還幫我找了條電線。首先，我用麥克筆在錫罐上畫了條龍；接著，我爸幫忙沿著我設計的圖，用鎚子和釘子敲出洞來；然後再幫我把蠟燭放到底部中央，我們用融化的蠟固定蠟燭。最後，我們裝上電線提把。

看來簡單，但其實很費功夫。完工時，我的手指痛死了，還長了幾個水泡。雖然過程很艱辛，但我們都玩得滿愉快的。最後，我們走到室外，在黑暗中點亮蠟燭。看起來其實不像龍，比較像條蛇，我們都大笑不止。

Part 2

Objects

Vocabulary

tin can 錫罐
baby formula 嬰兒奶粉
wire (n.) 電線
blister (n.) 水泡

Long Answer

For Lantern Festival, which is right after Chinese New Year, it's the tradition to make lanterns. I've made several paper lanterns, **but I'm going to describe** one I made with a tin can.

I think it was when I was in year five, and I made it with my dad. You need a tin, some wire, a hammer, a nail and a candle. We rummaged through my grandfather's tool shed to find a hammer, a nail and wire. I got a large baby formula tin from my neighbour, and my mother gave me a candle.

The idea is to make a design by poking holes into the can, **and then** when light shines through the holes, the design can be seen. **So, first,** I drew a dragon on the can with a marker **because** it was the year of the dragon. **Then,** my father helped me hammer in the nail to make holes along the lines I had drawn. **But** every time we hammered in the nail, we dented the can! **By the time** we were done, the can was deformed. We hammered out the bigger dents, but it wasn't very smooth. **Anyway, then** my dad dripped some hot wax onto the bottom of the can, and I stuck the bottom of the candle to it. I held it in place until the wax dried. **Finally,** we attached the wire to the top of the tin to make a handle. It seems like a simple project, but it was actually a lot of work. I had blisters on my fingers to show for it!

In the end, we took the lantern outside to light the candle in the dark. My design didn't really look like a dragon at all—it was more like a snake! We had a good laugh, but I still thought it was quite lovely, the way the candle light flickered through the holes. **As they say**, 'Beauty is in the eye of the beholder!'

Vocabulary

rummage (v.) 翻找
shed (n.) 小屋，棚
dent (v.) 使凹陷
deformed (adj.) 變形的
flicker (v.) 閃爍

在中國新年後緊接登場的元宵節，有做燈籠的傳統。我做過幾次紙燈籠，但我要說的是我用錫罐做的燈籠。

我想那是在我五年級的時候，和我爸一起做的。你需要一個錫罐、一些電線、一把鎚子、一根釘子和一根蠟燭。我們翻遍爺爺的工具房，找出鎚子、釘子和電線，我從鄰居那裡要到一個大的嬰兒奶粉罐，而我媽給了我一根蠟燭。

我想在罐子上戳洞設計出圖案，所以當亮光從洞裡照出來，圖案就會顯現出來。所以我一開始用麥克筆在罐子上畫了條龍，因為那年是龍年。然後父親幫我用釘子沿著我畫的線敲出一個個的洞。但我們每次敲釘子，都會把罐子敲凹！等我們做完的時候，罐子已經變形。我們把比較大的凹陷敲平，但不是非常平整。接著，我爸在罐子底部滴了一些熱蠟，我再把蠟燭底部固定上去，我一直扶著蠟燭直到蠟變乾。最後，我們把電線固定在罐子上方當作提把。看來是個簡單的任務，但其實很費功夫。我的手指還因此長了好幾個水泡！

最後我們把燈籠拿到室外，在黑暗中點亮蠟燭。我的設計看來其實一點也不像龍，比較像蛇！我們都笑到不行，但我還是認為蠟燭光透過那些洞閃爍的樣子很美。這就是所謂的「情人眼裡出西施」吧！

Part 2

Objects

一梗多用之變化形

- your favourite photograph
- an indoor activity you did in your childhood
- your hobby

Question 2

Describe a car or other motor vehicle you want to buy in the future.

You should say:
    what kind of vehicle it is
    what it would look like
    how you would pay for it
and explain why you would like to own this means of transport.

描述你未來會想買的汽車或其他機動車。

你要提到：
        它是哪種車
        它的外表
        你要如何付錢
並解釋你為什麼想要擁有這種交通工具。

如果想講汽車可能需要車輛領域相關字彙，除非是車迷，不然不太好講。為求保險，選擇單字相對簡單的機車來講可能比較容易。

一些相關點子

- hoverboard 漂浮滑板
- self-balancing electric scooter 電動平衡車
- motorcycle 摩托車 / Harley-Davidson 哈雷
- scooter 速克達機車 / electric scooter 電動機車 / Gogoro Gogoro 電動機車
- saloon 房車；轎車
- SUV (sport utility vehicle) 休旅車
- RV (recreational vehicle) 露營車
- sports car 跑車
- supercar 超跑
- convertible 敞篷車

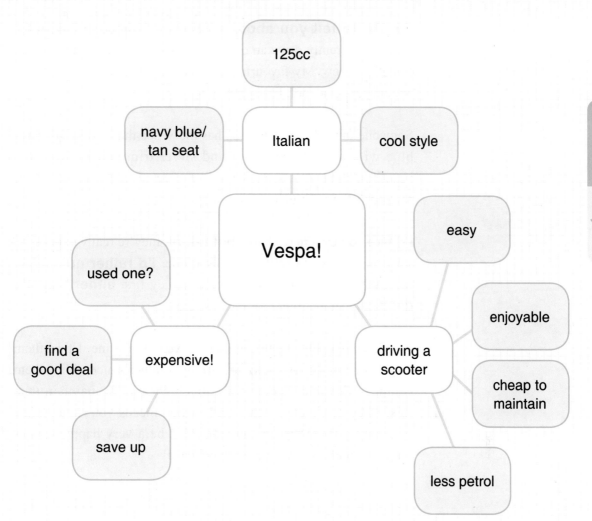

I'd like to tell you about a Vespa that I hope to buy in the future. I currently drive an old Kymco scooter, but I'd love to buy something new. My favourite scooters are Vespas. They're Italian, and they have a cool, European style.

Someone in my neighbourhood has the Vespa that I want. It's navy blue with a tan leather seat and silver trim and mirrors. It's beautiful, and I'm so jealous! I'd like to get at least a 125cc engine **so that** it's powerful and fast.

I'd like to buy a new Vespa, **but I think** they're really expensive, **so** I might have to settle for a used one. **I'd rather not** go into debt, **so** I'll have to save up some money first **either way**. **I'd definitely** shop around for the best deal.

A scooter is really the best choice of vehicle for me. I find them easy to ride in the city, **and**, **when** the weather's nice, riding them is quite enjoyable. Scooters are much cheaper to maintain than cars. They don't use much petrol, which means you save money and don't pollute the air too much. I'd be a very happy scooter driver if I had a shiny blue Vespa to drive!

我想談一談我未來想買的偉士牌機車。我目前騎的是一台老舊的光陽機車,但我很想買新車。我最喜歡的機車是偉士牌,那是義大利品牌,很酷、很有歐洲的風格。

我鄰居就有我想要的偉士牌機車。海軍藍的車身,配上棕褐色的皮革座墊以及銀色鑲邊和後照鏡。看起來很漂亮,我好嫉妒!我想買至少 125cc 引擎的車,這樣才夠力夠快。

Vocabulary

scooter (n.) 機車
settle for 勉強接受
deal (n.)(交易)價格
maintain (v.) 維修,保養
petrol (n., BrE) 汽油(美式英語為 gasoline/gas)

我想買新的偉士牌,但我覺得真的很貴,所以我可能必須退而求其次接受二手車。我不想負債,所以我想總之我得先存點錢,而且我一定會四處比價,找到最划算的價格。

對我來說,機車真的是最好的選擇,因為在市區騎乘容易,而且天氣好的時候騎車很舒服。機車的保養比汽車便宜,用的汽油也不多,這表示可以省錢,而且不會太汙染空氣。如果有台閃亮的藍色偉士牌機車,我會是個非常開心的機車騎士!

Long Answer

When I saw this topic, I initially thought of a sports car or a luxury vehicle like a Jaguar. **But** I would never actually buy one **because** I'm not a millionaire! A more realistic dream vehicle for me is a Vespa.

Like many people in Taiwan, I drive a scooter. It's just an old Kymco, nothing special. It gets me where I need to go, but I'd love to upgrade someday. The nicest scooters I've seen are Vespas. They're Italian and very well made. I love their cool retro style.

Someone in my neighbourhood has a shiny new Vespa that I've been drooling over. It's navy blue with a tan leather seat and silver trim. It's gorgeous. I'm willing to consider other colours, but that's the one I'm dreaming of. I'd love to get a 125cc or bigger engine, **so that** it's powerful and fast.

I'm not sure how much a Vespa costs, but they're not cheap—at least a hundred grand. **So, I'd definitely** shop around and wait for the best deal. **For example**, when the new models come out, the previous year's models will probably go on sale. I don't feel the need to own the latest model. **I wouldn't mind** buying a used one **as long as** it was still in very good condition. **Either way**, I'll probably have to save up for a long time before I can afford one.

A scooter is really the best choice of vehicle for me. They don't use much petrol, which means you save money and don't pollute the air too much. There are scooter shops everywhere, and scooters are much cheaper to maintain than cars. You spend less time sitting in traffic **because** you can go around the cars and buses. I find driving a scooter to be easy **and**, **when** the weather's nice, very enjoyable. It would be even more enjoyable if I had a shiny blue Vespa to drive!

Vocabulary

upgrade (v./n.) 升級
retro (adj.) 復古的
drool over 垂涎
gorgeous (adj.)
極好的；極美的
grand (n., slang) 一千
（通常用在表示金額）
come out 上市

119

當我看到這個主題，一開始想到跑車或像捷豹那類的豪華轎車。但我絕不可能真的買一台，因為我不是個百萬富翁！對我來說，比較實際的夢想交通工具是偉士牌機車。

就像台灣的許多人，我也騎機車，不過只是一台舊光陽機車，沒什麼特別的。它能載我去我要去的地方，但我希望有天能升級。我看過最好的機車是偉士牌，那是義大利品牌，做工精細，我喜歡它們酷炫的復古風格。

我鄰居有人擁有一台閃亮的新偉士牌機車，讓我大流口水。海軍藍車身配上棕色皮革座墊和銀邊，美極了。如果是其他顏色我也可以接受，但那就是我夢寐以求的車了。我想買 125cc 或更大的引擎，這樣才夠有力且夠快。

我不確定一台偉士牌機車要多少錢，但它們不便宜，至少要十萬（美）元。所以我一定會四處比價，等待最划算的價格。舉例來說，當新款上市時，前一年的款式或許會特價。我覺得沒必要買最新款式，我不介意買二手車，只要車況良好。不管怎樣，我或許得存很久的錢才買得起一台。

對我來說，機車真的是最好的選擇，耗油量不高，這表示可以省錢，而且不會太汙染空氣。到處都有機車店，而且機車的保養比汽車便宜多了。另外，困在車陣裡的時間比較少，因為你可以在汽車和公車間穿梭。我覺得騎機車很容易，而且當天氣好的時候，是件非常享受的事。如果有台閃亮的藍色偉士牌機車，那就更享受了！

一梗多用之變化形

- a gift you received
- something expensive or valuable that you bought
- a piece of equipment (besides a computer) which you often use at home or work

Question 3

Describe something you bought but seldom use.

You should say:
> what it was
> where you bought it
> how much it cost

and explain why you seldom use it.

描述一件你買了但鮮少使用的物品。

你要提到：
> 它是什麼
> 你在哪裡買的
> 花了你多少錢

並解釋為什麼你很少使用它。

一些相關點子
- folding bike 小折腳踏車
- hula hoop 呼啦圈
- juicer 果汁機
- fountain pen 鋼筆
- suitcase 行李箱
- cosmetic 化妝品

Last year, it was my New Year's resolution to lose weight. I used to enjoy going to a spinning class, but I wasn't a member of that gym anymore. **Instead of** joining again, **I thought** it might be a good idea to buy my own exercise bike.

I went to a big sporting equipment store—just to look—and saw an exercise bike I liked. I didn't have enough money, but the store offered a payment plan, and the salesman convinced me to buy it right away. He said, 'the sooner you get it, the sooner you'll get in shape'!

At first, I used it at least a couple of times a week. **But later**, I got busy, **and I guess** I lost interest. Cycling in my living room wasn't nearly as fun as cycling in a spinning class.

Now, it's where I hang my clothes at the end of the day. Sometimes, I forget it's there until I get a bill from that sports equipment shop. It's almost paid off now, but what a waste! I haven't decided if I'm going to sell it or not. **After all**, I still want to lose weight!

去年，我的新年願望是減重。我以前喜歡去上飛輪課，但我已經不是那家健身房的會員了。我想與其再次加入會員，倒不如去買台自己的運動腳踏車。

我去一家大型運動用品店，只是去逛逛，看到一台我喜歡的運動腳踏車。我的錢不夠，但店家提供付款方案，業務員說服我立刻買下它。他說：「愈快買，愈快塑身！」

一開始我每週至少使用兩次，但後來變忙了，而且我應該是失去興趣了。在客廳騎車實在遠不如在飛輪教室騎車有趣。

現在，那裡最終成了我掛衣服的地方。我有時根本忘了它的存在，只有在收到運動用品店的帳單時才想起來。那筆帳現在快付完了，真是浪費錢！我還沒決定要不要賣了它，畢竟，我還是想減重！

Part 2

Objects

Vocabulary

New Year's resolution
新年願望
spinning/spin class
飛輪課
at the end of the day
到最後
pay off 付清

Last year, it was my New Year's resolution to get in shape. I enjoyed the spinning class I used to go to at the gym, **so I thought** about doing something like that. My gym membership had long since expired **so I thought,** 'Why not invest the money in an exercise bike?' **After all**, a bike would cost less than a year's membership at the gym, and it could last for a decade!

I went to a big sporting equipment store, tried out the exercise bikes, and found one I liked. I had planned to return once I had enough money. **However**, the salesman was very persuasive and convinced me that I shouldn't procrastinate about getting fit. He said he could put me on an instalment plan and give me a discount if I didn't wait.

When my exercise bike was delivered the next day, I was really excited to get started. I tried out a few of its many different settings, trying to remember what we had done in spinning class. I kept going for about fifteen minutes. **Then** I got bored and tired.

In the first month that I had the exercise bike, I probably used it every other day. Sometimes, I tried to go fast, but usually, I just cycled on a low setting while watching TV. **In the second month**, I barely used it at all. I just lost my motivation **for some reason**. It's a lot easier when you're in a class and the instructor is yelling and everyone is doing it with you!

Now, it's just an expensive coat rack—**I mean**, it's where I throw my clothes at the end of the day. I generally ignore it, but **whenever** I get a bill from that sports equipment shop, I feel terrible. What a waste! I should really sell it to try to get some of my money back, but I keep thinking I'm going to get motivated and start using it again.

Vocabulary

get in shape 塑身
expire (v.) 到期
procrastinate (v.) 拖延
instalment (n.) 分期付款
every other day 每隔一天
motivation (n.) 動機
關 motivated (adj.) 有動機的
　　motivate (v.) 刺激

去年，我的新年願望是塑身。我以前去健身房時喜歡上飛輪課，所以我想做類似的運動。我的健身房會員早就過期了，所以我想，「為何不投資買台健身腳踏車？」畢竟，一台腳踏車的費用比一年健身房會員費低，而且它可以用十年！

我去了一家大型運動用品店，試用了幾台健身腳踏車後，找到一台我喜歡的。我打算等我有足夠的錢再回來，但是業務員非常會說話，說服我健身不能拖延。他說他可以讓我分期付款，如果馬上買的話還可以給我折扣。

隔天健身腳踏車一送到，我就迫不及待開始運動。我試了許多不同的設定，試著記起在飛輪課做過的練習，我持續了大概十五分鐘，然後就覺得無聊又好累。

剛買健身腳踏車的第一個月，我大概每隔一天就會使用，有時候會騎快一點，但通常只是在看電視時用低速騎車。第二個月，我就幾乎沒碰過它了。不知為何，我就失去了動機。當你在教室裡，有教練在吶喊，大家也一起練習時，騎車容易多了！

現在它只是一台昂貴的衣帽架，意思是，那裡最終成了我掛衣服的地方。我基本上無視於它的存在，但每當收到運動用品店寄來的帳單，我就感覺很糟糕，真是浪費！我應該賣掉它，試著拿回一些錢，但我一直想振作起來再開始使用它。

一梗多用之變化形

- an advertisement
- something expensive or valuable that you bought
- something that broke down in your house
- a new activity you did recently

Question 4

Describe a toy you had when you were a child.

You should say:
      what the toy was
      who bought it for you
      how you played with it
and explain how you felt about this toy.

描述你小時候的一樣玩具。
你要提到：
      是什麼玩具
      誰買給你的
      你怎麼玩這個玩具
並說明你對這個玩具的感覺。

一些相關點子

- stuffed animal 填充動物玩偶
- Barbie 芭比娃娃
- Power Rangers 金鋼戰士
- dollhouse 娃娃屋
- Nintendo video game console 任天堂遊戲機
- PlayStation/Game Boy 遊戲機
- handheld digital pet 電子寵物（雞）

multi-coloured

plastic bricks

small blocks

LEGO

best friend

grandparents

role-play — ways to play

toy shop — parents

stories

me

creative

buildings

monsters

cars

One kind of toy I played with a lot during my childhood was Lego blocks. They're small multi-coloured plastic bricks that you can make just about anything out of.

I had a pretty large collection. Sometimes, I bought small Lego sets, **like** car sets, with my own money. Sometimes, I got Lego for my birthday from my parents. **One time**, my grandparents bought me a cool Lego castle.

I usually played with my Lego **either** by myself **or** with my best friend from school. We would spend a couple of hours building a whole town **and then** role-playing with the little Lego people. We made up some crazy stories for them. I still remember some of the names we gave to the figures. **Now that I think about** it, it's just really funny!

I guess the reason I liked them so much **is that** you can do so many things with them. You can follow the instructions, or you can design your own building or monster or vehicle or whatever. You never have to make the same thing or play in the same way. **I guess** that's why I continued to play with Lego throughout my childhood, **even after** I lost interest in my other toys.

我童年很常玩的其中一個玩具是樂高積木。那是彩色的塑膠小方塊,幾乎什麼都能拼出來。

我收藏了很多。有時候我會用我自己的錢買汽車之類的小樂高組。有時候爸媽會送我樂高當生日禮物,有一次爺爺奶奶買了一組很酷的樂高城堡給我。

我通常自己玩樂高,或是和學校的好朋友一起玩。我們會花幾個小時打造一整個城鎮,然後用小樂高人偶玩角色扮演。我們還為他們編些瘋狂的故事。我還記得一些我們幫小人偶取的名字。現在想起來,真的好好笑!

我想我這麼喜歡樂高的理由,是因為你可以用它們做出許多東西。你可以依照說明書組合,也可以設計自己的大樓、怪獸、汽車什麼的,你不必做出同樣的東西,或用同樣的方式玩。我想這就是我童年一直都在玩樂高的原因,即使我已經對其他的玩具都失去興趣了。

Vocabulary

block (n.) 方塊
role-play (v.) 角色扮演
figure (n.) 人物,塑像
關 action figure/figurine
  公仔,小塑像
  figurine (n.) 小塑像
instructions (n.) 說明(書)

Long Answer

Well, the toys I played with the most when I was a kid were definitely my Lego blocks. **I'm sure** you know what they are **because** children all over the world have played with them for decades. They're small multi-coloured plastic bricks that snap together, **so** you can make just about anything out of them.

Over the years, I amassed quite a large Lego collection. I was always eying the big playsets I saw in toy stores—I remember seeing a restaurant that came with little Lego pizzas. Sometimes, I spent my pocket money on Lego, but I only ever managed to save enough for a small set, **like** a car **or** something. My parents often gave me Lego for my birthday or as a reward for doing well in school. **One time**, my grandparents bought me a Lego castle. I was thrilled!

The great thing about Lego **is that** you can follow the instructions to put together a set or you can just be totally free and creative and design your own building or monster or vehicle or whatever. I usually played with my Lego **either** by myself **or** with my best friend from school, who was just as obsessed with Lego as I was. We would get so absorbed in the process that we didn't even notice until later that our hands were getting sore from digging through my bin of blocks, pulling old structures apart, and putting new ones together. We could easily amuse ourselves for a couple of hours building a whole town **and then** role-playing with the little Lego people.

Because they're so versatile, they're the only toy I continued to play with throughout my childhood, **even after** I had outgrown some of my other toys. I still keep them around for when my younger cousins come to visit. **To tell you the truth**, I still get some enjoyment out of helping them make things and watching their excitement.

Vocabulary

snap (v.) 喀地一聲合上
amass (v.) 收集
eye (v.) 注視，打量
pocket money (BrE) 零用錢
（美式英語為 allowance）
thrilled (adj.) 興奮的
be obsessed with 著迷
absorbed (adj.) 全神貫注的
versatile (adj.) 萬用的；多功能的
outgrow (v.) 長大而不再適用
關 outlast (v.) 比⋯活得長
outlive (v.) 比⋯活得長
outdo (v.) 勝過

我小時候最常玩的玩具絕對是我的樂高積木。我相信你一定知道那是什麼，因為數十年來，全世界的兒童都在玩。那是彩色的塑膠小方塊，可以組合在一起，拼出任何你想做的東西。

多年來，我收藏了很多樂高，到玩具店時我總是會看大型的玩具組合，我記得看過有小型樂高披薩的餐廳。有時候我會用零用錢買樂高，但只夠買小型組合，像是車子之類的。我爸媽常在我生日時送我樂高，或是當作學校表現優良的獎勵。有一次，我爺爺奶奶買給我一組樂高城堡，我樂壞了！

樂高最棒的一點，是你可以依照說明書組合，也可以完全自由創作，設計你自己的大樓、怪獸、汽車等等。我通常自己玩樂高，或是和學校的好朋友一起玩，他們也跟我一樣瘋樂高。我們會全神貫注於過程中，甚至沒注意到我們的手因為在積木箱裡翻找、拆散舊結構、組成新結構而酸痛。我們可以樂在其中好幾個小時，打造一整個城鎮，然後用小樂高人偶玩角色扮演。

因為樂高如此萬能，所以成為唯一能讓我整個童年都在玩的玩具，甚至在我已經長大不再對其他一些玩具有興趣之後。我現有還保留著積木，這樣我的堂弟表妹來訪時就可以玩。說實話，幫他們組樂高，看著他們興奮的樣子，我依然樂在其中。

一梗多用之變化形

- a gift
- an activity you did in your childhood
- an old thing your family keeps

Question 5

Describe a piece of clothing that you often wear.

You should say:
        what the item of clothing is
        where and when you bought it
        when you wear it
and explain why you like wearing it.

描述一件你經常穿戴的衣物。

你要提到：

        它是哪種衣物

        你在何時何地買的

        你什麼時候會穿

並解釋你為什麼喜歡穿。

字典裡對於 clothing 的定義通常是 clothes（衣服），但其實 clothing 可以包含配件，例如 tie（領帶）或 high heels（高跟鞋）。

但若題目問的是 **clothes**，那就只能講衣服類，例如 jersey（球衣）、T-shirt（T恤）、hoodie（帽T）、jeans（牛仔褲）等。

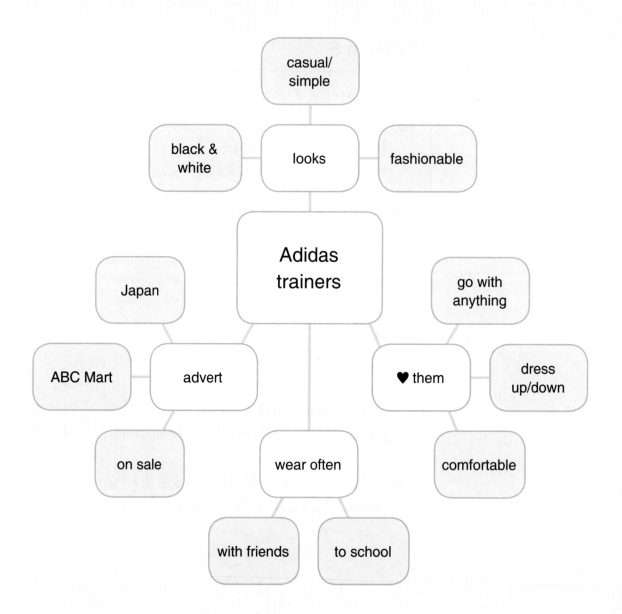

This is an easy question for me to answer because there's something I wear almost all the time—my Adidas Superstar Originals trainers. They're casual, simple shoes, but they're **also** really fashionable. They come in many colours, but mine are black and white.

I **first** noticed these shoes in an advertisement. David Beckham and other celebrities were wearing them. **I thought** 'Wow, they look cool!' **I thought about** buying them online, **but of course**, they were really expensive. **A few months later**, I travelled to Japan and saw them on display in a shop called ABC Mart. **And** they were on sale for less than 3000NT! That's something like 30 percent off the regular price. Trainers like these don't often go on sale, **so** I bought them right away.

They're probably the best investment I've ever made **because** they are so comfortable and stylish. I wear them whenever I go out, if I can. Usually, I wear them with jeans, and if I add a blazer or a nice shirt, I can look quite smart. **When** I go out with my friends, they go with anything I throw on. **Now**, many of my friends are wearing them **too**. I highly recommend them to anyone!

這對我來說是很容易回答的問題,因為有樣東西我幾乎無時無刻穿在身上,我的 Adidas Superstar Originals 運動鞋。那是一雙很休閒、簡單的鞋子,但也很時尚。這款鞋有推出許多顏色,我那雙是黑白相間的。

我一開始是在廣告上注意到的,貝克漢和其他明星穿著這款鞋,我心想「哇,看來真酷!」我原本想在網路上買一雙,但想當然爾非常昂貴。幾個月後,我到日本旅遊,在一家名叫 ABC Mart 的商店看到正在展示這款鞋,特價不到三千台幣!大概是定價的七折,這類運動鞋並不常有折扣,所以我馬上就買了一雙。

這或許是我做過最好的投資,因為它們舒適又有型,只要可以,不管何時出門我都穿著這雙鞋。通常我會搭牛仔褲,如果再加件輕便外套或好看的襯衫,看來就很時髦。當我和朋友出去,隨便穿什麼都跟這雙鞋很搭。現在我有很多朋友也穿這款鞋。我真的非常推薦!

Vocabulary

trainer (n.) 運動鞋
come in 以⋯形式出現
celebrity (n.) 名人
blazer (n.) 輕便外套
smart (adj.) 時髦的
關 classy (adj.) 時髦的
polished (adj.) 優美的
sophisticated (adj.) 精緻的

Long Answer

This is an easy question for me to answer because there's something I wear almost every day. They're my Adidas Superstar Originals trainers. They're casual and simple, and mine are mostly white with black trim. I first noticed these shoes in an advertisement, and they were modelled by various celebrities, **both** male and female. The person I really remember is David Beckham, and he made them look so effortlessly cool.

I didn't really think about buying the shoes **because** I assumed they would be out of my price range. I checked online anyway, and I was right—they were nearly 4000NT! **But a few months later**, I was in Japan and I found them in an outlet store. Trainers like these don't normally go on sale, **but I guess** it was the end of the season and Japanese customers only want the newest designs. They were less than 3000NT! **I thought** it was an unbeatable price—and I actually needed a new pair of casual shoes—**so** I bought them right away.

Luckily, I'm a student, and I seldom need to dress up in formal or professional clothes, **so** I wear them pretty much all the time. I usually wear them with a T-shirt and jeans, but if I need to dress up a bit, I can add a blazer and look very smart. I really think they go with just about any outfit or occasion.

My Adidas shoes were a great investment **because** they're both fashionable and comfortable. **Even if** I do a lot of walking, they don't hurt my feet. I hardly wear any of my other shoes! **Now**, many of my friends have purchased similar Adidas trainers in various colours, **so I guess** I'm a trend-setter. They're great for girls, guys, whoever. They're a great item to have in your wardrobe, whether you've got a feminine, masculine or androgynous look. I'm going to have to start saving for a new pair for when these get worn out!

Vocabulary

effortlessly (adv.) 輕鬆地
out of one's price range
超過某人能承受的價格範圍
反 within one's price range
　在某人能承受的價格範圍內
unbeatable (adj.) 無敵的
trend-setter (n.)
引領潮流的人
wardrobe (n.) 衣櫥；（個
人的）全部衣服
feminine (adj.) 女性的
masculine (adj.) 男性的
androgynous (adj.)
中性化的

134

這對我來說是個很容易回答的問題，因為有樣東西我幾乎每天都穿，我的 Adidas Superstar Originals 運動鞋。那是一款很休閒、簡單的鞋子，我的那雙是幾乎全白帶黑色線條。我一開始是在廣告上注意到這款鞋，他們找了許多名人當模特兒，男女皆有。我記得很清楚其中一位是貝克漢，這雙鞋被他隨便一穿就很酷。

我當時沒真的想買這款鞋，因為我想應該很貴我根本買不起。我上網一查，果不其然，將近四千台幣！不過幾個月後，我去日本在一家暢貨中心看到這雙鞋，這類運動鞋通常沒有折扣，但我想當時是季末，加上日本消費者只想買最新款，所以售價不到三千！我覺得那是無敵的價格了，而且我也真的需要一雙新的休閒鞋，所以馬上買了一雙。

幸運的是，我是個學生，很少需要穿著正式或專業的衣服，所以我幾乎無時無刻穿著這雙鞋。我通常穿 T 恤和牛仔褲搭配，但如果需要打扮一下，我可以加件輕便外套，看來就很時髦。我真的認為這雙鞋可以搭配任何衣服或場合。

我的這雙 Adidas 鞋是非常好的投資，因為它們既時尚又舒適。即使我走很多路，腳也不會痛。我幾乎不穿我其他的鞋了！現在我有很多朋友也買了類似的 Adidas 運動鞋，只是顏色各不相同，所以我想我引領了潮流。這雙鞋適合女孩、男孩等所有人，是服裝搭配的絕佳單品，無論你是女性化、男性化或是中性造型都適合。我得開始存錢，等這雙穿壞了再買一雙！

一梗多用之變化形

- an advertisement
- a famous company you know
- something you bought recently
- an item of clothing bought for you

Question 1

Describe a paid job you or someone you know had.

You should say:
> what the job was
> how you/this person found the job
> how long you/this person had this job
and explain how you/this person felt about this job.

描述一個你或你認識的人曾做過的計薪工作。

你要提到：
> 那是什麼樣的工作
> 你或這個人是如何找到這份工作的
> 你或這個人做這份工作多久
並說明你或這個人對這份工作的感覺。

對於問及考生親身經歷的題目，考生如果缺乏該經歷，可以談別人的經歷。針對本題，缺乏工作經驗的考生除了可以談其他人的工作經驗，也可以講自己實習的經驗。

一些非正式的工作

- Cooperative Education System 建教合作
- school placement 實習（教育學程的一部分）
- apprentice(ship) 學徒
- summer intern(ship) 暑期實習
- research assistant 研究助理

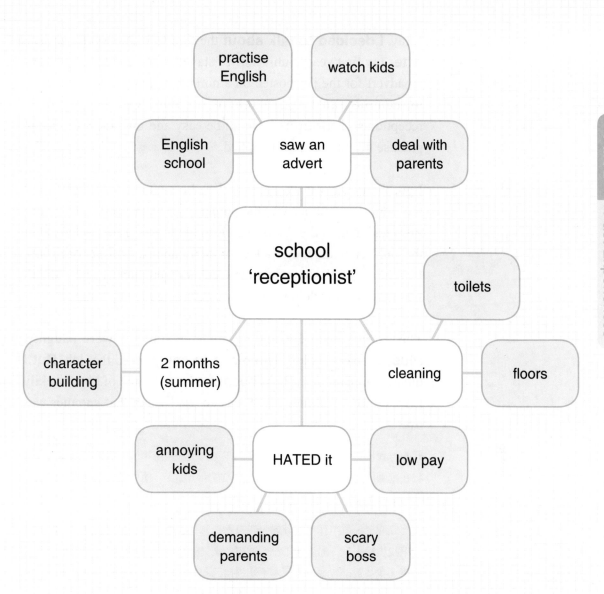

Okay. **I decided to talk about** the first full-time job I ever had. **After** my first year at university, I stayed in the city to work. I saw an advert for the job posted on a noticeboard at the student centre on campus; an English school for kids was looking for a receptionist. **I thought** it would be easy and give me a chance to practise my English, **so** I applied.

I got the job, but it wasn't easy. I had assumed I would just sit at the front desk and answer the phone. I was surprised to find out I **also** had to mop the floors and clean the toilets! I had to look after the children while they waited for their parents, **and sometimes**, I even taught classes when the teachers were sick. I really didn't know what I was doing, and they didn't give me any training!

The parents were demanding, and the students were naughty. **Plus**, the pay was low. **Needless to say**, I hated that job. **But** I didn't complain to the boss **because** I was scared of him. Luckily it was only a summer job. I was so glad when that summer was over!

好的,我決定談談我的第一份全職工作。大一學期結束後,我留在市區工作,我在校園學生中心的告示板上看到徵人廣告,那是一所兒童英語學校在徵櫃台人員。我想這工作可能很輕鬆,也有機會練習英文,就去應徵了。

我被錄取了,但工作並不輕鬆。我原本以為只要坐在櫃台接電話就好,卻意外發現我也得拖地、掃廁所!小朋友等待家長時,我得照顧他們,有時候老師生病時,我甚至得教課。我根本不知道自己在做什麼,而且他們也沒給我任何訓練!

家長的要求很高,學生又頑皮。而且,薪水很低。不用說,我討厭那份工作,但我沒有跟老闆抱怨,因為我很怕他。還好那只是一份暑假工作,暑假結束時我好高興。

Vocabulary

advert (n., BrE) 廣告
(英式英語縮寫,美式英
語的縮寫為 ad)
demanding (adj.)
要求高的
needless to say
顯然,自不待言
關 obviously (adv.) 顯然地

Long Answer

Okay, right then. I'm going to talk about the first full-time job I ever had. **After** my first year at university, my parents and I decided that I should stay in the city and work for the summer instead of going back to my small hometown, where there wasn't much for me to do. There were some adverts for summer jobs posted on a noticeboard at the student centre on campus. The one that caught my eye was for a receptionist at an English school for kids. It sounded pretty easy, **and I thought** it might give me a chance to practise my English, **so** I applied.

I had imagined I would, **you know**, greet adorable children, answer the phone, maybe do some light paperwork. **But after** I got the job, I learnt that it entailed much more than that. **Besides** being a receptionist, you could say I was a maid, babysitter, teacher and customer service representative. I had to mop the floors and scrub the toilets. I looked after the kids after class, and sometimes covered for sick teachers, which I wasn't qualified to do!

I hated it. The students were out of control and annoying. The toilets were disgusting. **But, believe it or not**, I actually preferred cleaning the toilets to dealing with the parents. They often called with questions I couldn't answer and many of them had complaints about the way the school was run. They were very demanding and some were very rude to me. I had no training whatsoever. Maybe I should have asked the boss for help, but he was really intimidating and had a bad temper. The pay was low, and nobody respected me or acknowledged my hard work. The teachers ignored me unless they needed something.

I wanted to quit after a few days, but my parents encouraged me to finish the summer. They thought it would build character or something. I was so glad when it was time to go back to university!

Vocabulary

catch one's eye
吸引某人的注意
adorable (adj.) 可愛的
entail (v.) 承擔;包含
whatsoever (adv.)
無論什麼
cover for（某人請假時）
代替某人做事
intimidating (adj.) 嚇人的
acknowledge (v.) 認可
build character 培養人格

Part 2　Past Experiences

好的,我要談談我的第一份全職工作。大一學期結束後,我爸媽和我都認為我應該留在城裡找份暑期工作,而不是回到我的家鄉小鎮,因為那裡沒什麼事可以做。校園裡的學生中心告示板上有些暑期打工廣告,其中吸引我注意的是一家兒童英語學校要招聘櫃台人員的工作。看起來很輕鬆,而且我以為我會有機會練習英文,就去應徵了。

我原本想像我的工作內容會是——迎接可愛的小朋友、接電話,或許做一點簡單的文書作業。但我被錄取後,才知道要做的事遠遠不止於此。除了當接待人員,你可以說我還是個女傭、保姆、老師和客服人員。我得拖地、刷廁所,下課後得照顧小孩,有時候還要幫生病的老師代課,而我根本沒有資格教課!

我討厭那份工作。學生不聽話又煩人,廁所很噁心,但是信不信由你,我寧願清廁所,也不要面對家長。他們經常打電話來問一些我無法回答的問題,而且很多人在抱怨學校運作的方式。他們要求很高,有些人還非常無禮。我沒接受過任何訓練,或許我該要求老闆幫忙,但他很嚇人,脾氣又差。我的薪水很低,沒人尊重我或注意到我的辛勤工作。老師除非需要什麼東西,否則根本不理我。

我做沒幾天就想辭職了,但我爸媽鼓勵我做完那個暑假,他們認為這可以培養人格什麼的。開學那天我真的好開心。

一梗多用之變化形

- a decision made by others that you disagreed with
- a small company you know
- a family member who has had an important influence on you

Question 2

> Describe an interesting speech you heard.
>
> You should say:
> > when and where it was
> > who gave the speech
> > what it was about
> and explain how you felt about this speech.

描述你曾聽過的一場有趣的演講。

你要提到:

> 在何時何地聽到
>
> 演講者是誰
>
> 演講內容是什麼

並說明你對該演講的感覺。

在準備考試期間最好大量收看英文演講,收集有趣的演講內容。
若曾聽過有趣的中文演講,也可以嘗試用英文說說看。

作者私心推薦演講

- Steve Jobs 2005 @Stanford University
  史丹佛大學畢業典禮演說
- Alanna Shaikh 2012 @TED
  我如何面對阿茲海默症的到來
- Jamie Oliver 2010 @TED
  給予孩童食品教育

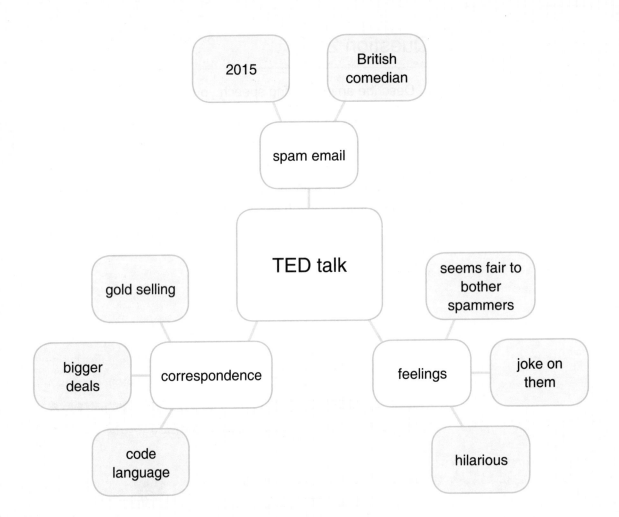

I saw an interesting TED talk recently called, 'This Is What Happens When You Reply to Spam Email'. **I think** it's from 2015, but I just watched it a few weeks ago. I don't remember the speaker's name **and I'm not sure** where the talk was originally given, but the speaker was a British comedian, **so** maybe it was in the U.K.

He told the story of how he once replied to a spam email. He got an email about a 'business opportunity' to sell gold and decided to reply as if he was interested. He kept in touch with the guy for a while, making the deal bigger and bigger and saying ridiculous things to see if he would go along with it. He started doing it with other spam emails, **too**. He says he's not being mean; he's just wasting their time, **so** they have less time to scam others.

Overall, it was really fascinating to know what actually happens when you reply to one of those emails. I didn't know they would keep replying for so long—**I guess** they didn't realise the joke was on them! I enjoyed the talk **because** it was funny and interesting.

我最近看了一個有趣的 TED 演說，題目是「回覆垃圾郵件時會發生的事」，我想那是二〇一五年的演說，但我是幾個星期前看的。我不記得演講者的名字，也不確定最初演說是在哪裡舉行的，但演講者是個英國喜劇演員，所以地點或許是在英國。

他說了一個故事，是關於有一次他回覆一封垃圾郵件的事。他收到一封電子郵件在介紹販賣黃金的「商機」，他決定回覆，表現得像自己感興趣的樣子。他和對方通信一段時間，讓那筆生意愈來愈大，然後說些可笑的話，看他是否附會。他也開始回覆其他垃圾郵件。他說他不是在做壞事，只是在浪費他們的時間，好讓他們沒空去詐騙其他人。

總而言之，能夠知道回覆那些郵件後究竟會發生什麼事，真的很有意思。我滿意外他們會通信那麼久，我猜他們並不知道自己被捉弄了！我喜歡那場演說，因為很好笑也很有趣。

Vocabulary

spam (n.) 垃圾郵件
comedian (n.) 喜劇演員
scam (v./n.) 詐騙
關 scammer (n.) 詐騙犯
　con (n./v.) 欺詐
fascinating (adj.) 有趣的

Part 2　Past Experiences

I haven't seen a live speech recently, but I've been watching TED Talks online as a way to improve my English. **One that was particularly interesting is called**, 'This is What Happens When You Reply to Spam Email'. **I think** it's from 2015, but I just watched it a few weeks ago. **I'm not sure** where the talk was originally given, but the speaker was British, **so** maybe it was in the U.K. The speaker was introduced as a comedian, **but I guess** not a very famous one **because** I didn't recognise him, and I don't remember his name.

Anyway, this comedian got an email about a supposed 'business opportunity' to sell gold. It was obviously a scam, but he decided to reply as if he was interested. Lots of emails went back and forth, and the correspondence was really funny. **For example**, the speaker made up a code language substituting types of sweets for words **like** 'gold' **or** 'bank account'. He insisted they use the code, which made the emails sound even more hilarious. **Of course**, the deal never went through **because** he was never going to give them his bank account information, which is generally what scammers are after. He started doing it with other spam emails **too**. He says he's doing a good deed by wasting spammers' time, **so** they have less time to scam others! It seems fair to me. He's giving them a taste of their own medicine.

It reminded me of a friend who had a similar experience. He got a suspicious phone call and basically played along, giving silly answers, until the callers realised he was joking and hung up on him! I've always wanted to do something like that.

Overall, it was really funny and interesting to know what actually happens when you reply to a spam email. I was surprised that the scammers kept responding for so long, **even after** it should have been obvious he was joking.

我最近沒聽什麼現場演講，但我一直都有看線上的 TED 演說來改善英文。其中有一個演說特別有趣，名稱為「回覆垃圾郵件時會發生的事」，我想那是二〇一五年的演說，但我是幾個星期前看的。我不確定演說原本在哪裡舉行，但演講者是英國人，所以或許地點是在英國。演講者的介紹說他是個喜劇演員，但我猜不是非常有名，因為我不認得他，也不記得他的名字。

總之，這個喜劇演員收到一封詐稱販賣黃金「商機」的電子郵件。那顯然是場騙局，但他決定回覆，表現得像自己感興趣的樣子。來來回回好幾封電子郵件，通信非常有趣。例如，演講者編造了代碼語言，用不同種類的糖果來取代像是「黃金」或「銀行帳號」等用字。他堅持要對方使用這些代碼，讓這些電子郵件看起來更可笑了。當然，這筆生意一直沒談成，因為他根本就沒打算把銀行帳號資訊交給他們，這就是一般來說詐騙者想取得的資訊。他也開始對其他垃圾郵件如法泡製。他說自己是在做善事，浪費那些寄垃圾郵件的人的時間，讓他們沒有時間去詐騙其他人！在我聽來很合理，他只是以其人之道，還治其人之身。

這也讓我想到一個朋友的類似經驗。他接到一通可疑的電話，基本上他就順著對方的話陪他玩，回答一些愚蠢的答案，直到對方發現他是在開玩笑，掛了他的電話！我一直也想做那種事。

總的來說，能夠知道回覆垃圾郵件後究竟會發生什麼事，真的很好笑又有趣。我很意外那些詐騙犯會一直回信，即使已經可以明顯看出對方是在開玩笑。

一梗多用之變化形

- an interesting conversation you had with someone
- an interesting story someone told you
- an article you've read recently

Question 3

> Describe a meeting you went to at work, college or school.
>
> You should say:
>   when and where the meeting was held
>   who was at the meeting
>   what the people at the meeting talked about
> and explain why you remember going to this meeting.

描述你在工作、大學或高中參加過的一場會議。

你要提到:

　　會議在何時何地舉辦

　　與會者是誰

　　與會者在討論什麼

並解釋你為什麼會記得參加過這場會議。

若真的想不起來自己曾經參加過哪個值得一提的會議,可以善用以下的 Wh- 字隨機應變,臨場編一個會議應對。這個用法也適用於被問到「物品」的相關題目。

- Who 與會者是誰
- What 討論什麼
- When 何時
- Where 何地
- Why 目的

最後再加上一個 conclusion,對這場會議提出你的看法或感覺來總結就可以了。

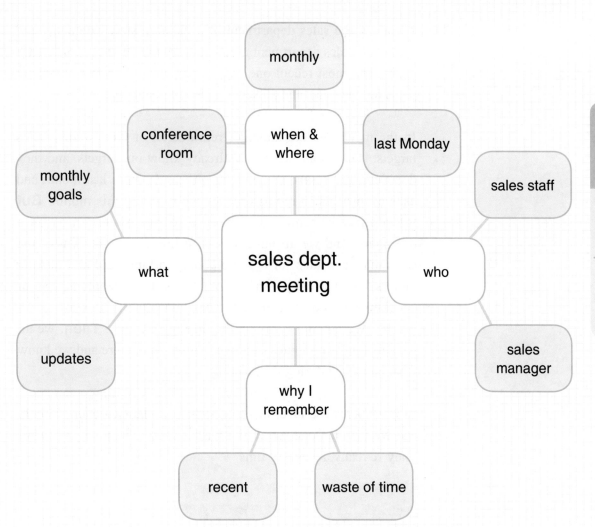

I work in the sales department of a medium-sized company, and we have a sales department meeting every month in the conference room. The most recent one was last Monday. The sales manager leads the meetings and all seven of us sales staff attend them.

In the meetings, the manager reminds us of the monthly sales targets. It's nothing new—we already know our targets, and they don't change. **Then**, she reviews our results from last month and asks each of us to report on how we're doing this month. **But** we're already required to keep a record of our sales on a document, and we all have access to this document. **Then**, the sales manager talks for a while about working hard and making more sales. It's really boring. Sometimes, I see people texting or checking Facebook on their phones under the table while she's talking. We take turns taking the meeting minutes. **Then**, we all have to sign the minutes to prove that we were there and we know what happened during the meeting.

I remember these meetings **because** they happen every month, and we just had one recently. I wish we could stop having them! They're really a waste of time.

我在一家中型公司的業務部工作,我們每個月都要在會議室開業務部門會議。最近一次是上週一,業務經理主持會議,而所有七名業務員都要參加會議。

在會議中,經理提醒我們每月業務目標。這不是什麼新鮮事,我們早就知道自己的目標,從來沒有變過。然後她檢視我們上個月的報表,叫我們每個人報告這個月的進度。但我們已經被要求將銷售紀錄製成文件,每個人也都可以看到這份文件。然後業務經理又說了一會兒有關努力工作、多多銷售的話,真的很無聊。有時候我會看到別人在她說話時,會在桌子底下用手機傳訊息或看臉書。我們會輪流做會議紀錄,然後大家都必須在紀錄上簽名,證明我們到場,並清楚了解會議的內容。

我記得這些會議,因為每個月都要開,而且我們最近才開過會。真希望不要再開會了,有夠浪費時間。

Vocabulary

conference room
會議室
text (v.) 傳訊息
minutes (n.) 會議紀錄

Long Answer

I'm a sales representative for a medium-sized company. Every month, we have a sales department meeting. The meetings are held in the conference room of our office, and all the sales staff are required to attend. Including the sales manager, who leads the meetings, there are usually eight people in attendance. This month's meeting was last Monday. **But** they're all the same, **so** describing one of them is like talking about all of them.

In the meetings, the manager usually begins by reminding us of the monthly sales targets, which is silly **because** we are all aware of them and they never change. She reviews our results from last month and asks each of us to report on how we're doing this month. **But** we're already required to keep a record of our sales on a spreadsheet, and we all have access to this spreadsheet on the server, **so** it's pretty pointless. **Then**, there's usually a lecture from the sales manager about how we should work harder and implement her favourite sales strategies. **Again**, it's never anything we haven't heard before. It's so boring that sometimes, I see people texting or checking Facebook on their phones under the table while she's talking. I don't dare to do that **because** the manager would be really angry if she found out. **But** sometimes, I doodle in my notebook.

I remember these meetings **because** they happen every month, and we just had one recently. They're **also** notable for how counterproductive they are, **in my opinion**. They don't seem to serve any purpose. A good meeting should be planned around goals, but we're never given goals or an agenda beforehand. We only take turns taking the meeting minutes. **Then**, we all have to sign the minutes as evidence that we were there and that we know what was covered during the meeting. All of this adds up to over an hour of time when we could be actually working and making sales.

Vocabulary

in attendance 出席
pointless (adj.) 無意義的
spreadsheet (n.)
（如Excel等）電子試算表
implement (v.) 實施
strategy (n.) 策略
doodle (v./n.) 塗鴉
notable (adj.) 值得注意的
counterproductive (adj.)
產生反效果的
agenda (n.) 議題
beforehand (adv.) 事前

我是一間中型公司的業務代表，我們每個月都要開業務部會議。會議在我們辦公室的會議室舉辦，所有業務員都被要求參加。包括主持會議的業務經理，與會者通常有八個人。這個月的會議在上週一，但會議千篇一律，所以描述其中一場就等於描述了所有會議。

在會議中，經理一開始通常會提醒我們每月的業務目標，這有點蠢，因為我們都很清楚，而且從來沒變過。她會檢視我們上個月的績效，然後叫我們每個人報告這個月的進度。但我們早就被要求將銷售紀錄製成報表，每個人也都能從伺服器上取得這份報表，所以根本沒有意義。然後通常業務經理會開始訓誡，說我們應該努力工作，實踐她心目中的業務策略。同樣地，這也不是我們前所未聞的事，實在很無聊，所以有時候在她說話時，我會看到有人在桌子下用手機傳訊息或看臉書。我不敢那麼做，因為如果經理發現了會很生氣。但有時候我會在筆記本上塗鴉。

我記得這些會議，因為每個月都會舉行，最近就剛開過一次。在我看來，這些會議顯然也會導致反效果，似乎根本起不了任何作用。好的會議應該針對目標訂定議程，但我們事先從沒取得目標或議程。我們只是輪流做會議紀錄，然後大家都必須在紀錄上簽名，以證明我們到場，並了解會議所包含的內容。這些會議程序總計超過一小時，這些時間原本大可用來工作和銷售。

一梗多用之變化形

- a small company
- a change that would improve your work/life
- a project you did with someone

Question 4

Describe something you did that made you feel
yourself.

You should say:
> what you did
> when you did it
> why you felt proud of what you had done

and explain how you felt when this happened.

描述一件讓你為自己感到驕傲的事。

你要提到：
> 你做了什麼
> 那是什麼時候的事
> 為什麼你為自己的行為感到驕傲

並說明你當時的感受。

一些相關點子

- lose a stone 減重（英式用法）
- quit smoking 戒菸
- enter a singing competition 參加歌唱比賽
- pass an exam 通過考試
- get a decent job 得到好工作
- get a promotion 獲得升遷

4 years ago

September

Taroko Marathon

7.5 miles

challenge

first time

pride

worked hard

wasn't in shape

training

stuck with a plan

felt

nervous

happy

exhausted

About four years ago, I ran in a 7.5-mile race, which is about 12 kilometres. It's something to be proud of **because** I find running long distances to be very challenging!

I heard about the race from a co-worker who was planning to do the full 26-mile marathon. I would never do that, but I once did a 3-mile race, and I wondered if I would be able to do a longer one. I noticed there was a 7.5-mile 'tiny marathon', **so** I decided to register.

I found a training plan online. It was a six- or eight-week schedule that tells you exactly what to do each day, **like** how far to run, **and** when to take a rest. I'm a bit lazy and not very athletic, but I managed to stick with the training program.

On the day of the race, I was a little nervous, but ready. I didn't run very fast, but at least I didn't stop to walk at all. **When** I finished, I felt exhausted but happy!

All in all, **the reason** I'm proud of this accomplishment **is because** I had to work hard for it, and I did something that I wasn't sure I'd be able to do.

大約四年前,我參加過一場 7.5 英里賽跑,大約是 12 公里。那是很值得驕傲的一件事,因為我發現長距離賽跑非常有挑戰性!

我是從同事那裡知道有這場馬拉松的,他準備要跑 26 公里全馬。我永遠不可能跑全馬,但我曾參加過三英里的比賽,有點想知道自己能不能完成更長距離的比賽。我注意到有個 7.5 英里的「迷你馬拉松」,所以我決定報名。

我在網路上找到訓練計畫,那是六或八週的計畫表,明確告訴你每天要做什麼事,例如跑多遠,什麼時候休息。我有點懶,而且沒那麼擅長運動,但我還是堅持執行這個訓練計畫。

比賽當天,我有點緊張,但已經準備好了。我跑得不是很快,但至少沒有完全停下來走路。當我跑完的時候,我感到筋疲力竭,但很開心!

總而言之,這項成就讓我感到驕傲的理由,是因為我得為此努力,而我也完成了原本不確定能否完成的事。

Vocabulary

athletic (adj.) 運動的
關 athlete (n.) 運動員
　athletics (n.) 體育運動
stick with something
堅持做某件事
accomplishment (n.)
成就

Generally speaking, I get a sense of pride whenever I achieve a difficult goal. **So, when I was thinking about this topic, the first thing that came to mind was** running in a 7.5-mile race **because** I find running long distances to be very challenging!

It was about four years ago. My co-worker was talking about joining the Taroko Marathon, and I was looking over her shoulder at the website. **I think** you have to be a little off your rocker to do a full 26-mile marathon, but I noticed they **also** had a 7.5-mile race, and it made me wonder if I could run that far. I was an occasional jogger, but I wasn't in great shape, and the furthest I had ever run was two or three miles.

After thinking about it for a while, I decided to register. I found a training plan online that was perfect for me. It was a six- or eight-week schedule that tells you exactly what to do each day, **like** how far or how long to run, **and** when to take a rest.

I actually surprised myself with how dedicated and consistent I was with my training. I remember going away to the beach one weekend. I'm not one of those people who likes exercising on holiday, but I still did my scheduled run!

The day of the race was pretty exciting. There were lots of people and the sun was shining. I was a little nervous, but ready. I set a slow pace at first **because** I wanted to make sure I had enough energy to finish the race. **So**, my time wasn't very impressive, but at least I didn't stop to walk at all. **When** I finished, I felt exhausted but happy!

As I said earlier, the reason I'm proud of this accomplishment is because I had to work hard for it, and I did something that I wasn't sure I'd be able to do.

Vocabulary

off one's rocker
精神失常，發瘋
關 crazy (adj.) 瘋狂的
dedicated (adj.) 專注的
pace (n.) 步調

一般說來，達成困難的目標，我就會感到驕傲。所以當我思考這個主題時，第一個想到的就是 7.5 英里的賽跑，因為我覺得長距離賽跑非常有挑戰性！

大約四年前，我的同事在討論參加太魯閣馬拉松，我站在她身後看那個網站。我想只有發神經才會跑 26 英里全馬，但我注意到他們也有 7.5 英里賽跑，讓我很好奇自己是否能跑那麼遠。我有時候會慢跑，但身體不是很強健，最遠也只跑過二或三英里。

經過考慮之後，我決定報名。我在網路上找到一個很適合我的訓練計畫，那是六或八週的計畫表，明確告訴你每天要做什麼事，例如跑多遠、跑多久以及什麼時候該休息。

真正出乎我意料的，是我對訓練的全心投入和毅力。我記得有次週末去海邊，我不是那種喜歡在假日運動的人，但還是照表操課跑完了！

比賽當天很令人興奮，現場有很多人，陽光閃耀。我有點緊張，但已經準備好了。我一開始先用慢速跑，因為我想確定自己有足夠的體力完賽，所以我的時間成績不太出色，但至少我完全沒停下來用走的。我跑完的時候感覺筋疲力竭，但很開心！

如我之前所說，這項成就讓我驕傲的理由，是因為我得為此努力，也完成了原本不確定能否完成的事。

一梗多用之變化形

- an athlete
- an activity you do to keep fit
- a sport you enjoy doing
- a goal you have for the future

Question 5

Describe a conflict that you had, or a time when you became angry.

You should say:
> when it happened
> why it happened
> how you resolved it

and explain how you felt about this experience.

描述你有過的一場衝突,或一次令你生氣的經驗。

你要提到:

> 那是什麼時候的事
> 為什麼會發生
> 你如何解決

並說明你對這個經驗的感覺。

基本上發生衝突或感到生氣一定是因為對某個人不滿,所以對於這類題目,先設定一個對象,再根據這個對象發展爭執的內容,再決定時間、地點,以及後續處理方式,會比較容易發展出一篇完整的小演說。

容易發生爭執的對象

- boyfriend/girlfriend 男女朋友
- spouse (wife/husband) 配偶
- colleague 同事
- classmate 同學
- boss/supervisor 老闆;主管
- stranger 陌生人

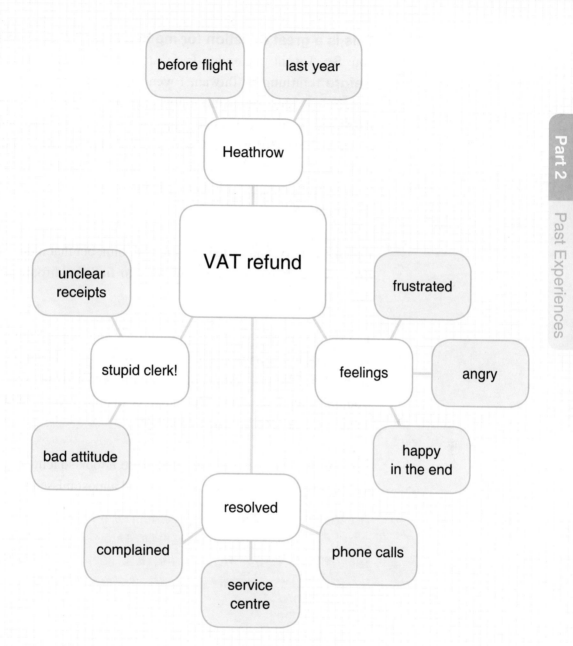

This is a great question for me because I've got a story for you. **So**, I went to London last year and did a lot of shopping. **Before** returning to Taiwan, I went to the tax refund office at Heathrow Airport **because** tourists are entitled to a VAT refund. **After** waiting in line and checking out a form, I gave the clerk all of my receipts. **But** the clerk said he couldn't accept them. I didn't really understand why. Some were hard to read but there was nothing really wrong with them. **I think** he was just having a bad day or something.

I got a bit angry, and I tried arguing with him, but that didn't work. **So**, I wrote down his name and went to find the airport service centre to complain.

The service centre staff were really nice and calmed me down. They made a few phone calls and said sorry to me. **Then**, I had to go back to the tax refund office again. **This time**, the clerk wouldn't even look at me. **But** he processed the receipts and gave me my refund. **So** I'm glad I complained.

After that, I was happier, **but**, **because** it took so long to get my refund, I had to run to catch my flight and almost missed it.

對我來說,這是個好問題,因為我有個故事可以分享。我去年去倫敦,買了很多東西。在回台灣之前,我去了希斯洛機場的退稅辦公室,因為觀光客有退稅資格。排隊等待、檢查表格之後,我將所有收據交給辦事員,但他說他不收,我不太明白為什麼。有些收據是看不太清楚,但並沒有什麼真的錯誤。我想他只是心情不好之類的吧。

我有點生氣,試著和他理論,但沒有用。所以我記下他的名字,去找機場服務中心投訴。

服務中心的員工真的很好,讓我冷靜下來。他們打了幾通電話,跟我說抱歉。然後我得再回退稅辦公室。這一次那個辦事員根本不看我,但他處理了收據,然後把錢退給我。所以我很高興自己去投訴了。

退稅之後,我開心多了,但因為花了很長的時間辦理退稅,我得快跑去趕飛機,還差點趕不上。

Vocabulary

tax refund 退稅
entitle (v.) 具有資格
calm someone down
讓某人冷靜下來

068

This is a great question for me because I've got a story for you. **So,** I went to London last year with my sister, and we had a great time. We spent too much money shopping, but we consoled ourselves with the knowledge that we'd at least be able to get a tax refund for our purchases. **I think** most countries have a law like that for tourists—you can show your receipts at the airport when you leave, and they'll give you back the VAT, which stands for value added tax. It's a pretty significant amount, about 15 or 20 percent.

So, **before** our flight back to Taiwan, we went to the tax counter at Heathrow Airport. We filled out a form and took a number. **When** it was our turn, we presented all the receipts we had. **But apparently**, the guy had got up on the wrong side of bed that morning. He grumbled and mumbled, saying he couldn't process our receipts. He gave some excuses, **like** they were hard to read **or** the amounts were too small **or** some information was missing **or something. But** I knew the law, and I was pretty sure we were owed a refund! I was getting angry and argued with him a little bit. **Then** I wrote down his name (it was on his nametag), and we went to find the airport service centre.

They made a few phone calls, sorted it out, and apologised for the inconvenience. **Then**, we had to go back to the tax refund office again. **This time**, the guy wouldn't even look at us. **But** he quickly processed our claim and gave us our refund.

It's not that I wanted to get the guy in trouble, but I really felt like an injustice was being done, and I had to speak up! That saying, 'the squeaky wheel gets the grease', is really true. **Anyway**, all that took a lot of time, and we had to run to catch our flight. **But** it was worth it!

Part 2 Past Experiences

Vocabulary

console (v.) 安慰
significant (adj.)
數量龐大的
get up on the wrong
side of bed 有起床氣
grumble (v.) 抱怨，嘟囔
mumble (v.) 含糊其辭
sort out 釐清，解決
injustice (n.) 不公正
反 justice (n.) 公正
the squeaky wheel
gets the grease 會吵的
孩子有糖吃

對我來說，這是個好問題，因為我有個故事可以分享。去年我和妹妹去倫敦，玩得很愉快。我們花了太多錢購物，但得知我們買東西買到可以辦理退稅，我們至少感到些許安慰。我想多數國家對觀光客都有這樣的法律，你可以在離境時，於機場出示收據，他們就會將 VAT——也就是增值稅退還給你。那是一筆很可觀的金額，大約百分之十五或二十。

所以，在飛回台灣之前，我們到希斯洛機場的稅務櫃台填寫表格、領取號碼牌。輪到我們時，我們出示了所有收據，但辦事員那天顯然有起床氣，他嘟嘟囔囔、含糊其辭，說他不受理我們的收據。他說了一堆藉口，例如太難辨認、金額太小，或是缺少某些資訊什麼的。但我知道相關法令，也很確定我們可以退稅！我很生氣，和他爭辯了一會兒。然後我記下他的名字（就在他的名牌上），然後去找機場的服務中心。

他們打了幾通電話，釐清事情，並道歉造成不便。然後我們還是得再回去退稅辦公室，這次那傢伙根本不看我們，但他快速處理了我們的申請，並給我們退稅款項。

我並不想讓那傢伙惹上麻煩，但我真的覺得很不公平，必須大聲說出來！那句「會吵的孩子有糖吃」千真萬確。總之，那些事花了我們很多時間，我們得快跑去趕飛機，不過很值得！

一梗多用之變化形

- a time when you experienced good service in a shop or restaurant
- an important conversation you had
- a useful piece of advice you received
- a time when you waited for someone

Question 1

Describe an elderly person you know.

You should say:
>　who this person is
>　how you know him/her
>　what he/she is like
and explain how you feel about him/her.

Tip

若這位長輩已經過世，要注意有關他 / 她的內容都要用過去式。

描述一位你認識的長輩。

你要提到：

>　他 / 她是誰

>　你是怎麼認識他 / 她的

>　他 / 她是怎麼樣的人

並說明你對他 / 她的感覺。

選擇的長輩不一定要是自己的家人，描述有特色或經常見到的長者，例如鄰居的阿公、公司前輩會比較容易。為了讓考官知道你有注意到細節，記得提一下這位長輩的年紀。

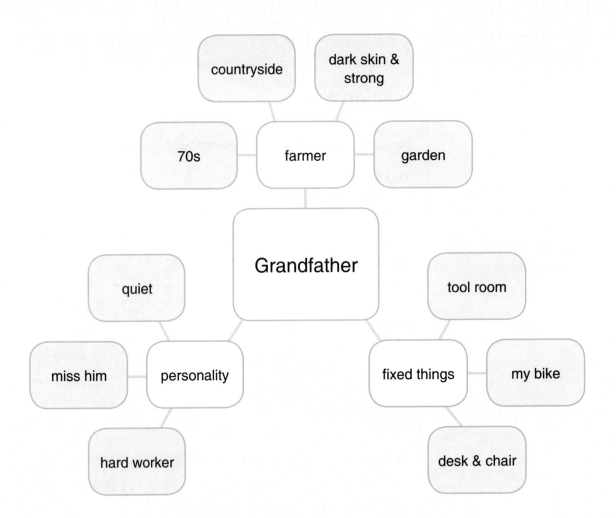

I'd like to tell you about my grandfather. **When** I was about ten years old, my parents sent me to live with my grandparents for the summer. They lived in the countryside, in a beautiful little village.

My grandpa was about 70 years old at the time. He was a farmer most of his life, **so** he had very dark skin. He was too old to manage a big farm anymore, but he still had a garden. I often helped him pull out weeds or pick vegetables for dinner. He didn't talk much—**maybe because** my grandma loved to talk non-stop. He was always working, **either** in the garden **or** around the house. He could fix almost anything. He even made me a desk and chair, and they're still there in my grandparents' house.

That was probably the best summer of my life. I loved playing with insects, dogs and other kids in the country. It was **also** special to me **because** I got to spend time with my grandfather. **Even though** he didn't talk much, I feel like I got to know him well. He passed away a few years ago, and I really miss him.

我想談談我的祖父。當我十歲左右，父母送我到祖父母家過暑假，他們住在鄉下一個美麗的小村莊。

我祖父當時大約七十歲，他大半輩子都是農夫，所以他的皮膚非常黝黑。他年紀太大，無法再管理大片農田，但他還是有個小菜園。我經常幫他拔草，或是摘蔬菜當晚餐。他的話不多，或許是因為我奶奶喜歡說個不停。他總是在工作，不是在菜園就是在屋子忙來忙去。他幾乎什麼都能修，他甚至為我做了書桌和椅子，現在還放在我祖父母家。

那或許是我人生中最美好的夏天，我喜歡和鄉間的昆蟲、狗與其他孩子玩。那段時間對我來說也很特別，因為我得以和祖父相處，即使他不多話，但我覺得我很了解他。他幾年前去世了，我真的很想他。

Vocabulary

countryside (n.) 農村
weed (n.) 雜草
non-stop (adv.) 不停地

I'd like to tell you about my grandfather. **When** I was about ten years old, my parents were very busy with their business, **so** they sent me to live with my grandparents for the summer. They lived in the countryside, in a beautiful little village.

My grandpa was in his seventies at the time. He had been a farmer most of his life, **so** he had dark, sun-tanned skin. He was thin and not very tall but was quite strong and muscular for his age. He was too old to manage a big farm anymore, but he still had a thriving garden. I often helped him pull out the weeds or pick fresh vegetables for dinner.

He was a man of few words. In my memories of him, he was always working quietly, **either** in the garden **or** around the house. He had a knack for fixing things. I saw where he put all his tools— it was a room as big as my bedroom! My grandma usually stayed in doing the housework and cooking. **At the same time**, she would gossip on the phone with her friends or chat to me. Maybe it's **because** my grandma loved to talk non-stop that my grandpa was so quiet!

That was probably the best summer of my life. **After that**, I moved back to the city, and I no longer had the opportunity to play with insects, dogs and other kids in the country. **Most importantly**, I really cherish the time I got to spend with my grandparents. **Even though** he didn't talk much, I feel like I got to know my grandfather well. He passed away **a few years ago**, **and** I really miss him. Sometimes, I wish I had spent more time with him when he was still around. I've been visiting my grandmother more often lately, **so that** I don't have the same regrets about her.

Vocabulary

muscular (adj.)
肌肉發達的
for one's age
就其年齡而論
thriving (adj.) 欣欣向榮的
關 thrive (v.) 繁榮
a man of few words
沉默寡言的人
have a knack for
有做…的訣竅
cherish (v.) 珍惜
pass away 過世

我想談談我的祖父。當我十歲左右，父母因為做生意非常忙碌，就把我送到祖父母家過暑假。他們住在鄉下一個美麗的小村莊。

當時我祖父七十幾歲，他大半輩子都是農夫，所以擁有日曬黝黑的膚色。他很瘦，不太高，但以他的年齡來說相當硬朗且很有肌肉。他年紀太大，無法再管理大片農田，但他還有片欣欣向榮的小菜園。我經常幫他拔草，或是摘新鮮蔬菜當晚餐。

他是個沉默寡言的人，在我對他的記憶裡，他總是靜靜工作，不是在菜園，就是在屋子忙來忙去。他很有修理東西的本事，我看過他擺放所有工具的房間，根本和我的臥室一樣大！我奶奶經常待在屋裡做家務和煮飯。同時，她還會打電話跟朋友聊八卦，或是和我聊天。或許是因為我奶奶喜歡說個不停，我爺爺才這麼安靜。

那或許是我人生中最美好的夏天。在那之後，我搬回市區，就再也沒有機會和鄉間的昆蟲、小狗與其他小孩玩了。更重要的是，我真的很珍惜和祖父母相處的時間。即使他不多話，我還是覺得自己很了解我祖父。他幾年前過世了，我真的很想他。有時候我希望他還在世時，自己能多花點時間和他相處。最近我比以前更常去探望奶奶，這樣我對她才不會有相同的遺憾。

一梗多用之變化形

● someone you've lived with

● someone you visited recently

● someone who is special or means a lot to you

Question 2

Talk about a famous person you would like to meet.

You should say:
>   who this person is
>   why he/she is famous
>   why you want to meet him/her
> and explain what you would do if you met him/her.

描述一位你會想見的名人。

你要提到：

>   他 / 她是誰

>   他 / 她為何有名

>   你為什麼想見他 / 她

並說明跟他 / 她見面時你會做什麼。

考生平常就要準備一些具有專業的名人，例如歌手、演員、商業巨擘、科學家、名醫或藝術家的背景資料，準備時可以以自己熟悉或有興趣的領域為基準。這些資料都可以一梗多用，例如被問到「偶像」時就可以派上用場。

一些相關點子

- writer 作家
- scientist 科學家
- athlete 運動員
- chef 主廚
- politician 政治人物
- blogger 部落客
- vlogger 影片部落客
- celebrity 名人
- entrepreneur 創業家

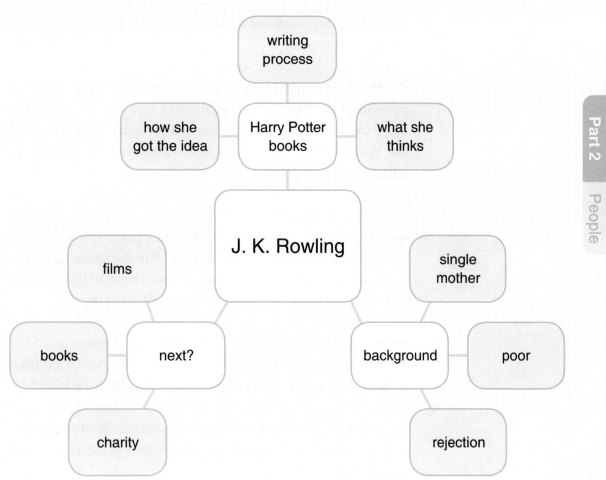

I would be very interested to meet J.K. Rowling, the author of the Harry Potter books.

When she was working on the first Harry Potter book, she was a poor single mother. Many publishers rejected her book, but somehow she found the confidence and strength to keep trying. I'd like to know if she has any advice about how to keep trying **even when** it seems hopeless!

The Harry Potter series is really amazing, and I have so many questions about it. Where did the idea come from? Did she plan all seven books before she started writing? Are the characters based on anyone she knows? **And** since her books have all been adapted into films, I'd like to know what she thought about the films!

Now, Ms. Rowling is super rich, and she's given a lot of her money to charity. I'd like to talk to her about that, **too. Of course**, I'd **also** love to find out about the next book she's going to write!

As you can probably tell, I'm a big fan of J.K. Rowling. If I ever get to meet her, I hope I have the chance to ask her some of these questions.

我會非常想見見《哈利波特》系列書的作者 J.K. 羅琳。

她在寫《哈利波特》第一集時，還是個貧窮的單親媽媽。當時，許多出版商拒絕了她的書，但不知為何，她還是找到信心和力量不斷嘗試。我想知道，對於如何在絕望時繼續嘗試，她是否有什麼建議！

《哈利波特》系列真的很棒，我有好多相關的問題。例如想法是從哪裡來的？她是否在動筆前就計畫好七本書？主角是以她認識的人為本嗎？還有既然她的書已經全部翻拍成電影，我想知道她對電影有什麼想法！

現在羅琳小姐已經超級富有，還捐了很多錢給慈善機構，我也想問問她這件事。當然，我還想知道她下本書要寫什麼！

你或許可以看出，我是 J.K. 羅琳的大粉絲。如果我可以見到她，希望有機會能問她一些這類問題。

Vocabulary

base on 以⋯為基礎
adapt (v.) 改編
charity (n.) 慈善事業

Long Answer

There are a lot of celebrities who I admire. In most cases, I'm happy just being a fan of their work, and I don't have a strong desire to meet them in person. **However**, one person who I think would be really interesting to meet is J.K. Rowling, the author of the Harry Potter books.

I'd love to hear her talk about her life experiences. I read that she was a poor single mother, **so** it must have been a real struggle to find time to work on her writing. **When** she finished her first book, many publishers rejected it. I want to know how she found the confidence and persistence to keep trying anyway. **I think** I would have given up sooner.

As I read the Harry Potter series, I became more and more curious about her writing process. The stories are so interesting and creative—I wonder where she got the inspiration. Did she plan all seven books before she started writing, **or** did she make it up as she went along? Are the characters based on anyone she knows? **And** since her books have all been adapted into films, I'd like to know what it's like to see her words come to life!

I'd **also** ask Ms. Rowling a little about her life since becoming famous. I read that she became a billionaire, **but then** donated so much money to charity that she's not a billionaire anymore! **So**, I'd like to ask her why she did that and how she decided which causes to support. **Of course**, I'd **also** love to find out about what books she's going to write next!

As you can probably tell, I'm a big fan of J.K. Rowling, and I have loads of questions to ask her. **The reality is**, if I got to meet her, I'd probably be too nervous to ask all my questions. **Anyway**, it would be an honour to just shake her hand and tell her how much I admire her.

Part 2

People

Vocabulary

persistence (n.) 毅力
關 persist (v.) 堅持
curious (adj.) 好奇的
come to life
賦予生命般動起來
billionaire (n.) 億萬富翁
cause (n.) 事業

我欣賞的名人很多。其中大多數，我樂於單純欣賞他們的作品，沒有強烈的欲望想當面見見他們。然而，我有個非常想要見的人，就是《哈利波特》系列書的作者 J.K. 羅琳。

我想聽聽她的人生經驗。我讀過報導說她曾是個貧窮的單親媽媽，所以要找出時間寫作一定很不容易。當她完成第一本書時，許多出版商都拒絕出版，我想知道她如何找到自信和毅力不斷努力，我覺得要是我應該很快就放棄了。

當我閱讀《哈利波特》系列時，我愈來愈好奇她的寫作過程。故事非常有趣又很有創造力，不知道她哪裡來的靈感。她是否在動筆前就計畫好七本書，還是她邊寫邊編故事？角色是以她認識的人為本嗎？而且既然她的書都已經全部翻拍成電影，我想知道看到自己的文字被賦予生命是什麼感覺！

我也想問羅琳小姐一些成名之後生活上的問題。我讀過報導說她成了億萬富翁，但後來捐了很多錢給慈善機構，因此又不是億萬富翁了！我想問她為何要那麼做，又如何決定要支持哪些事業。當然，我還想知道她下本書要寫什麼！

你或許可以看出，我是 J.K. 羅琳的大粉絲，我有一堆問題想問她。事實上，如果我真的能見到她，我或許會緊張到無法問出所有問題。反正，只要可以握到她的手，告訴她我有多麼崇拜她，就是我的榮幸了。

一梗多用之變化形

- a good leader
- an athlete
- someone with an important job

Question 3

Describe a quality you admire in a person you know.

You should say:
> what quality it is
> who the person is
> how he/she exemplifies the quality

and explain why you admire this quality.

描述某個你認識的人所具有的優秀特質。

你要提到：

> 是什麼樣的特質
>
> 那個人是誰
>
> 他／她如何展現該特質

並解釋你為什麼欣賞這個特質。

這個題目很容易被誤認為是要描述「一個人」，看仔細了，題目是問 Describe a quality ... in a person，是要描述「人格特質」，例如 patience、determination、persistence、positivity 等，可別講成這個人的外型或其他無關的事情了。為避免不斷重複使用相同字彙，要交替運用一個字的名詞、形容詞、同義字、反義字等。另外，作答時盡量著重在一種特質上就好，以免主題散亂，連貫性盡失。

One quality I really like in a person is a sense of adventure. One of my best friends Ann definitely has it, and it makes her life so interesting! She always challenges herself. **Let me give you two examples.**

A few years ago, Ann joined a cycling club. They went cycling every weekend. She bought an expensive mountain bike and loads of equipment: helmets, gloves, waterproof shoes, you name it. She told me that they were going to go on a four-day bike trip from Taizhong to Taidong. **I thought** that was a crazy idea **because** it was around Chinese New Year. **At that time of the year**, the weather is usually cold and wet, but Ann was excited about it anyway. During the trip, she called me from a place called Dulan. I don't even know where Dulan is!

Apart from cycling, Ann **also** loves swimming. In September, she decided to join the Sun Moon Lake swimming competition. I met her as soon as she got back, and her face and shoulders were badly sunburnt. She didn't even care. She was just happy about her accomplishment. I looked at her and thought she's the coolest person I know!

我很喜歡的一種人格特質是勇於冒險。我最好的其中一個朋友，安，她就百分之百擁有這個特質，而且這讓她的人生充滿樂趣！她總是勇於挑戰自我，讓我告訴你兩個例子。

幾年前，安加入自行車俱樂部，他們每個週末都會去騎腳踏車，她買了一輛昂貴的登山腳踏車以及很多設備：安全帽、手套、防水鞋，應有盡有。她告訴我，他們要進行四天的單車之旅，從台中騎到台東，我覺得那是個瘋狂的想法，因為時值中國新年。每年那個時候，天氣通常都又冷又濕，但安還是很興奮。在旅程中，她從一個叫都蘭的地方打電話給我，我根本不知道都蘭在哪裡！

除了騎腳踏車，安也熱愛游泳。她在九月時決定參加日月潭游泳比賽。她一回來我們就見面，她的臉和肩膀都嚴重曬傷，但她根本不在乎，她對自己的成就很滿意。我看著她，覺得她是我所認識最酷的人！

Vocabulary

you name it 應有盡有
關 anything you can think of 任何你能想到的事
sunburn (v.) 曬傷，曬紅

My friend Ann is someone I'm really proud of. She has lots of good qualities, **but I think** the one I admire most is her sense of adventure. She never backs down from a challenge, and she doesn't do anything halfway. **Let me give you two examples.**

A few years ago, Ann spent a fortune on a mountain bike and joined a cycling club. They went cycling every weekend. **One time**, I went to her place and I was amazed by how much equipment she'd bought: helmets, gloves, waterproof shoes, you name it. She told me that they were going to go on a four-day bike trip from Taizhong to Taidong. **I thought** that was a crazy idea **because** it was around Chinese New Year. **At that time of the year**, the weather can be quite unpleasant and unpredictable, but Ann wasn't discouraged—**quite the opposite**; she was excited about it. **A few weeks later**, I had forgotten about her trip, and I got a call out of the blue from a place called Dulan. I don't even know where Dulan is, but she had ridden her bike there!

Aside from cycling, Ann **also** loves swimming. In September, she joined the Sun Moon Lake swimming competition. **Although** she invited me to join her, **I'm sure** she knew I'd turn her down. I can't swim, and I'm afraid of water! I met her as soon as she got back, and her face and shoulders were badly sunburnt. She didn't even care. She said she had forgotten to take sunscreen, **but since** they were in the water for more than four hours, the sunscreen would've been washed off anyway. I looked at her and thought she's the coolest person I know.

This sense of adventure carries over into other areas of her life, **too**, **such as** work and travel. **Whenever** I'm afraid to try something new, I think, 'What would Ann do?'

Vocabulary

back down 放棄
spend a fortune
花了一大筆錢
關 make/cost/come into a
fortune
賺／花／繼承一大筆錢
unpleasant (adj.) 討厭的
unpredictable (adj.)
不可預測的
discouraged (adj.)
沮喪的；氣餒的
out of the blue 突然地
關 unexpectedly (adv.)
出乎意料地
carry over 繼續存在

我的朋友，安，是一個讓我感到很驕傲的人。她有很多優秀特質，但我認為最讓我崇拜的，是她勇於冒險的精神。她面對挑戰從不退卻，而且絕不半途而廢。讓我告訴你兩個例子。

幾年前，安花了一大筆錢買登山腳踏車，還加入了自行車俱樂部。他們每週都去騎腳踏車，有次我去她家，被她買的那一大堆設備嚇到：安全帽、手套、防水鞋，應有盡有。她說他們要去一趟四天的單車之旅，從台中騎到台東。我覺得那是個瘋狂的想法，因為那時正值中國新年，每年那時候的天氣都很不舒適又很不穩定。但安並未因此退卻，相反地，她很迫不及待。幾個星期後，我都忘了她去旅遊了，卻突然接到她從都蘭打來的電話，我連都蘭在哪都不知道，但她已經騎著腳踏車到那裡了！

除了騎腳踏車，安也熱愛游泳。她在九月參加了日月潭游泳比賽。雖然她邀請我一起參加，但我敢說她早知道我會拒絕。我不會游泳，又怕水！她一回來我們就見面，她的臉和肩膀都嚴重曬傷，但她根本不在乎。她說她忘了帶防曬乳，但反正他們待在水裡超過四小時，就算擦防曬乳也早就被沖掉了。我看著她，覺得她是我認識最酷的人。

這種勇於冒險的精神也存在於她生活的其他領域，例如工作和旅遊。每當我害怕嘗試新鮮事時，我就會想「安會怎麼做呢？」

一梗多用之變化形

- your best friend
- an unforgettable trip
- an exciting event you did with a friend

Question 4

Describe an intelligent person you know.

You should say:
    who this person is
    what he/she does
    what he/she is like
and explain how you feel about him/her.

描述你認識的一位聰明人士。
你要提到：
    他 / 她是誰
    他 / 她從事什麼工作
    他 / 她是什麼樣的人
並說明你對他 / 她的感覺。

為了精確回答問題，一定要說明清楚這個人到底有多聰明，可以透過介紹他 / 她的（教育）背景、工作或學業上的特殊表現來佐證。或者也可以朝情緒管理 (emotional control) 的方向作答。

開始作答時，可以先定義一下你認為的 intelligent 的人是什麼樣子，例如 calm、witty、humourous、knowledgeable、composed、quick thinker、problem solver 等，接下來會比較好延伸答案。

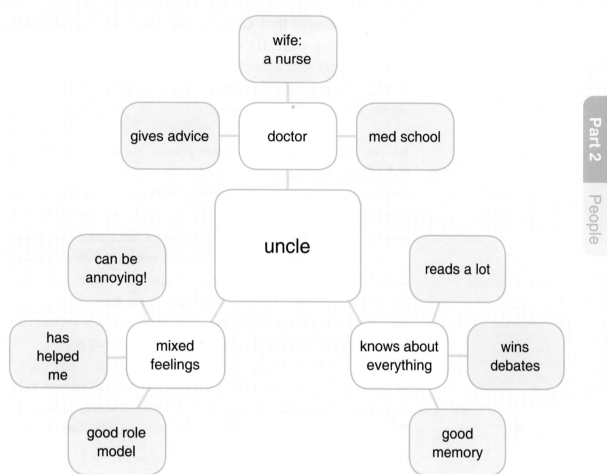

Short Answer

The first person that came to my mind when I saw this topic was my uncle. He's a doctor. I was very young when he was in medical school, but I can remember he was very smart. He was the first person in my family to study medicine and became a doctor.

It's not just medicine that he knows about. He has a small library in his home, and there are thousands of books about many different subjects **like** literature, philosophy **and** even architecture. He reads a lot and has a good memory, **so** he has an answer for just about any question you can think of! I asked him so many questions **as a kid**, and he could always come up with an answer. **One time**, he helped me make a volcano for a science project, and I won a prize! He's not someone you'd want to get into a debate with **because** he usually wins. **But** I don't want to make him sound too arrogant. He doesn't look down on anyone.

I admire his intelligence a lot. Intelligence alone isn't enough to be successful, **though**; you have to work hard and stay motivated. **So**, he's a good role model for me and everyone who knows him.

看到這個主題，我第一個想到的人是我叔叔。他是個醫生，他念醫學院的時候我還很小，但我記得他非常聰明。他是家族中第一個讀醫學、成為醫生的人。

他懂的不只醫學，他在家裡有個小圖書館，裡面有數千本書，涵蓋各種不同主題，例如文學、哲學，甚至是建築。他大量閱讀，記憶力超強，所以你能想到的問題他幾乎都有答案！我小時候問了他很多問題，他總是能回答。有一次他幫我一起做火山的科學作品，我還得了獎！他不會是你想辯論的對象，因為贏的通常是他。但我並不想把他說得太傲慢，他不會看不起任何人。

我非常崇拜他的聰明才智，但光是聰明並不足以成功；你必須努力工作、保持積極態度。所以對我和所有認識他的人來說，他都是很好的榜樣。

Vocabulary

come to one's mind
腦袋浮出想法
come up with 想出
debate (n./v.) 辯論
arrogant (adj.) 傲慢的
look down on 看不起
role model 榜樣

178

The first person that came to mind when I saw this topic was my uncle. He's my dad's younger brother, and he's a doctor. I was very young when he was in medical school, but I can remember my relatives being impressed that he had decided to become a doctor and that he was doing well in school. He's the only person in my family to have become a doctor. He has worked as a doctor in a few different countries.

It's not just medicine that he knows about. He has a small library in his home which **houses** thousands of books on a huge variety of subjects **like** literature, philosophy **and even** architecture. He reads a lot and has a good memory, **so** he has an answer for just about any question you can think of! I asked him so many questions **as a kid**, and he could always come up with an answer. **When** I was in grade three, he helped me make a volcano for my science project. We used different materials to **portray** the structures and layers of the volcano, and I won a prize! **But** he's not someone you'd want to get into a debate with **because** he usually—no, always—wins. He knows lots of facts and quotes that back up his arguments. **Even if** you make a good counterargument, he brings up more information to prove his point. **Mind you**, I wouldn't say he's overly arrogant. He certainly doesn't **despise** anyone.

It can be annoying that he's such a know-it-all, but he's my uncle, **so of course** I love him anyway. He has succeeded in a difficult field, **not just because of** his intelligence **but because of** his hard work **and** strong motivation. **Even more than** his hard work and his intelligence, the thing I admire most about him is his passion for helping people. **Overall**, I'd say he's a good role model for me and everyone who knows him.

Part 2 People

Vocabulary

house (v.) 屋內收藏有
portray (v.) 表現，呈現
quote (n.) 引述，引證
counterargument (n.) 用來反駁的論點
despise (v.) 輕視
know-it-all (n.) 萬事通

看到這個主題，我第一個想到的人是我叔叔。他是我爸的弟弟，是個醫生。他上醫學院的時候我還很小，但我記得我的親戚對他決心當個醫生，以及他的學業表現優異都很佩服。他是家族裡唯一當醫生的人，他還到一些不同的國家行醫。

他懂的不只醫學，他家有個小圖書館，裡面有數千本書，主題包羅萬象，例如文學、哲學，甚至是建築。他大量閱讀、記憶力超強，所以你能想到的任何問題，他幾乎都有答案！我小時候問了他很多問題，他總是能回答。當我三年級的時候，他幫我一起做火山的科學作品，我們用不同的材料呈現火山的結構和層理，我還得了獎！他不是你會想辯論的對象，因為贏的人經常是——不——總是他。他知識豐富又能引經據典來支持他的論點，即使你反駁的論點很好，他也會提出更多資料來證明他的看法。請注意，我不是說他過度傲慢，他絕不會輕視任何人。

他這樣的萬事通實在很煩人，但他是我叔叔，所以我當然還是愛他。他在不同的領域獲得成功，不只是因為他的聰明才智，更因為他努力工作又有強烈的動機。除了他的努力和聰明，我最崇拜的是他助人的熱情。總而言之，我會說他對我和所有認識他的人來說，都是好榜樣。

一梗多用之變化形

- a leader
- someone who can speak another language well
- someone who does something really well

Question 5

> Describe a historical figure.
>
> You should say:
>   who this person was
>   when he/she lived
>   why he/she became famous
> and explain why he/she is important.

描述一位歷史人物。
你要提到：
    他／她是誰
    他／她活在什麼時代
    他／她為什麼有名
並解釋為什麼他／她很重要。

題目若沒有限制一定要是「本國」的歷史人物，可以講的對象就很多了。本題的答題範例是為了示範可以一梗多用，而選擇台灣的道教人物「媽祖」。或許有人會認為媽祖是宗教人物，但媽祖在歷史上真有其人，所以把她當作歷史人物也說得通。

其他點子

● Liu Mingchuan（劉銘傳）

Today he is remembered for his efforts in modernizing Taiwan during his tenure as governor.（資料引自 Wikipedia）

● Li Chunsheng（李春生）

Active in Qing-era Taiwan. Li was not only a great businessman, but also a man of public spirit. He donated money enthusiastically, and also took part in supervising to build Taipei City.（資料引自 Wikipedia）

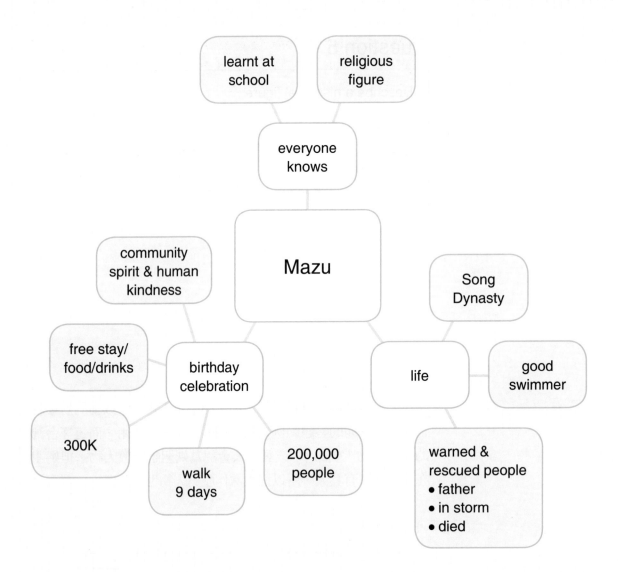

I'll try my best to describe Mazu, who is both a historical and a religious figure. I'm not that religious, but everyone living in Taiwan knows Mazu, the Chinese sea goddess.

We learnt about her at school, **so** I'll tell you what I can remember. **I think** she was born in the Song Dynasty, in the year 906. She had the ability to predict the weather. She became a very good swimmer and often rescued people from the sea, **even** in bad weather. Some people say she died **because** she went out into the sea during a storm to try to find her lost father. **After** her death, her family and sailors and fishermen started to pray for her help in dangerous weather.

Every year, her birthday is celebrated all around central Taiwan. It's one of the greatest religious festivals in the world. 200,000 pilgrims walk for nine days and carry a statue of Mazu in a wooden chair. The total journey is about 300 kilometres long. On the way, many local people offer their living rooms or garages for visitors to rest in. **In addition to** free resting places, free food and drink are **also** provided. **I think** the Mazu Festival is an amazing show of community spirit and human kindness!

我會盡我最大努力描述媽祖,她是歷史人物,也是宗教神祇。我並不篤信宗教,但生活在台灣的每個人都知道媽祖,也就是中國的海上女神。

我們在學校學過關於她的事蹟,我來講講我還記得的部分。我想她出生於宋朝,西元九〇六年。她有預測天氣的能力,泳技很好,經常拯救海上的人,甚至甘冒惡劣天氣。傳說她的死因,是由於她在暴風雨中,出海尋找她失蹤的父親。在她死後,她的家人和水手、漁夫開始在惡劣的天氣中祈求她的協助。

每一年她生日時,中台灣都會有慶祝活動,那是世界上最大的宗教慶典之一。二十萬名香客扛著坐在木轎上的媽祖神像,連走九天,旅程大約三百公里。在途中,許多地方民眾都會提供客廳或車庫供遊客休息。除了提供免費的場所,還有免費的食物和飲料。我覺得媽祖慶典展現了驚人的團結精神和人情味!

Vocabulary

rescue (v.) 拯救
pilgrim (n.) 朝聖者,香客
statue (n.) 雕像,塑像

I'll try my best to describe Mazu, who is both a historical and a religious figure. I'm not that religious, but everyone living in Taiwan knows Mazu as a Chinese sea goddess.

We learnt about her at school, and from what I can remember, she was born in the Song Dynasty, around the year 906. She had a mysterious ability to predict weather, and she often warned sailors against going to sea when the weather would be rough. She became a very good swimmer and would rescue people from the sea, **even** in the harshest weather. **Legend says** that Mazu's father was lost at sea and that she went out to search for him during a terrible storm. Hours passed, but still she couldn't find her father. She refused to give up and eventually died of exhaustion. **After** her death, her family and sailors and fishermen started to pray for her heroic acts. Starting from Fuijian, the worship of Mazu spread to the neighbouring coastal provinces. **Later**, Chinese immigrants brought the worship of Mazu to Taiwan. People began to build temples dedicated to Mazu all over the world.

Every year, her birthday, which **I believe** is in the third month of the lunar calendar, is celebrated widely in central Taiwan at temples in Dajia and Beigang. The 'Mazu pilgrimage' is recognised internationally as a world heritage event. It's one of the greatest religious festivals in the world. Huge groups of pilgrims walk for nine days, carrying a statue of Mazu in a wooden sedan chair. The journey covers 300 kilometres. On the way, many local people offer their living rooms or garages for visitors to rest in. **In addition** to free stays, free food and drink are **also** provided. **I think** it's amazing!

Mazu is not just a historic figure. **To this day**, she inspires countless followers, and her festival has become an event that shows great community spirit and human kindness. It's part of local Taiwanese culture now.

Vocabulary

mysterious (adj.) 神祕的
exhaustion (n.) 體力耗盡
worship (n./v.) 敬神
coastal (adj.) 沿海的
immigrant (n.) 移民
pilgrimage (n.) 朝聖
heritage (n.) 遺產
sedan (n.) 轎子

我會盡我最大努力描述媽祖，她是歷史人物，也是宗教神祇。我並不篤信宗教，但生活在台灣的人都視她為中國的海上女神。

我們在學校學過她的事蹟，就我記憶所及，她出生於宋朝，西元九〇六年。她有預測天氣的神祕能力，當天氣即將轉趨惡劣時，她時常警告水手不要出海。她的泳技很好，經常拯救海上的人，甚至甘冒惡劣天氣。傳說媽祖的父親在海上失蹤，她在狂風暴雨中出海找他，幾個小時過去，她還是沒能找到父親，她不願放棄，後來力盡而亡。在她死後，她的家人和水手、漁夫感佩她的英勇，開始祭拜她。對媽祖的崇拜始於福建，一直擴及到鄰近沿海省分。後來，來自中國的移民將媽祖信仰帶到台灣，人們也開始在全世界興建供奉媽祖的廟宇。

每年媽祖聖誕，我想是在農曆的三月，中台灣大甲和北港的廟宇會舉辦盛大的慶祝活動。「媽祖繞境」被國際認證為世界遺產活動，是世界上最大的宗教節慶之一。數量龐大的香客團扛著坐在木製神轎上的媽祖神像，連走九天，旅程大約三百公里。在途中，許多地方民眾會提供客廳或車庫供遊客休息。除了提供免費住宿，還供應免費的食物和飲料。我覺得很不可思議！

媽祖不只是歷史人物，時至今日，她鼓舞了無數的追隨者。她的節慶也成為展現強大團結精神和人情味的活動，現在已成為台灣地方文化的一部分。

一梗多用之變化形

- a historic event in your country
- a tradition in your country
- a story you read in your childhood

Question 1

> Describe your favourite part of your town/city.
>
> You should say:
>   where it is
>   what you do there
>   how often you go there
> and explain why you like that place.

描述你所居住城市中，你最喜愛的地方。

你要提到：

　　是什麼地方

　　你在那裡做什麼

　　你多久去一次

並解釋你為什麼喜歡那個地方。

要描述一個自己喜愛的地點時，可以使用大量的形容詞及名詞。為了讓答案更豐富，可以加入聽覺、視覺與嗅覺等各方面的感受。這樣會比僅僅描述地理位置、環境、可進行的活動生動多了！

一些相關點子

- café 咖啡店
- bookshop 書店
- the tallest building 最高的大樓
- the nature 自然景觀
- theme park 主題樂園
- a quiet place 安靜的地方

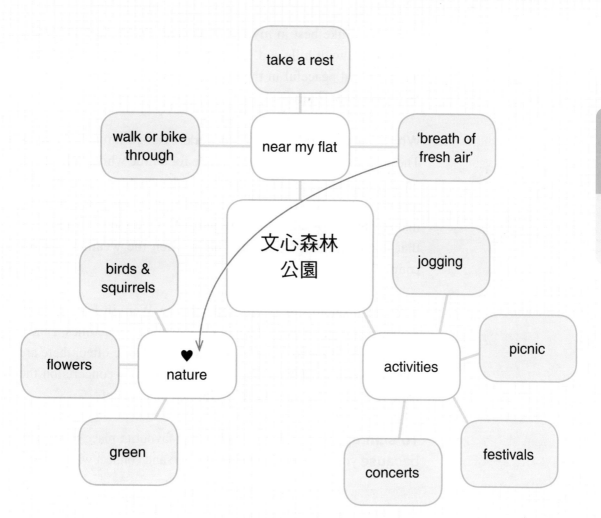

The place I like best in my city is Wenxin Forest Park. It's a big green space with hills and trees. It's near some busy streets, **but** it's quiet and peaceful in the middle. There are flowers and birds and sometimes squirrels.

When I walk or ride my bike to work, I can go through the park. The air is fresh ... I can get into nature for a little while. **When** I'm on my way home and not in a hurry, I sometimes stop to take pictures of the flowers or take a short rest on the grass. It really makes me feel good, especially when I'm stressed. I usually do that in the autumn **because** that's when the weather is most comfortable.

You can do many different activities in Wenxin Forest Park. Sometimes, I go jogging there in the evenings. Sometimes, I meet friends to do some exercise or have a picnic. Quite often, there are special events, **such as** the Lantern Festival or concerts on the park's stage. Lady Gaga **even** performed there once!

To sum up, Wenxin Forest Park is my favourite place in my city **because** you can have fun there, exercise and connect with nature.

在我居住的城市裡，我最喜歡的地方是文心森林公園。那是一大片綠地，有山丘還有樹林，鄰近交通繁忙的街道，但公園內部十分安靜平和。裡面有花、有鳥，有時候還有松鼠。

當我走路或騎腳踏車去上班時，我可以穿過公園，空氣很清新……我可以稍微親近一下大自然。如果回家不趕時間，有時候我會停下來拍攝花朵，在草地上休息一下。這會讓我真正覺得身心舒暢，特別是我有壓力的時候。秋天時我經常這麼做，因為那是天氣最舒適的時節。

在文心森林公園可以做許多不同的活動，有時候我會在晚上去慢跑，有時候會和朋友在那裡做運動或野餐。那裡也經常有特別的活動，例如元宵節或舞台音樂會，甚至連女神卡卡都曾在那裡表演過！

總而言之，在我居住的城市當中，文心森林公園是我的最愛，因為那是個能開心玩樂、運動，同時接觸大自然的地方。

Vocabulary

stressed (adj.)
精神緊繃的

Long Answer

I live in Taizhong. Like most big cities, it's somewhat polluted, noisy and busy. **But** it **also** has some decent parks, and Wenxin Forest Park is one of the best. It's my favourite place in Taizhong. **Although** it's surrounded by busy streets, it's quiet and peaceful in the middle. It's a big green space with hills and trees. There are flowers and birds there, and even some squirrels.

Wenxin Forest Park is near my flat, **so** I see it every day. If I walk or ride my bike to work, I always cut through it. **It's like** ... I'm escaping the city for a few minutes. It's literally a breath of fresh air. Being there, even for a short time, makes me feel more relaxed and connected to nature. In the autumn, **when** the weather is pleasant, I often stop to take a short rest in the park on my way home.

Wenxin Park is great for all sorts of activities. Sometimes, I go jogging there in the evenings. Almost every month, I meet friends there for a picnic or just to walk around. They host special events, **such as** the Lantern Festival, **too**. It's fun to see the lanterns and displays, but my favourite part of those events is the food stalls. I can always find some tasty snacks! Sometimes, there are concerts in the amphitheatre. **Rather than** sitting in the amphitheatre seats, **however**, I like sitting on the hillside and enjoying the show from a distance, perhaps with a drink in my hand from the nearby convenience store.

To sum up, Wenxin Forest Park is my favourite location in Taizhong **because** it provides lots of opportunities for entertainment **and** socialising **as well as** for getting some physical exercise **and** connecting with nature. **I think** it's really important for any big city to have places like this for its residents.

Part 2 Places

Vocabulary

decent (adj.) 不錯的
literally (adv.) 真正地
a breath of fresh air
清新的空氣，使人耳目一
新的事物
stall (n.) 小攤子
amphitheatre (n.)
圓形劇場
socialise (v.) 社交

我住在台中，那裡就跟多數大城市一樣汙染、嘈雜又忙碌。但這裡也有些不錯的公園，而文心森林公園算是數一數二。那是我在台中最喜歡的地方。雖然四周都是忙碌的街道，但公園內部十分安靜平和。那是一大片綠地，有山丘還有樹林，有花、有鳥，甚至還有松鼠。

文心森林公園在我的公寓附近，所以我每天都可以看到它。如果我走路或騎腳踏車去上班，總會穿過公園，就像是……暫時逃離這城市，真的可說是名副其實地感受清新的空氣。在那裡，即使只待一下下，都能讓我放鬆下來，感受大自然。秋天時天氣宜人，我常在回家路上，在公園裡停下來稍作休息。

文心公園很適合各種活動。有時候我會在晚上去慢跑，幾乎每個月，我都會找朋友到那裡野餐，或散散步。那裡也會舉辦特殊活動，例如元宵節。看花燈展很有趣，但我最喜歡的部分是美食攤，那裡總是能找到美味的點心！有時候，圓形劇場會有音樂會。然而，比起坐在圓形劇場的椅子上，我更喜歡坐在山坡上，從遠方欣賞，或許手裡還拿著旁邊便利商店買的飲料。

總而言之，文心森林公園是我在台中最喜歡的地方，因為那裡提供很多娛樂和社交的機會，同時也能做運動、接觸大自然。我想對任何大城市來說，讓居民擁有這類地方都是很重要的。

一梗多用之變化形

- a picnic
- an attraction in your country
- a place with open air which makes you feel relaxed

Question 2

Describe a historical site you've been to.

You should say:
      where it is
      how old it is
      what you can do there
and explain why it is significant.

描述一個你造訪過的歷史古蹟。

你要提到：

      位於何處

      歷史多悠久

      在那裡可以做什麼

並解釋該處為什麼很重要。

描述歷史景點一定要提到相關歷史：距今多久？有哪些人參與了這段歷史？跟歷史有關的比例要足夠，答案才算完整。如果講太多目前該地的商業活動（有什麼吃的、喝的或可以買的東西），答案就離題了。

一些相關點子
- Longshan Temple 龍山寺
- Confucian Temple 孔廟
- Fort San Domingo 紅毛城
- National Palace Museum 故宮
- Dragon and Tiger Pagodas 龍虎塔
- The Lin Family Mansion and Garden 林家花園
- Anping Small Fort 安平小砲台

Honestly, I'm not very interested in history. I don't visit historical sites very often, but there is an old cultural and historical town I like called Jiufen. It's in northeast Taiwan, on a mountain near the ocean. You can get there by train and bus.

Jiufen is a beautiful old mining town. It became famous when gold was discovered there more than a hundred years ago. **I think** the gold mine was run by the Japanese in the beginning. Around 1970, it was closed **because** there was no more gold. **Now** Jiufen is mainly a tourist town.

The narrow, dark streets are charming. People like to take pictures with the old Japanese buildings in the background. You can find many vendors and restaurants selling traditional Taiwanese food. My favourite snack to eat there is the taro balls. There are **also** lots of old tea houses, which are popular with the tourists and older people. **And** a lot of people visit the Gold Museum. I prefer to just walk around the souvenir shops and check out the cute wooden toys that children used to play with a long time ago.

I think Jiufen is a nice place to visit if you want to know a bit more about the history of Taiwan.

老實說，我對歷史不是很有興趣，也不太常去參觀歷史遺址，但我喜歡一個古老的文化歷史小鎮，名叫九份，位於台灣東北角，靠近海邊的一座山上。搭火車和公車就能抵達。

九份是個美麗的礦業古城，一百多年前在那裡發現了黃金因而聲名大噪。我想金礦一開始是由日本人經營，在一九七〇年左右，因為不再產金而關閉。現在九份主要是旅遊小鎮。

那些狹窄、幽暗的街道很迷人，大家喜歡以日式舊建築當背景拍照，你可以找到很多販售傳統台灣食物的攤販和餐廳。我在那裡最愛吃的點心是芋圓。那裡有很多老茶屋，很受觀光客及老人家的歡迎。很多人也會去黃金博物館，但我比較喜歡逛禮品店，看看一些很久以前小孩子玩的可愛木製玩具。

如果有人想更了解台灣的歷史，我覺得九份是個好去處。

Part 2

Places

Vocabulary

mining (n.) 採礦
mine (n.) 礦坑
vendor (n.) 攤販
souvenir (n.) 紀念品

To tell you the truth, I'm not very keen on history, and I don't visit historical sites very often. Luckily, I do remember a place I've been to a couple times called Jiufen. It's a famous cultural and historical town in northeast Taiwan. It takes about two hours to get there by public transport (first a train, and then a bus) from Taipei, **but I'm sure** you can drive there in under an hour.

I'm not sure how old Jiufen is, but it became famous when gold was discovered in the area over a hundred years ago. Many people were attracted there at that time by the prospect of finding gold. The Japanese used to manage the place, and you can still see some evidence of Japanese colonisation. In about 1970, the gold mine was closed, and the workers all left. **Now**, it mainly attracts tourists, photographers and foodies.

Jiufen sits on a mountainside overlooking the Pacific Ocean, **so** there are lots of steps and hills to climb, but you get rewarded with beautiful views. It's a charming, quaint town with old brick houses and narrow, dark alleys. **Although** it's often rainy, it's a great place to take pictures. There are lots of vendors and restaurants selling traditional Taiwanese foods. One of my favourite things to eat there is a dessert called yuyuan, which is a dish of little chewy balls made of taro. **Another popular thing to do there is** to visit one of the old tea houses, but they're always crowded. The Gold Museum is pretty interesting, but I've already been there, **so** I usually just walk around the souvenir shops. They sell interesting handicrafts and traditional wooden toys, which remind me of my childhood.

Even though I'm not really into history, I actually enjoy going to Jiufen. It's great to get away from the city for the day and experience a little of what Taiwan might have been like a century ago.

Vocabulary

prospect (n.) 預期
關 prospective (adj.) 預期的
colonisation (n.) 殖民化
foodie (n., slang) 美食家，吃貨
quaint (adj.) 古雅的
chewy (adj.) 有嚼勁的
handicraft (n.) 手工藝品

跟你老實說，我對歷史不太感興趣，也不常去參觀歷史古蹟。還好，我記得有個去過幾次的地方，叫做九份，那是台灣東北角有名的文化歷史小鎮，從台北搭乘大眾運輸（先搭火車再轉公車）到那裡大約需要兩小時，但我確定開車去不必一小時。

我不確定九份有多久的歷史，但一百多年前那裡因發現黃金聲名大噪，當時吸引了許多懷著淘金夢的人前往。那裡原本由日本人經營，現在還能看到日本殖民的證據。大約一九七〇年，金礦關閉，工人也全都撤離了。現在九份吸引的主要是觀光客、攝影師和美食愛好者。

九份座落在能俯瞰太平洋的山坡，所以得爬很多階梯和山丘，但有美景作為回報。這個古雅的小鎮有老磚房、狹窄幽暗的巷弄。雖然那裡常下雨，依然是個拍照的好地方。那裡有很多攤販和餐廳，販售傳統台灣食物，我在那裡最喜歡吃的其中一樣甜點是芋圓，是用芋頭做的小球，很有嚼勁。那裡另一項受歡迎的活動，是參觀老茶房，但總是人滿為患。黃金博物館挺有趣的，不過我去過了，所以我通常只會逛逛禮品店。店內販賣有趣的手工藝品和傳統木製玩具，總讓我想起我的童年。

即使我不太迷歷史，還是很喜歡去九份。可以遠離城市一天，稍微體驗一下一世紀前的台灣樣貌，是很棒的事。

一梗多用之變化形

- a photograph
- an attraction in your country
- a museum you've visited
- a place you visited as a child
- a souvenir you've bought

Question 3

Describe a house you'd like to live in.

You should say:
    where it is
    what it looks like
    how big it is
and explain why you would like to live there.

描述一間你想居住的房子。

你要提到：

位在哪裡

外觀長什麼樣子

房子有多大

並解釋為什麼你想住在裡面。

若還沒想過自己夢想中的房子，可以翻一翻 IKEA 型錄或逛一逛 Muji 店面，欣賞其中的室內設計，想想是哪些地方吸引你？

另外，Pinterest 網站也是一個找靈感的好地方，輸入 dream house 就可以看到各種不同風格的房子，還可以順便學學不同風格的英文用法。

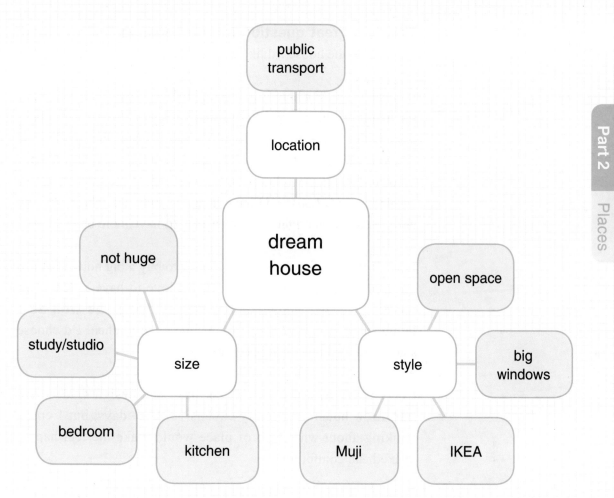

This is a great question for me because I've got a lot of ideas about the house I'd like to live in!

It doesn't matter where it is located. I'll live anywhere in the city **as long as** there is public transport nearby. What I care about more is the whole atmosphere of the house. I love the simple style that you can see in IKEA catalogues. I love light and space, **so** it needs to have big windows and high ceilings. I might want to buy an old flat or a house and have it re-designed. I'd take down any unnecessary walls right away **in order to** have more open space.

I don't think I'll ever have the money to buy a big house, **so** I'm not too picky about the size of it. I'd love to have at least two rooms—one for sleeping and one for studying—**as well as** a living room area **and** a small but functional kitchen. I'd choose some cool furniture in light colours.

I may never own my own place that I can design or decorate **because** housing is really expensive these days, but I enjoy thinking about what type of place would make me feel happy, relaxed and comfortable.

對我來說,這是個很好的問題,因為我對想住的房子有很多想法。

房子的地點不重要,只要是在市區且附近有大眾運輸工具我都可以接受。我更在乎的是房子的整體氣氛。我喜歡簡單的風格,就像在 IKEA 型錄上看到的那樣。我喜歡明亮、寬敞,所以需要大窗戶和挑高的天花板。我可能想買間舊公寓或舊房子,再加以重新設計,直接拆掉任何不必要的牆面,好擁有更多開放空間。

我不認為自己會有錢買大房子,所以不會太挑剔房子的大小。我希望至少有兩個房間,一間臥室、一間書房,還要有客廳以及一間功能齊全的小廚房。我還會選一些色彩明亮的酷炫家具。

或許我永遠不會擁有可以隨意設計、裝潢的房子,因為現在的房子非常昂貴,但我喜歡想像哪種房子會讓我覺得快樂、放鬆和舒適。

Vocabulary

catalogue (n.) 目錄
picky (adj.) 挑剔的

This is a great question for me because I often daydream about my ideal home!

The location isn't important, **as long as** there is public transport nearby and I can easily get to work. **However**, if I had a choice, I'd prefer a quiet neighbourhood to a noisy one.

What I care about more is the inside of the house or flat and the impression it gives people. I love light and space, **so** I'd prefer a loft-style home, with big windows and high ceilings. I might want to buy an old flat or a house, hire an interior designer, and renovate it. Small rooms and dark colours make a place feel cramped. **So** the first thing I'd do is knock down any unnecessary walls in favour of a more open floor plan. **Then** I'd probably paint everything white.

Then of course, I'd get some furniture, but I wouldn't clutter up the place. I love the minimalist style and always admire the model houses in IKEA catalogues. **Over the past few years**, I've **also** been really into simple Japanese interior design. There's a shop I like called Muji, which is famous for its wooden furniture and good quality kitchenware.

I don't think I could ever afford to buy a big house, **so** I'm realistic and not too picky about the size of it. **But** I'd love to have at least two bedrooms—one would be the master bedroom, and the other would be a multi-purpose guest room, study, and studio. I **also** want a small but functional kitchen and enough space to entertain a few guests. Those would be my basic requirements. A bathtub or hot tub sounds really appealing **too**, but it would probably take up too much space.

I think it'll be really difficult to have my own place **due to** the high housing costs these days, but it would be brilliant to live in a place that makes me feel relaxed and comfortable.

Part 2

Places

Vocabulary

loft (n.) 無隔間住宅（最
早是利用廠房、倉庫改建）
interior (adj.) 內部的
renovate (v.) 整修
cramped (adj.) 狹窄的
in favour of 有利於
clutter up 使雜亂
minimalist (adj.)
極簡主義的
kitchenware (n.) 廚具
appealing (adj.) 吸引人的

對我來說，這是個很好的問題，因為我常做白日夢想像理想中的房屋！

房子的地點不重要，只要附近有大眾運輸工具，可以方便上班即可。然而，如果我能選擇，我偏好安靜的社區，而不是嘈雜的地方。

我更在乎的是房屋或公寓的內部，還有它給人的印象。我喜歡明亮、寬敞，所以我偏好無隔間風格，有大窗戶和挑高天花板那種。我可能想買間舊公寓或舊房子，雇用一名室內設計師，然後重新裝修。小房間和深顏色都會讓空間顯得擁擠，所以我首先要做的就是拆掉不需要的牆以營造一個更開闊的空間。然後，我大概會把整個空間都漆成白色。

當然，再來我會買些家具，但不會把整個空間塞得亂七八糟。我喜歡極簡風格，一直都很欣賞 IKEA 型錄裡的模型屋。近幾年，我也很迷簡約的日本室內設計，有間叫 Muji 的店我很喜歡，那間店以木製家具和高品質廚房用具聞名。

我不認為自己會有錢買大房子，所以我很實際，不會太挑剔房子的大小。但我希望至少有兩間臥房，一間是主臥室，另一間是多功能客房，兼作書房和工作室。我還想要一間麻雀雖小五臟俱全的廚房，另外還要有足夠的空間能接待一些客人，這些是我的基本要求。浴缸聽來也很吸引人，但或許會占太多空間。

因為近來的高房價，我覺得要擁有自己的房子非常困難，但能住在一個讓我感到放鬆又舒適的地方，一定是很棒的事。

一梗多用之變化形

- a place to relax
- a magazine you like to read
- someone who just moved house
- someone who you visited

Question 4

> Describe a restaurant you like.
>
> You should say:
>> where it is
>> what kind of food it serves
>> how often you go there
> and explain how you feel about this place.

描述一間你喜歡的餐廳。

你要提到：

> 位在哪裡
>
> 提供什麼樣的食物
>
> 你多久去一次

並說明你對這家餐廳的感覺。

這種題目看似很簡單，但變化形很多。有時會問一間你**常去的餐廳**（那就要用現在式），有時會問你**曾去過的**一間餐廳（部分內容就要用過去式）。一定要注意看清楚題目。

可以用五種感官來延伸答案：

look：餐廳裝潢、餐點擺盤

taste：餐點口感、味道

feel：餐廳氣氛、服務生品質

sound：餐廳音樂、客人音量

smell：餐點香味、廁所（臭）味

I've chosen to describe the Italian restaurant I went to last weekend. **I think** it's called Mario's.

I don't go there often. **Actually**, Saturday evening was my first time. Some friends and I wanted to have dinner together, and my friend Shannon suggested Mario's. Shannon also picked me up and drove to the restaurant, **so** I don't know the address, but it's in the city centre.

I ordered the spinach ravioli. It had a spicy red sauce, and it was delicious. They had other kinds of pasta **as well as** other dishes **like** pizzas **and** salads. It was an interesting menu, with lots of things I'd like to try. It's a bit expensive, **but I think** it's worth it. The chef is definitely talented and adds his own creative, modern touch to traditional Italian dishes.

The decor, **on the other hand**, isn't modern at all. Sitting in the restaurant, you feel like you could be in Italy, but Italy a long time ago. The lights were dim. All the tables had chequered tablecloths and candles on them. There was Italian opera music playing softly in the background. **Actually**, it was very romantic—a good place for a date. My friends and I really enjoyed it.

我選擇談談上週末去的義大利餐廳，我想是叫做 Mario's。

我不常去那裡。事實上，週六晚上是第一次去。我和幾個朋友晚上想要一起聚餐，其中一個朋友夏倫推薦 Mario's，她還開車接我去餐廳，所以我不知道地址，但位在市中心。

我點了菠菜義大利餃，配上辛辣紅醬，非常美味。他們還有其他種類的義大利麵及餐點，像是披薩和沙拉。菜單很吸引人，上面有很多我想嘗試的食物。價格有點貴，但我認為很值得。主廚真的很有才華，他在傳統的義大利料理當中，加入自己的創意及現代的料理手法。

另一方面，裝潢則一點也不現代。坐在餐廳裡，就像身在義大利，不過是年代久遠的義大利。燈光有些昏暗，所有的桌巾都是格子花紋，上面還擺了蠟燭，並播放著輕柔的義大利歌劇音樂。事實上，那裡非常浪漫，是個約會的好地方，我朋友和我都很喜歡。

Part 2

Places

Vocabulary

pasta (n.) 義大利麵（通稱）
touch (n.) 潤飾
decor (n.) 裝潢
chequered (adj.) 格紋的

Since it's fresh in my memory, I've chosen to describe the Italian restaurant I went to last weekend. **I think** it's called Mario's or Marino's. **Anyway**, it was definitely named after an Italian man.

Last Saturday, a few friends and I had a small gathering to celebrate **because** one of them recently got a promotion. Another of my friends suggested Marino's and gave me a ride there, **so** I don't know the actual address, but it was somewhere in the city centre. It's in the basement of an average-looking building.

It was a good thing we had a reservation **because** the restaurant was full and there was a waiting list to get a table. **After** trying the food, I can see why! I ordered the spinach ravioli. It came in a spicy red sauce, and it was to die for. They **also** had other kinds of pasta, various pizzas, and salads. It was an interesting menu, **actually**, not just your typical Italian food. I got the impression that the chef enjoys adding his own creative, modern touch to traditional Italian dishes. **For example**, one of my friends ordered a pizza with goat's cheese, apples, and walnuts on it! He said it was amazing.

The decor, **on the other hand**, is definitely traditional. Stepping into the restaurant, you're immediately transported back in time and across to Italy. The lights are dim. All the tables have red and white chequered tablecloths and tall candles. There was Italian opera music playing softly in the background. It created a very romantic ambience.

All in all, I really have no complaints. It was a little pricey but definitely worth it. It's a lovely restaurant with amazing food. The service was excellent, **too**. I can't believe I had never heard of this restaurant before. That was my first time, but it won't be my last!

Vocabulary

gathering (n.) 聚會
關 gather (v.) 聚集
to die for 極好的
typical (adj.) 典型的
walnut (n.) 核桃
ambience (n.) 氛圍
pricey (adj.) 昂貴的

因為記憶猶新，我選擇描述上週末去的義大利餐廳，好像叫做 Mario's 還是 Marino's。反正，肯定是用義大利人的名字命名的。

上週六，幾個朋友和我有場小聚會，慶祝其中一位朋友最近升職了。我另一個朋友建議 Marino's，並載我到那裡，所以我不知道正確的地址。不過是在市中心的某處，位於一棟外觀平常的大樓地下室。

還好我們有訂位，因為餐廳客滿，還有多組客人在候位。吃過那裡的餐點之後，我可以理解為何會如此熱門！我點了菠菜義大利餃，搭配辛辣紅醬，好吃極了。他們還有其他種類的義大利麵、各種披薩和沙拉。菜單很吸引人，事實上，不只有典型的義大利菜。我感覺主廚很喜歡加入自己的創意，為傳統義大利菜增加現代感。例如，我其中一位朋友點的披薩上有羊奶乳酪、蘋果和核桃！他說非常好吃。

另一方面，裝潢就是完完全全的傳統風格。走進餐廳裡，你馬上像回到舊時光的義大利，燈光昏暗，所有桌子都鋪上紅白格紋的桌巾，上面還有高蠟燭，背景播放著輕柔的義大利歌劇音樂，創造出非常浪漫的氛圍。

總而言之，我想不到哪裡可以抱怨。價格是有點貴，但絕對值得。這是家令人愉快的餐廳，有非常好的食物，服務也很棒，我不敢相信之前從沒聽過這家餐廳。那是我的第一次，但不會是最後一次！

一梗多用之變化形

- a place to relax
- something you ate for the first time
- an important conversation you had with someone
- an occasion when you received good service from a restaurant or shop

Question 5

Describe a country you hope to visit.

You should say:
>   where it is
>   what it's like
>   what you can do there
and explain why you want to go there.

描述一個你希望造訪的國家。

你要提到：

>   位在哪裡
>   那裡是什麼樣子
>   在那裡可以做什麼

並解釋為什麼你想去那裡。

描述自己想造訪的國家時，不要只提美食或購物等千篇一律的內容，可多著墨在該國特殊的文化、景觀、風土民情，如此也可使用到較多樣的字彙，較能讓考官留下深刻印象。

一些相關點子

- traditional dancing 傳統舞蹈
- museums and galleries 博物館與藝廊
- handicrafts 手工藝品
- architecture 建築
- cooking class 烹飪課程
- trekking 長途健行
- scuba diving 水肺潛水

One place I've wanted to go for a while now is Greece. It's in Europe, **of course**, by the Mediterranean Sea. I **first** became interested in visiting Greece when I was at university. I met a Greek exchange student who showed me pictures of her hometown. **Later**, I saw some travel programmes about Greece on TV. I'm very interested in Greece now.

In my imagination, Greece is always warm and sunny, with historical sites and beaches everywhere. I used to have a calendar hanging on my wall which had pictures of beautiful scenery from different Greek islands. The only one I can remember is Santorini. The houses there all have white walls and blue roofs. I heard that poor people painted their houses white **because** coloured paint was expensive. **I thought** that was so interesting.

There's lots to do in Greece. **One thing** I know most people do is island hopping. I would love to do some sunbathing and shopping on the islands—**oh, and** eating! There are some new Mediterranean restaurants in my town, and I really love the fried squid and different salads I've tried. **Anyway**, I hope I can make my dream of going to Greece come true soon.

目前我想去待一陣子的地方是希臘。希臘位於歐洲，當然啦，濱地中海。我最早開始想去希臘玩是在念大學時。當時我遇到一名希臘的交換學生，她給我看她家鄉的照片。後來，我在電視上看到一些去希臘的旅遊節目，我現在對希臘非常感興趣。

在我的想像中，希臘總是溫暖又晴朗，到處都是歷史遺跡和海灘。我牆上曾掛過一份月曆，上面有希臘各島嶼的美麗風景照。我唯一記得的是聖托里尼島，那裡的房子都是白牆藍屋頂。我聽說窮人會將房屋漆白，是因為彩色油漆很貴。我覺得好有趣。

在希臘可以進行很多活動。我知道多數人會跳島旅遊。我會想做日光浴，在島上購物，喔，還有大吃特吃！我居住的城市裡有些新開的地中海餐廳，我吃過炸魷魚和幾種沙拉都很喜歡。反正，希望我可以早點夢想成真，去希臘旅遊。

Vocabulary

exchange student 交換學生
island hopping 跳島旅遊
squid (n.) 魷魚

Long Answer

One place I've wanted to go for a while now is Greece. It's located in southern Europe, by the Mediterranean Sea. I **first** became interested in visiting Greece when I was at uni. I was a member of the international club, and I met a Greek exchange student who told me a lot about her home country. **Before that**, I had only thought about Greece as an ancient civilization. More recently, I've seen some travel programmes about Greece on TV. I'm totally fascinated by Greece now.

Although it may not be true, I imagine Greece to be sunny all the time. I used to have a calendar hanging on my wall which featured beautiful scenery from different Greek islands. The only one I can remember by name is Santorini. It's famous for its houses on the hillside which all have white walls and blue roofs that match the blue sky. I heard that only rich people had colourful houses and the poor could only paint their houses white. **I guess** that would explain it, but I bet those houses are worth a lot of money these days.

There's loads to do in Greece. **Of course**, there are plenty of historical sites from ancient Greece. It would be a shame to go all the way to Greece and not see the Parthenon and a few other key places. **But** I'd like to spend most of my time on the islands. Island hopping is a popular tourist activity. I'd do plenty of sunbathing on the beaches and probably some shopping. Mediterranean food is becoming more common here in Taiwan, and I really love the fried squid and different salads I've tried. **So, I'm sure** if I go, I'll eat plenty of authentic, local Greek food.

I've looked into going to Greece and it's not cheap, **so** I probably won't go in the very near future. **But** I'm saving money, **so** hopefully, I'll get there in the next few years.

Part 2

Places

Vocabulary

uni (n.) 大學（university 的縮寫，英式口語）
ancient (adj.) 古老的
fascinate (v.) 著迷
feature (v.) 以…為特色
authentic (adj.) 道地的
look into 調查，研究

209

目前我想去待一陣子的地方是希臘。希臘位於歐洲南部，濱地中海。我最開始想去希臘玩是在念大學的時候。當時我是國際社團的成員，認識了一名希臘交換學生，她告訴我許多她家鄉的事。在那之前，我以為希臘就只是個古文明國家。最近，我在電視上看了去希臘的旅遊節目，我現在完全迷上希臘了。

雖然不一定是真的，我想像中的希臘總是陽光普照。我曾在牆上掛一份月曆，上面有希臘各島嶼的美麗風景。我唯一記得是聖托里尼島，山丘上的白牆藍屋頂與藍天相輝映，非常有名。我聽說以前只有富裕人家有彩色房屋，窮人只能將房子漆成白色。我想這就說得通了，但我敢說那些房子現在值很多錢。

在希臘可以進行很多活動。當然，那裡有許多古希臘的歷史遺跡，如果大老遠跑去希臘，卻沒參觀帕德嫩神廟和其他重要景點，就太可惜了。但我想把多數時間花在島上，跳島是很受觀光客歡迎的旅遊方式，我想要在海灘上大做日光浴，或許也會去逛街購物。地中海食物在台灣愈來愈普遍，我吃過炸魷魚和幾種不同的沙拉都很喜歡，所以我確定如果去到那裡，我會去吃很多正統、在地的希臘食物。

我查過去希臘旅行不便宜，所以我近期內或許不會去。但我正在存錢，希望再過幾年可以成行。

一梗多用之變化形

- a place to relax
- a colourful place you went to
- something you ate for the first time
- a television programme you enjoyed watching

Part 3
考試技巧大揭密

題目類型

Part 3 的問題會跟 Part 2 的卡片題有些微關連，但問題通常會比較有深度，也會比較抽象，不過都是一些常見的主題，例如健康、娛樂、教育、科技、環境議題等。Part 3 的問題有以下五種類別：

1. Quick question
快問快答類

這類題目要求考生直接回答，後面再加幾句話延伸說明。例如：

Is pollution a big problem in your country?
汙染在你的國家是個很嚴重的問題嗎？

What sorts of things do you do with friends?
你和朋友在一起時會做些什麼事？

2. Opinion
看法類

詢問考生對某事物或某觀點的看法，考生需要提出個人看法並延伸說明。例如：

Is it better to buy clothes in small shops/online?
在小店 / 網路上買衣服比較好嗎？

Some people say that it is more important to be able to learn new things now than it was in the past. Do you agree or disagree? Why?
有些人說，現在能夠學習新事物比起過去更加重要。你是否同意？為什麼？

**3. Compare &
Contrast
比較類**

詢問兩件事的差異處與相似點，或比較兩個時期的狀況。例如：

How do you think school life differs from university life?
你認為中學生活和大學生活有什麼不同？

Do you think children and adults learn to do new things in the same way? How are their learning styles different?
你認為小孩和成人是用同樣的方法學習新事物嗎？他們的學習模式有什麼不同？

**4. Cause and Effect
因果關係類**

詢問某事的原因、影響或解決方式。例如：

What are some of the causes of water pollution?
水汙染的部分原因是什麼？

What effects can watching television have on children?
看電視對兒童有什麼影響？

**5. Hypothetical
假設類**

這類題目是在問假想性的問題。例如：

If you could choose any country to live in, which one would you choose?
如果你可以選擇居住的國家，你會選擇哪個國家？

What would happen if there were no Internet?
如果沒有網路，會出現什麼情況？

Part 3 的問題無法像 Part 1 那樣反射性快答，Part 3 的問題考驗考生的思辯能力，作答時需要解釋、舉例、總結或提出其他解決方案，所以一個問題往往需要用到好幾句話才能完整回答。

Part 3 的問題沒有正確答案，重點在於考生是否有能力捍衛自己的想法、深入探討話題。考官不在乎考生的意見為何，考生的意見就算跟考官的想法不同也不會失分。

AEC 三步驟答題法

Part 3 除了快問快答的問題，其他類型的問題建議至少都要回答 3～4 句，才能讓回答聽起來夠深入完整。以下介紹 **A → E → C 三步驟答題法**，只要記得這三個步驟，就可以讓 Part 3 的答案聽起來完整、有連貫性又有深度。

直接回答
Answer

↓

解釋或舉例
Explanation or **E**xample

↓

讓步或結論
Concession or **C**onclusion

Answer
直接回答

一聽到問題，**馬上直接回答，不需要開場白**。例如：

問題

Do you think your country would benefit from more tourists?
你覺得你的國家會因為有更多觀光客而受益嗎？

Part 3 的回答不要太常使用一些累贅說法（例如 Well, that's an interesting question），盡量清楚明確地回答問題，例如：

回答

Definitely not!
完全不會！

Explanation or Example
解釋或舉例

直接回答問題後，可以繼續提供進一步的**「解釋」**，讓答案往下延伸。

例如上一個問題，在回答 Definitely not! 之後，便可以進一步**解釋**，為什麼你覺得你的國家並不會因為有更多觀光客而受益，例如：

回答　Definitely not! Taiwan is very small, and there are a lot of people living here. If we have more tourists, we won't even be able to leave our homes!
完全不會！台灣非常小，有很多人住在這裡。如果有更多觀光客，我們甚至可能會出不了門。

有些問題則是需要**「舉例」**才能讓你的回答更清楚易懂。例如：

問題　How does advertising influence what people choose to buy?
廣告如何影響人們購買的選擇？

若你只回答：In many ways.（有很多方式。）

這樣的回答就講得不清不楚，很多方式是什麼方式呢？不必等考官問，自己主動舉例比較好。例如：

In many ways. Advertisements can really make a product look irresistible. For example, people generally have a positive response when they see their favourite celebrity endorsing a product.
有很多方式，廣告真的能讓產品看起來令人無法抗拒。例如，人們若看到產品是他們喜歡的名人所代言，通常就會對該產品有好的評價。

偶爾也可以用**解釋＋舉例**，但注意這樣的組合容易給人重複感，若一定要這麼使用時，使用的字彙要盡量有所變化。

如果你講完一個答案之後，覺得話有點講太滿了，或是失之偏頗，就可以接幾句**「讓步」**的句子，讓言論聽起來不那麼武斷。例如：

問題

Who goes to coffee shops in your country?
在你的國家，哪些人會去咖啡店？

若你的答案是：

回答

Young people. Young people like to hang out in coffee shops.
年輕人。年輕人喜歡到咖啡店消磨時間。

後面接的這句話就是讓步：

But I guess more and more older people are going to coffee shops.
Nowadays, you see people from all walks of life in cafés.
但我猜有愈來愈多年紀比較大的人也去咖啡店。現在咖啡店裡可以看到形形色色的人。

walk of life

回答除了可以用讓步作結，也可以利用**「結論」**作結，而且有時方法很簡單，只要把前面講過的話換句話說即可。例如：

問題

What is the best way to learn a foreign language?
學習外國語言，最好的方式是什麼？

回答

You need a good teacher—a teacher who knows what your problems are and can answer all your questions. Without someone to guide you, it's just a waste of time. **You can't really learn a language without a good teacher.**
你需要一位好老師。一位知道你的缺點，而且可以回答你所有問題的老師，沒有人指導，只是浪費時間。缺少好老師，你無法真正學會一種語言。

Tip

AEC 步驟像積木一樣，可以混合搭配，有很多排列組合，考生可以靈活運用。

- Answer + Explanation
- Answer + Explanation + Example
- Answer + Explanation + Concession
- Answer + Explanation + Conclusion
- Answer + Example
- Answer + Example + Conclusion
- Answer + Example + Concession
- Answer + Example + Explanation + Conclusion

在練習初期，考生可以先在紙上寫下自己想講的順序，但習慣之後就要把這個步驟搬進腦子裡，因為 Part 3 考試時不但沒有紙筆，也沒有時間讓考生琢磨答案的。

現在，我們來實際練習一下。若被問到這個題目：

問題

Which social media apps or websites are most popular in your country?
在你的國家，哪個社群應用程式或網站最受歡迎？

你會怎麼用 AEC 三步驟組織你的答案呢？

Answer 1: Answer + Explanation + Concession

A 回答	E 解釋	C 讓步
Facebook	Everyone is on it	Instagram

Without a doubt, the most used social network in Taiwan is Facebook. Everyone I know is on it, even my grandmother! My friends and I use it to keep in touch. These days, Instagram is also gaining in popularity, but I believe Facebook still has more users.

無庸置疑地，台灣最普遍使用的社交媒體是臉書。我認識的每個人都有用臉書，連我奶奶都有！我朋友和我藉此保持聯繫。最近 IG 也愈來愈受歡迎，但我相信臉書的使用者還是比較多。

Answer 2: Answer + Example + Conclusion

A 回答	E 舉例	C 結論
American	Facebook and Instagram	old-fashioned

I would say that American social networks are extremely popular, not just in my country, but all over the world. Facebook and Instagram, for example, have billions of users worldwide. You'd be considered old-fashioned if you weren't on at least one of them!

我想美國的社交媒體極受歡迎，不只在我的國家，而是舉世皆然。例如臉書和 IG 在全世界有數十億使用者。如果沒有至少使用其中一個，會被認為跟不上時代。

Answer 3: Answer + Example + Example

A 回答	E 舉例	E 舉例
Facebook	Instagram	Twitter

It's hard to say. It was Facebook, but I think Instagram and Twitter have been gaining in popularity lately. I downloaded Instagram just last year, and it's pretty addictive! It's really fun to post pictures and messages on it. I'm using it more than Facebook now. I also have a Twitter account, but I don't use it much.

很難說，本來是臉書，但我想 IG 和推特最近也很有人氣。我去年才下載 IG，非常令人上癮！上傳照片和訊息非常好玩。比起臉書，現在我更常用 IG。我也有推特帳號，但不常用。

Part 3 應試小提醒

1. 預先準備好各種問題及答案

要在 Part 3 表現出色，平常準備時就要大量涉獵有深度的問題，設想這些問題會如何延伸發展，並假想考官會再深入探討哪些問題。

例如 coffee shops 這個主題，如果套用到 Part 3 的五大常見題目類型：Quick question（快問快答）、Opinion（看法）、Compare & Contrast（比較）、Cause and Effect（因果關係），以及 Hypothetical（假設），可能出現的問題就會有：

快問快答
Who goes to coffee shops?
誰會去咖啡店？

看法
Why do people go to coffee shops?
為什麼人們要去咖啡店？

比較
Do you think young people go to coffee shops more than old people?
你覺得年輕人比老年人更常去咖啡店嗎？

因果關係
Do you think more and more people are going to coffee shops these days because of the influence of Western culture?
你認為現在有愈來愈多人去咖啡店是受到西方文化的影響嗎？

假設
Would you like to be the owner of a coffee shop?
你想開咖啡店嗎？

每一種主題都試著想一輪可能出現的問題和作答方式，這樣考試時就能隨機應變。

2. 練習換句話說

Part 1 的問題通常比較簡單，答案也相對比較直接，換句話說會顯得累贅，但 Part 3 的問題通常需要比較深入回答。換句話說是延伸答案的方法之一，考生一定要多多練習換句話說的能力。

3. 練習批判性思考的能力

很多考生因為缺乏深入思考的訓練，被問到問題時，常會不假思索地「同意」考官提出的問題，或是丟出一個「大眾型」答案。例如被問到：

Do you think traffic is a big problem in your city?
在你所居住的城市中，交通是個大問題嗎？

就馬上回答 Yes。或是聽到：

What is the biggest problem in your city?
在你所居住的城市中，最大的問題是什麼？

就只會想到 traffic jams（塞車）。不是說回答 traffic jams 不行，因為可能考生居住的城市，塞車真的是個很嚴重的問題，但回答交通問題的考生比例相當高，使用的單字同質性也很高。平時應該多收集多樣性的答案，例如這一題若能改成回答 housing（居住）、few job opportunities（缺少工作機會）或是 lack of public transport（缺乏大眾運輸）等，再加以延伸，就會給考官耳目一新的感覺。

「大眾型」的答案不容易出錯，或許也能得到不錯的分數，但想要精益求精的考生，可以藉由提升思考能力突破瓶頸，取得進一步的高分。

Part 3 口說高分練習題

五大常考主題　　常考主題 1：Internet 網路

常考主題 2：Reading 閱讀

常考主題 3：Weather 天氣

常考主題 4：Television 電視

常考主題 5：Shopping 購物

練習方法　　接下來，我們要實際運用前面學過的技巧。每一類常考主題都會有五個問題，每一個問題都會提供兩種不同的答題示範。建議考生先不要看答案，試著自己用 AEC 三步驟答題法作答，最後再參考答案範例。

答案中的粗體字是讓語意更流暢連貫的指標詞，考生可以仔細觀察使用位置，學習如何使用指標詞讓 AEC 的銜接順暢且合乎邏輯，讓你的英文聽起來更道地。

Part 3

Question 1

Which social media apps or websites are most popular in your country?
在你的國家，哪個社群應用程式或網站最受歡迎？

Answer 1 答題步驟：Answer + Explanation + Concession

A

I'd say the most widely-used one is Facebook.
我想使用最廣泛的是臉書。

E

Everyone I know is on it, **so** it's easy to stay in touch with friends and acquaintances. People like it **because** it's an all-purpose social-media app. It's useful for posting photos and links, promoting events and sending private messages.
我認識的每個人都有用臉書，所以很容易和親朋好友保持聯繫。大家喜歡用臉書，因為那是全方位的社群應用程式，很方便用來上傳照片和連結、促銷活動以及傳私訊。

C

Other than that, I think more and more people are starting to use Instagram, but it's still not as popular as Facebook.
此外，我想有愈來愈多人開始使用 IG，但仍不如臉書普遍。

● acquaintance (n.) 熟人

Answer 2 答題步驟：Answer + Example 1 + Example 2

A

It's hard to say. It was definitely Facebook for a long time, **but I think** Instagram and Twitter are gaining in popularity lately.
很難說。一直以來都是臉書，但我想 IG 和推特最近也很有人氣。

E1 I downloaded Instagram just last year, and it's pretty addictive! It's really fun to post pictures and messages on it. I'm using it more than Facebook now.

我去年才下載 IG，非常令人上癮！上傳照片和訊息非常好玩，現在比起臉書，我更常用 IG。

E2 I **also** have a Twitter account. I know a lot of people tweet every day, but I don't use it much.

我也有推特帳號。我知道很多人每天都會發推文，但我不太常用。

● account (n.) 帳號

🎧 090 Question 2

Do you think young people are spending too much time on the Internet?
你認為年輕人花太多時間上網嗎？

Answer 1 答題步驟： Answer + Explanation + Conclusion

A **Probably**.
大概吧。

E I often see teenagers with their eyes glued to their smartphones **and I don't think** it's healthy. They should be reading a book or spending time with people in the real world.
我常看到青少年緊盯著他們的智慧型手機，我覺得這樣不太健康。他們應該看書或花時間與現實生活中的人多多相處。

C **So all in all, I think** it's a problem, and **I'm afraid** it's getting worse.
總而言之，我認為這是個問題，而且恐怕會愈來愈糟。

● glue (v.) 緊黏

A **Well**, they're online a lot, but it's a fact of life now. **And** it's not just young people.

這個嘛，他們經常上網。但這就是現實生活，而且不只是年輕人如此。

E Everyone uses the Internet to do work and keep in touch with friends. Without it, it's difficult to know what's going on.

每個人都使用網路工作以及和朋友保持聯繫。沒有網路，就很難知道外界的情況。

C **But I guess** it can be annoying to see people using their phones in meetings or at the dinner table. Sometimes people aren't even aware of their excessive phone use.

但我覺得在開會或餐桌上看到有人使用手機，是蠻討厭的。有時候大家根本沒注意到自己過度使用手機。

● keep in touch with 與⋯保持聯絡　● excessive (adj.) 過度的

091 Question 3

How has the Internet changed the way people interact socially?

網路如何影響人們的社交互動？

Answer 1 答題步驟：Answer + Example + Conclusion

A **Well**, the most obvious change is that there's less face-to-face interaction and more written communication.

這個嘛，最明顯的改變是面對面的互動減少了，文字溝通變多了。

E We're more likely to send a text message than have a real chat with a friend. Instead of giving someone a compliment in person, we just 'like' their photos online.

比起真正和朋友聊天，我們更常傳訊息，而且我們不會當面稱讚別人，只會幫朋友的照片按「讚」。

C

I have to say that I miss the old days when people had better social skills.
我必須說，我懷念過去人們的社交比較高明的日子。

- interaction (n.) 互動   - compliment (n.) 讚美

Answer 2 答題步驟：Answer + Example + Concession

A

I actually think that the Internet has improved social interaction in a lot of ways.
其實，我認為網路在許多方面讓社會的互動變得更好了。

E

Thanks to Facebook and email, I'm in touch with a lot of old friends and acquaintances that I wouldn't otherwise interact with. My friends and I use the Internet to organise events and get-togethers, **so** it's a good thing for me.
多虧了臉書和電子郵件，我能和許多老朋友或熟人保持聯絡，否則我並不會跟他們有所互動。我和朋友會使用網路安排活動和聚會，所以網路對我來說有所助益。

C

We just need to remind ourselves that the Internet should help us communicate, not stop us.
我們只需要提醒自己，網路應該幫助我們溝通，而非阻礙溝通。

- get-together (n.) 聚會

092 Question 4

Should companies monitor their employees' online activity?
公司應該監看員工的網路活動嗎？

Answer 1 答題步驟：Answer + Explanation + Conclusion

A

Sure. I can understand why a company would want to, and I have no strong objection.
當然。我能明白公司為何想這麼做，我也不會強烈反對。

E **I mean**, if employees aren't doing anything against the company rules, they have nothing to hide. **After all**, the company pays for their employees to work and be productive, not for them to do online shopping at work.

我是說，如果員工所為不違反公司規則，就沒什麼好隱藏的。畢竟，公司付薪水給員工，是要他們工作並有生產力，不是讓他們在工作時線上購物的。

C **Personally**, I don't care if they monitor me.

就我個人來說，我不在乎他們是否監看我。

● monitor (v.) 監視　● objection (n.) 反對

Answer 2 答題步驟：Answer + Explanation + Concession + Conclusion

A **Hmm** ... I would feel uncomfortable if I knew my company was checking how I'm spending my time at work.

嗯……如果我得知公司在查看我工作時間做了什麼，我會覺得不舒服。

E **I mean**, if I can finish my work and not delay anything, I think my company should trust me.

我是說，如果我能完成工作，沒有延誤，我認為我的公司應該信任我。

C **But** I do have a colleague who spends a lot of time surfing and going on social media sites. **I'm sure** it affects his productivity, **so I think** the company has the right to stop him.

但我的確有同事花很多時間上網亂逛或上社交網站。我確定這會影響他的生產力，所以我認為公司有權利制止他。

C **So, I guess** it really depends on the employees' performance.

所以我想，這實在是取決於員工的表現。

● surf (v.) 上網瀏覽

Question 5

Not everyone in the world has access to the Internet. What are the main disadvantages of not being able to get online?

世界上不是每個人都能使用網路。不能上網的主要缺點是什麼？

Answer 1 答題步驟： Answer + Example + Explanation + Conclusion

A I can hardly imagine what that would be like! They're missing out on so much information and so many opportunities.

我不能想像那會是個什麼樣的世界！他們會錯過許多資訊和很多機會。

E If you didn't have Internet access, you wouldn't be able to quickly find the answers to all the questions you have. Running a business would be extra hard without being able to use online banking.

如果不能上網，遇到問題就不能很快找到答案。不能使用網路銀行，經營事業也會更加困難。

E **Basically**, you'd be isolated from the world! It'd be like living in prehistoric times!

基本上，你與世隔絕了！就好像活在史前時代！

C **I think** we should do whatever we can to bridge the digital divide.

我認為我們要盡全力消除數位落差。

● bridge (v.) 縮短距離 ● divide (n.) 分歧

Answer 2 答題步驟： Answer + Explanation + Example + Conclusion

A **I suppose** most people would say not having the Internet is bad, but I **actually** think it could be a good thing.

我想多數人會說沒有網路很糟，但我其實認為這是件好事。

E **I mean**, the Internet is useful, but it hasn't made people happier.

我是說，網路很有用，但它沒有讓人更快樂。

E A lot of people use it to waste time, spread harmful ideas, or even con people out of their money.

很多人上網浪費時間，散播有害的想法，甚至詐騙他人金錢。

C **So**, what people think is a disadvantage could **actually** be an advantage.

所以，人們認為有害之處其實是益處。

● con (v.) 詐欺

Now you try:

1. Do you think the government should provide free Wi-Fi for everyone?
2. How can we find reliable information on the Internet?
3. Should young children be allowed to use the Internet?
4. How has the Internet changed the way we work?

1. 你認為政府應該為所有人提供免費無線網路嗎？
2. 我們在網路上要如何找到可靠的資訊？
3. 應允許幼童上網嗎？
4. 網路如何改變我們工作的方式？

095

Question 1

Why do you think some children don't read books very often?
你認為有些兒童為何不常看書？

Answer 1 答題步驟： Answer + Example + Conclusion

A
I think it's because of the popularity of electronic devices.
我認為這是因為電子產品的普及。

E
Kids nowadays all seem to have smartphones or iPads. I see them watching cartoons or videos wherever I go. I never see kids reading books anymore.
現在的小孩似乎都有智慧型手機或 iPad。不管去到哪裡，我都會看到他們在看卡通或影片，再也沒看到有小孩在看書了。

C
But to be honest, I myself don't read much either. **I guess** it's just more interesting to watch videos than read books.
但老實說，我自己也不太看書了。我覺得看影片比看書有趣多了。

Answer 2 答題步驟： Answer + Explanation + Conclusion

A
I blame their parents, **to be honest**.
老實說，是他們的父母不對。

E
It's the parents' job to instil the habit of reading in their children. They should provide books, set aside time for reading, read with their children and restrict TV time.
養成小孩的閱讀習慣是父母的責任。父母應該提供書籍，安排時間和小孩一起看書，並且限制看電視的時間。

C My parents did that for me, **and I think** that's why I became an avid reader.

我的父母就是這麼對我的，我認為這是我愛讀書的原因。

- instil (v.) 逐漸灌輸　　● set aside 撥出（時間）　　● avid (adj.) 貪心的；渴望的

Question 2

Do you read a lot? What sort of things do you usually read?

你經常閱讀嗎？你通常讀哪種書？

Answer 1 答題步驟： Answer + Example + Concession

A **Yeah, I'd say** reading is one of my hobbies. I've always loved reading, especially fiction.

對，閱讀可以說是我的嗜好之一。我一直喜歡看書，特別是小說。

E I mostly read novels—some classics and some newer stuff. My favourite author at the moment is Haruki Murakami. He's Japanese, but his books are translated into Chinese and other languages.

我大多看小說，部分是經典小說，部分是較新的小說。我目前最喜歡的作者是村上春樹，他是日本人，但他的書被翻譯成中文和其他語言。

C **But** I have to admit, the last novel I read was a couple of months ago. I've been occupied with working and studying recently.

但我得承認，我最近一次看小說是在幾個月前，最近時間被工作和上課占滿了。

Answer 2 答題步驟： Answer + Explanation + Conclusion

A I'm not a book lover at all.

我完全不是個愛書人。

E **I guess it's because** as a child I was only encouraged to study, and the only books I read were textbooks! **Honestly**, that totally killed my interest in books.
我想這是因為小時候只被鼓勵用功讀書，我看的書都只有教科書！老實說，那完全扼殺了我對書本的興趣。

C If I have a child one day, I will try to do things differently. **I think** reading is a good habit. It can broaden your horizons. I wish I loved reading.
如果有天我有小孩，我會嘗試不同的做法。我認為閱讀是種好習慣，能擴展一個人的眼界，但願我喜歡閱讀。

097 ## Question 3

Do you think reading novels is more interesting than reading factual books?
你認為看小說比讀科普類書籍更有趣嗎？

Answer 1 答題步驟： Answer + Explanation + Concession

A **Not at all. I think** non-fiction is fascinating.
完全不會。我認為非小說作品很有趣。

E I like reading about amazing events that actually happened. **As they say**, truth is stranger than fiction.
我喜歡閱讀真正發生過的驚人事件，俗話說「真實奇於小說」。

C Novels can **also** be interesting, **I suppose**. I just think there's more value in knowing about facts and historical events.
我想小說也很有趣，我只是覺得了解事實和歷史事件更有價值。

Answer 2 答題步驟： Answer + Explanation + Conclusion

A **Definitely.** Novels let you escape reality for a while.
當然。小說可以讓你暫時跳脫現實。

E Fiction writers can create their own worlds where anything can happen. They have such good imaginations.
小說作者能創造自己的世界，在那個世界裡什麼都可能發生，他們有很好的想像力。

C Real life is pretty boring in comparison.
真實生活相較之下很無聊。

Question 4

Are there any occasions when speed-reading is a useful skill to have? What are they?
有沒有任何情況，速讀是很有用的技巧？是哪些情況？

Answer 1 答題步驟： Answer + Example + Conclusion

A **Hmm** ... yes ... it could be useful.
嗯……有……它可以很有用。

E **For example**, **when** you're taking the IELTS exam, you have to read everything quickly, and understand everything clearly!
例如，當你在考雅思時，你必須快速閱讀所有文字，並清楚了解。

C I'm a slow reader, **even when** I read in Chinese. **Whenever** I try to read too quickly, I don't retain much of the information. **I guess** I never learnt to read properly, and it's a big disadvantage.
我閱讀很慢，連讀中文也是。當我想讀快一點，就記不住太多資訊。我想我從來沒有學好如何好好閱讀，這是個很大的缺點。

● retain (v.) 保留

Answer 2 答題步驟： Answer + Example + Concession

A Students **definitely** benefit from being able to read quickly.
學生絕對會因速讀而獲益。

E I'm a fast reader, luckily. **When** I was at university, my professors would assign loads of reading for homework and it was not that difficult for me. **I mean**, I didn't struggle **like** some of my classmates.
很幸運地，我是個看書很快的人。我大學時，教授會指派大量讀物作為回家作業，那對我來說並不特別困難。我是說，我不像某些同學那麼費勁。

C **But** reading at a high speed isn't always the best way. **When** I read for pleasure, I don't read fast, **because** I want to enjoy what I'm reading.
但速讀不一定總是最好的方法。當我為了娛樂而閱讀，並不會讀得很快，因為我想享受正在閱讀的內容。

099 Question 5

Are there any jobs where people need to read a lot? What are they?
有工作需要人們大量閱讀嗎？是什麼工作？

Answer 1 答題步驟： Answer + Explanation + Conclusion

A **Of course**, especially in academia.
當然，特別是在學術圈。

E Researchers and professors definitely have to read a lot. They need to stay up to date on the latest developments in their field.
研究者和教授一定得大量閱讀，他們需要隨時與領域中的最新發展維持同步。

C **Then**, they make us students read a lot **too**!
然後他們會叫我們學生也大量閱讀！

● stay up to date 與最新資訊同步

A

I think most jobs require some reading, but **definitely** some more than others.

我想大多數的工作都需要讀點東西，但有些工作絕對比其他工作多。

E1

Editors and publishers probably spend most of their time reading.

編輯和出版商或許大多數時間都在閱讀。

E2

I have a lot to read at my job **as well**: emails, memos, daily reports, weekly reports, monthly reports and even annual reports!

我的工作也需要看很多東西：電子郵件、備忘錄、每日報表、每週報表、每月報表，甚至是年度報表。

C

All in all, reading is just something everyone needs to do!

總而言之，閱讀是每個人都必須做的事。

(100)

Now you try:

1. Are libraries becoming a thing of the past?
2. Are there any disadvantages to reading ebooks instead of paper books?
3. Do you think it's the government's role to ban or censor certain books?
4. What's the difference between reading a book and watching a film?

1. 圖書館已成為過去式了嗎？
2. 比起紙本書，閱讀電子書有什麼缺點嗎？
3. 你認為該由政府出面禁止或審查某些書嗎？
4. 讀書和看影片有什麼不同？

(101) Question 1

> What types of weather do people in your country most dislike? Why is that?
>
> 在你的國家，大家最不喜歡哪種天氣？為什麼？

Answer 1 答題步驟： Answer + Explanation + Conclusion

A Doesn't everyone in the world hate the rain? It rains a lot in my hometown, and it can be kind of depressing, not to mention inconvenient.

不是全世界的每個人都討厭下雨嗎？我的家鄉經常下雨，會讓人有點憂鬱，更別說會造成不便了。

E **One reason** we don't care for the rain **is because** most of us drive scooters, and it's no fun to drive a scooter in the rain. I hate having wet shoes and socks.

我們不喜歡下雨的其中一個原因是多數人騎機車，而在雨中騎車一點也不有趣。我討厭鞋子和襪子溼答答的。

C I always feel more cheerful on sunny days.

天氣晴朗的日子我的心情總是比較好。

● not care for 不喜歡

Answer 2 答題步驟： Answer + Explanation + Concession

A I hate it **when** it gets really hot in the summer.

我討厭夏天很熱的時候。

E **I find it** extremely uncomfortable when the temperature gets to 36 degrees and the humidity is high. It gets very sticky, and I feel like staying in my room with the A/C on all the time.

當溫度高達 36 度，濕度又高時，我會覺得非常不舒服。到處都又濕又黏，我只想一直待在隨時有空調的房間裡。

C

But I'm sure there are people who love the heat. **I guess** summer in Taiwan is just not for me.

但我確定有人喜歡炎熱的天氣，我想只是台灣的夏天不適合我。

● humidity (n.) 潮濕

Question 2

Are there any important festivals in your country that celebrate a season or type of weather?

你的國家有什麼重要的節慶是在慶祝某個季節，或某種氣候嗎？

Answer 1 答題步驟：Answer + Explanation + Concession

A

Let me see ... oh yeah, we have the Mid-Autumn Festival.

我想想……喔有，我們有中秋節。

E

It's **also** called the Moon Festival, and it celebrates harvest and the full moon. The weather is usually nice, maybe just starting to get cool. We always celebrate by having a barbecue.

也稱為月亮節，是為了慶祝豐收和滿月。那時的天氣經常相當宜人，可能剛開始轉涼，我們總是會烤肉慶祝。

C

There are certainly other seasonal festivals, but at the moment, I can only think of the Moon Festival.

當然還有其他季節節慶，但目前我只能想到中秋節。

Answer 2 答題步驟： Answer + Explanation + Conclusion

A
When it comes to festivals, my favourite one is Dongzhi, the Winter Solstice Festival in December.
說到節慶，我最喜歡的是十二月的冬至。

E
Generally speaking, the significance of this festival is that it's a time for family reunions. **Because** the weather is cool then, we celebrate by eating tangyuan, balls of glutinous rice in hot soup.
一般來說，這個節慶的重點在於全家團聚。因為天氣涼爽，大家會一起吃湯圓，那是用糯米丸煮成的熱湯。

C
We really love eating here in Taiwan, and every season seems to be associated with some kind of food, if not a full-on festival. **I bet** some people probably don't even remember why we're eating those foods.
我們台灣人真的很喜歡吃，每個季節——就算沒有大節慶，也似乎都和某種食物有關聯。我猜有些人或許根本不記得為何要吃那些食物。

● reunion (n.) 團圓

Question 3

How important do you think it is for everyone to know what the next day's weather will be? Why?
你認為大家可以知道隔天的天氣如何有多重要？為什麼？

Answer 1 答題步驟： Answer + Explanation + Conclusion

A
Hmm ... I do sometimes check the forecast, but I wouldn't say it's important.
嗯……我有時是真的會看天氣預報，但我也不會說那很重要。

E
You can't always trust the weather predictions, **so** I just always carry a small umbrella in my bag.
你不能完全相信氣象預報，所以我包包裡總是會帶把小傘。

C In Taiwan, **the reality is** that you just have to be ready for any kind of weather!

在台灣，實際的情況是你必須隨時準備迎接不同的天氣。

Answer 2 答題步驟：Answer + Explanation + Concession

A It's really important to know when severe weather is coming.

知道惡劣天氣什麼時候開始很重要。

E We get strong typhoons in Taiwan, and you have to prepare for them. Schools and workplaces need to decide whether or not to close, and airlines need to know if they'll have to cancel flights.

台灣有強烈颱風，所以大家必須做好準備。學校和公司必須決定要不要關閉，航空公司也需要知道是否得取消航班。

C On an ordinary day, **though**, it might be nice to know what the weather's going to be like, but it's not really necessary.

在一般日子裡，知道天氣會如何或許不錯，但也不是絕對必要。

(104) # Question 4

How easy or difficult is it to predict the weather in your country? Why is that?

在你的國家，預測氣候是件容易或困難的事？為什麼？

Answer 1 答題步驟：Answer + Explanation + Example + Conclusion

A I'm not a meteorologist, **but I think** it's pretty hard.

我不是氣象學者，但我覺得很困難。

E The weather here can vary a lot, especially in the spring.

這裡的天氣多變，特別是在春天。

E Yesterday, it was cloudy all day and everyone predicted rain, but it never came. **And** we often have typhoon holidays but the expected typhoon never comes!

昨天整天多雲，大家都預測會下雨，卻一直沒下。我們也常放颱風假，結果颱風卻沒來！

C **So**, you always have to take the weather forecast with a grain of salt.

所以你總是得對氣象預報打點折扣。

● meteorologist (n.) 氣象學家　● with a grain of salt 持保留態度

Answer 2 答題步驟： Answer + Example + Concession

A Older Taiwanese people always seem to know what the weather is going to be like.

老一輩的台灣人似乎總是知道天氣將有什麼變化。

E I remember one time I put away my winter duvet too quickly—a few days later, it got cold again. My grandma laughed at me and said always wait until Dragon Boat Festival. Folk wisdom apparently works **when it comes to** weather forecasting!

我記得有次我太快收起冬季羽絨被，幾天後又變冷了，我奶奶笑我，說一定要等到端午節。民俗智慧在氣象預測這方面顯然有效！

C **I'm not saying** my grandma could give an accurate hourly forecast, but **apparently**, it's not hard to predict general weather patterns if you know the seasons well.

我不是說我奶奶可以準確預測每小時的天氣，但如果你夠了解季節變化，顯然預測大致氣候模式並不難。

● duvet (n.) 羽絨被

Question 5

Do you think there is anything we can do to prevent bad weather?

你認為我們是否有辦法阻止惡劣氣候？

Answer 1 答題步驟： Answer + Explanation + Concession

A No way! All we can do is try to be prepared for it.

不可能！我們能做的只有盡力做好準備。

E Thanks to climate change, bad weather is a fact of life now, especially in certain parts of the world. **As far as I know**, it's too late to do anything about it.

因為氣候變遷，惡劣的氣候現在已經是無法逆轉了，世界上某些地區尤其嚴重。就我所知，現在做什麼都於事無補了！

C Maybe someday scientists will come up with a good solution to climate change and bad weather, but I doubt that will be any time soon!

或許有天科學家會想出好方法，解決氣候變遷及惡劣氣候的問題，不過我想應該不可能太快就是了。

Answer 2 答題步驟： Answer + Explanation + Concession

A **Well** no, **but I think** we can keep it from getting worse.

不能，但我想我們能阻止情況變得更糟。

E Scientists say that we're having more storms and droughts these days because of global warming. **So**, if we could stop producing so much carbon dioxide, we'd hypothetically have less bad weather.

科學家說因為全球暖化，暴風雨和乾旱愈來愈多。所以如果我們能停止製造太多二氧化碳，壞天氣說不定可以少一些。

C Easier said than done, **though**.

不過，說時容易做時難。

- carbon dioxide 二氧化碳　● hypothetically (adv.) 假設地

Now you try:

1. Do you think the weather/climate can affect people's mood?
2. Why do people live in places where the weather can sometimes be very bad?
3. Do you think people's personalities are influenced by the type of weather they usually experience?
4. Have there been any changes in your country's weather or climate in the last fifty years?

1. 你認為天氣 / 氣候會影響人的情緒嗎？
2. 為什麼人們要住在氣候有時可能會十分惡劣的地方？
3. 你認為一個人的個性會因經常身處於某種氣候類型而受到影響嗎？
4. 近五十年來，你們國家的天氣或氣候有什麼改變？

Question 1

What are the most popular kinds of television programmes in your country? Why is this?

在你的國家，最受歡迎的電視節目類型是什麼？為什麼？

Answer 1 答題步驟： Answer + Example + Concession

A Dramas!
戲劇！

E Loads of people I know—**well**, mostly women—watch Korean and Chinese soap operas, **as well as** other kinds of dramas.
我知道很多人——嗯，大多是女性，會看韓國和中國的肥皂劇以及其他種類的戲劇。

C I'm not really into them myself, but I often hear my friends discussing the latest episodes of their favourite TV dramas.
我自己沒什麼興趣，但我常聽朋友討論他們喜歡的電視劇的最新劇情。

Answer 2 答題步驟： Answer + Explanation + Conclusion

A **Well, I'm not sure!** I don't watch television, but **I know** we have a lot of talent shows and game shows.
這個嘛，我不太確定！我不看電視，但我知道我們有很多選秀節目和遊戲節目。

E People like these shows **because** they feature ordinary people.
大家喜歡看這些節目，因為演出的大多是素人。

C A lot of young singers have risen to fame because of these shows, **so** many young people are interested in them and dream of becoming famous **too**.
很多年輕歌手因此成名，所以很多年輕觀眾喜歡這些節目，也夢想可以成名。

108

Question 2

Do you think children should be allowed to watch a lot of television?
你認為應該允許小孩花很多時間看電視嗎？

Answer 1 答題步驟： Answer + Explanation + Conclusion

A **It's hard to say** how much is too much ... **I guess** a few hours a day is fine.
很難界定多少是太多……我想一天看幾個小時應該還好。

E **I think** it really depends on what kind of programmes they're watching. Some shows aren't suitable for kids while others are very educational.
我覺得其實要取決於他們看哪種節目，有些節目不適合小孩，但有些節目很有教育性。

C **So, what I'm saying is, as long as** their television viewing is supervised by a parent to be sure the content is suitable, it should be okay.
所以我的意思是，只要看電視時父母有確認內容合適，應該就沒問題。

● supervise (v.) 監管

Answer 2 答題步驟： Answer + Explanation + Concession

A No, **I don't think** children should watch much television at all.
不，我覺得小孩實在不該看太多電視。

E Kids should be playing, doing art, reading books, exercising and doing other activities. Sitting in front of a box probably isn't good for their mental or physical development.
小孩應該玩樂、畫畫、看書、運動或做其他活動，坐在電視機前應該不利於他們的身心發展。

C

I know busy parents might need to put their kid in front of the TV for a while **so** they can take a break. **But** children's TV time should be restricted as much as possible, **in my opinion**.

我知道忙碌的父母或許需要暫時將孩子放在電視前，好讓他們能喘口氣。但依我的意見，小孩的電視時間應該盡可能受到限制。

🎧 Question 3
109

Do you think television is the main way for people to get the news in your country? What other ways are there?

你認為在你的國家，電視是取得新聞的主要管道嗎？還有什麼其他管道？

Answer 1 答題步驟： Answer + Example + Explanation + Conclusion

A

Definitely. Most people would have no idea what was going on in the world if we didn't have televisions.

當然。如果不看電視，多數人不會知道世界發生了什麼事。

E

We **also** have newspapers and websites, but those things require a little more effort.

雖然我們也有報紙和網站，但使用這些管道比較費力。

E

It's easy to catch the news on television when you're in a restaurant or a waiting room. In my family, we usually watch the news while we eat dinner.

但無論你是在餐廳或等候室，從電視上看新聞都很方便。在我家，我們晚餐時大多會邊看新聞。

C

I never go out of my way to watch the news, **but I think** I always see the most important news stories **because** they get repeated a lot on TV.

我從沒特意去看新聞，但我想我總是能看到最重要的新聞，因為它們會在電視上一直重複播放。

● go out of one's way 費盡力氣（去做某事）

A **Honestly**, mainstream television news drives me crazy. They always report the least important things.
老實說，主流的電視新聞會讓我發瘋，他們總是報導最不重要的事。

E Restaurants reviews, **for example**, shouldn't be in the news, but that's what you see all the time. Some of my foreign friends thought food-based shows were the only programmes we have on TV in Taiwan.
例如餐廳的評比就不該出現在新聞中，但你無時無刻都會看到。我有些外國朋友以為台灣電視只有這些跟食物有關的節目。

C **Personally**, I don't want to watch rubbish, **so** I always go to reliable news websites to read news.
個人來說，我不想看一些垃圾，所以我總是到可靠的新聞網站看新聞。

● mainstream (adj.) 主流的

Question 4

Do you think that people pay attention to adverts on TV? Why do you think that is?
你認為人們會注意電視廣告嗎？為什麼你這麼覺得？

Answer 1 答題步驟：Answer + Explanation + Concession

A **Hmm** ... not really. Most adverts are really boring. I don't suppose many care about TV commercials.
嗯……不太會。大部分的廣告都很無聊。我覺得不會有太多人特別注意廣告。

E Like many people, I stream or download my favourite programmes without the adverts. **When** I do watch television, I usually change the channel, check my phone or go to the toilet when the adverts come on.
跟很多人一樣，我會上網看或下載我喜歡的節目，這些節目都沒有廣告。如果我看電視時，廣告時間我通常會轉台、滑手機或去上廁所。

C

The only time I pay attention is when it's particularly funny or well-made, or if there's a celebrity I really like.

我唯一會注意的廣告是很好笑或拍得很好的廣告，或出現我很喜歡的名人時。

Answer 2 答題步驟： Answer + Explanation + Example

A

Companies spend lots of money on television advertising, **so** they must think so. **And** a lot of people do fall in to the trap.

企業花很多錢在電視廣告上，所以他們必須這麼相信。很多人也的確會掉進陷阱裡。

E

You don't even really have to be paying attention for them to be effective. Some TV commercials in Taiwan are really, really old. I've seen them **since** I was a child, and to a great extent, the jingles and slogans do get stuck in your head.

我們根本不用特別去注意這些廣告，它們就有效果了。台灣有些電視廣告真的非常古老，從我小時候就有了，那些配樂和標語會緊緊卡在你的大腦裡。

E

My grandma buys medicine and cough syrup simply because of the adverts she saw, **and I don't think** she's even aware of that.

我奶奶會因為看到某個廣告，就去買藥或咳嗽糖漿，但我覺得她根本沒注意到她是受到廣告的影響。

● commercial (n.) 電視廣告　● jingle (n.) 簡短易記的廣告歌曲

🎧 111 Question 5

How important are regulations on television advertising?

電視廣告的規範有多重要？

Answer 1 答題步驟： Answer + Explanation + Conclusion

A

Of course you need some rules. You can't just let companies say whatever they want.

當然需要一些規範，我們不能讓廠商隨意製播。

E The main thing is, you can't allow adverts to make false claims about their products, especially products **like** medicine **or** weight loss equipment.

最重要的是，我們不能允許廣告替產品做不實宣傳，特別是藥品或減肥用品。

C Many people I know buy useless things because of what they see on television, **and I think** someone has to stop exaggerated television advertising.

我知道許多人會因為看到電視廣告，就買些無用的東西，我想必須有人阻止誇張的電視廣告。

Answer 2 答題步驟：Answer + Example + Conclusion

A **Hmm** ... **I guess** some regulations are essential, especially for certain products.

嗯……我想某些規範是必要的，尤其是特定類型產品。

E **I think** it's great that we no longer allow cigarettes to be advertised on TV, **for example**. **But** I don't know why alcohol adverts are still around.

例如，我覺得不再允許香菸在電視打廣告就很好，但我不知道為什麼還可以播放酒類廣告。

C The main consideration in making these laws should be that children watch television. Harmful products shouldn't be advertised, at least during the times when children might be watching.

制定這些法律的主要考量應該是兒童會看電視。不該宣傳有害的產品，至少在兒童可能看電視的時段不該出現。

Now you try:

1. How has television changed our lives?
2. What are the advantages and disadvantages of not having a television in your home?
3. Do you think television can influence a person's thinking or behaviour?
4. Do people on television have a responsibility to be role models to their viewers?

1. 電視如何改變了我們的生活？
2. 家裡沒有電視有什麼優缺點？
3. 你認為電視能影響人的思想或行為嗎？
4. 電視上的人有沒有責任作為觀眾的行為榜樣？

Question 1

> What kind of shops are big in your country?
> 你的國家有哪種大型商店？

Answer 1 答題步驟：Answer + Example + Conclusion

A
Oh, there are plenty of them! **I think** the biggest shops are supermarkets and warehouse-type stores.
喔，有很多種！我想最大的商店是超市和倉儲量販店。

E
Costco is huge, and Carrefour isn't far behind.
好市多很大，家樂福也不小。

C
I actually think they're too big. I always feel tired after shopping at those places.
其實，我覺得它們太大了，我在那些地方買完東西總是覺得很累。

Answer 2 答題步驟：Answer + Explanation + Conclusion

A
Well, some stores are physically large, **like** department stores **and** supermarkets. Others may be small shops, but they are still large businesses.
這個嘛，有些商店是實體店面很大，例如百貨公司和超市。有些則是實體店面或許很小，但生意做得很大。

E
What I mean is, chain stores **like** 7-Eleven are everywhere in Taiwan. They're big businesses that get a lot of customers.
我是指像 7-11 的連鎖店，在台灣到處都是，它們是擁有龐大顧客的大企業。

C
So, it depends on what you mean by a big shop.
所以這要看你所謂的大型商店是什麼。

Why do some people choose to visit small shops instead of large ones?

為什麼有些人選擇到小店購物，而非大型商店？

Answer 1 答題步驟： Answer + Example + Concession

A

It takes a lot less time and energy to buy something from a small shop. They're called 'convenience stores' for a reason!

在小店買東西省時省力多了，它們被稱為「便利商店」是有原因的。

E

We have hardware shops, greengrocers, 7-Elevens, and other little shops in every neighbourhood, on almost every corner.

我們所有的住宅區街頭巷尾幾乎都有五金行、蔬果店、便利商店或其他小店。

C

But sometimes, they don't have everything you need, **so** you have to visit a bigger shop. **Actually, I think both** big shops **and** small shops are losing customers to online shopping.

但有些時候，需要的東西在小店並不齊全，就必須到大一點的商店。不過，我想商店無論大小，都因為線上購物而流失顧客。

Answer 2 答題步驟： Answer + Explanation + Conclusion

A

I think there are several reasons to visit small, local shops.

我認為到小型地方商店購物有幾個原因。

E

It's **generally** easier, especially if you don't have a car. **And** it's a more pleasant shopping experience **because** they're usually not crowded and the staff are friendly. **But for me**, **the most important reason is that** I like to support small businesses.

一般來說比較輕鬆，特別是沒開車的情況下。購物經驗也比較愉快，因為通常不會太擁擠，員工也很友善。但對我來說，最重要的理由是我喜歡支持小型企業。

C

I'd rather my money go to a local family than a big, international corporation.

我寧願讓錢留在地方上的家庭，也不要流入大型國際企業。

Question 3

Do you think there's anything the government should do to help small businesses?
你認為政府需要採取任何措施支持小型企業嗎？

Answer 1 答題步驟：Answer + Explanation + Concession

A The government should stay out of business as much as possible.
政府應該盡可能不干涉企業。

E **I really believe in** the free market. If the business is well-run, it will survive. It's not a charity that needs government support.
我真的相信自由市場。如果企業運作無礙，它會存活下來，它不是需要政府支持的慈善事業。

C The government should only make sure nobody is cheating the system or creating a monopoly.
政府只應確認沒有人在系統中作弊，或是壟斷市場。

● stay out of 不介入　　● monopoly (n.) 獨占事業

Answer 2 答題步驟：Answer + Example + Conclusion

A **Sure.** I'm not an expert in business or economics, **but I agree that** big businesses sometimes have an unfair advantage.
當然。我不是商業或經濟專家，但我同意大企業有時候擁有不公平的優勢。

E Maybe small businesses could pay lower taxes or something.
或許小企業可以付較少的稅金之類的。

C People who open a small shop or start a business are taking a big risk, **so** a little government support would be great.
開設小商店或創業的人承擔很大的風險，所以政府的一點支持都會是很棒的。

Question 4

What can small shops do to attract customers?
小商店要怎麼吸引顧客？

Answer 1 答題步驟：Answer + Example + Concession

A **The main way to** attract customers **is** through advertising, right?
吸引顧客的主要方式是透過廣告，對吧？

E Small shops need local customers, **so I guess** they should advertise locally with posters, flyers and discount coupons. Word of mouth is **also** super important.
小店需要當地的顧客，所以我想他們應該利用海報、傳單或折價券，在地方進行宣傳。口碑也超重要。

C Some shops try to attract customers by shouting over a loudspeaker, but **to me**, that's a turn-off.
有些商店會用擴音器吸引顧客，但對我來說，反而讓我沒興趣。

● word of mouth 口碑，口耳相傳　● turn-off (n.) 讓人失去興趣的事物

Answer 2 答題步驟：Answer + Example 1 + Example 2

A **Well, I think** the appearance and the location of the shop are the most important things.
這個嘛，我認為商店的外觀和地點是最重要的。

E1 A small shop relies on passers-by deciding to go in and take a look. **So**, it needs to be in a place with a lot of foot traffic, **like** in a busy street **or** in a shopping centre. **And** it needs to look bright and have a welcoming vibe.
小店仰賴經過想進去逛一下的過路客，所以需要在有人潮的地方，像是在繁忙街道上或在購物中心內。另外，還需要看起來明亮以及有熱情好客的氣氛。

E2 There are a couple of shops I regularly stop into just **because** they're on my way home and they always have nice music and decor.

有幾家店因為剛好在我回家的路上，所以我經常去，它們播的音樂都很棒而且裝潢也漂亮。

- passer-by (n.) 路人，過路客　● foot traffic 人潮　● vibe (n.) 氣氛

Question 5

Do you think we'll have fewer shops in the future?
你認為未來商店會變少嗎？

Answer 1 答題步驟：Answer + Explanation + Conclusion

A No, **it seems to me** that more and more shops keep springing up.
不，在我看來，會有愈來愈多商店冒出來。

E Everywhere I go, there's a new shoe shop or convenience store or something. This is a growing economy, and people here love shopping.
不管我去到哪裡，都會看到有新的鞋店或便利商店什麼的。目前經濟正在成長，而且這裡的人喜歡購物。

C **In short**, I don't see this trend reversing any time soon.
簡單來說，我看不出最近會有什麼逆轉的趨勢。

- spring up 迅速增長　● trend (n.) 趨勢　● reverse (v.) 反轉

Answer 2 答題步驟：Answer + Concession + Conclusion

A **Of course**, **because** online shopping is becoming more common.
當然，因為線上購物愈來愈普及。

C **I mean**, we'll still have just as many shops, if not more, but there will be fewer bricks-and-mortar shops and more online ones.
我是說，商店只會有增無減，但實體商店會變少，線上商店會變多。

Eventually, we won't have to physically go out shopping for anything unless we want to.

最終，我們將不須親自出門購物，除非是我們想要出門。

- bricks-and-mortar (adj.) 實體的

Now you try:

1. Do you think a shop's location is important?
2. Why do some people want to start their own business?
3. Do you think local businesses are important for a neighbourhood? Why?
4. How do large shopping malls and commercial centres affect small shops?

1. 你認為商店的地點重要嗎？
2. 為什麼有些人想要創業？
3. 你認為地方企業對鄰里重要嗎？為什麼？
4. 大型購物中心和商業中心如何影響小型商店？

更多問題

以下提供更多 Part 3 的口說練習題，考生可多多練習。

Skills and Abilities

1. What skills and abilities do people most want to have today? Why?
2. Which skills should children learn at school? Are there any skills which they should learn at home? What are they?
3. Which skills do you think will be important in the future? Why?

技巧與能力
1. 今日人們最想擁有什麼技巧和能力？為什麼？
2. 兒童在學校應學習哪些技能？有什麼需要在家學習的技能嗎？是什麼？
3. 你認為未來哪些技能很重要？為什麼？

Salaries for skilled people

1. Which kinds of jobs have the highest salaries in your country? Why is this?
2. Are there any other jobs that you think should have high salaries? Why do you think that?
3. Some people say it would be better for society if everyone got the same salary. What do you think about that? Why?

技術人才的薪資
1. 在你的國家，哪些工作的薪水最高？為什麼？
2. 你認為還有其他工作應該享有高薪嗎？你為什麼這樣想？
3. 有些人說如果所有人同薪對社會比較好，你的想法為何？為什麼？

Children and Parents

1. How much time do children spend with their parents in your country? Do you think that it's enough?
2. How important do you think spending time together is for the relationships between parents and children? Why?
3. Have relationships between parents and children changed in recent years? Why do you think that is?

兒童和父母

1. 在你的國家，兒童和父母相處的時間有多少？你認為足夠嗎？

2. 你認為相處時間對親子關係有多重要？為什麼？

3. 近年來，親子關係有改變嗎？你覺得是為什麼？

Children's free-time activities

1. What are the most popular free-time activities with children today?
2. Do you think the popular free-time activities children do today are good for their health?
3. How do you think children's activities will change in the future? Will this be a positive change?

兒童的自由活動

1. 現今最受兒童歡迎的自由活動是什麼？

2. 你認為現今最受兒童歡迎的自由活動對他們的健康有益嗎？

3. 你覺得兒童的活動在未來會有什麼改變？是正向的改變嗎？

Owning things

1. What types of things do young people in your country most want to own today? Why is this?
2. Why do some people feel the need to own a lot of things?
3. Do you think that owning lots of things makes people happy? Why/Why not?
4. Do you think television and films can make people want to acquire new possessions? Why do they have this effect?
5. Are there any benefits to society of people wanting to get new possessions? Why do you think this is?
6. Do you think people in the future will consider that having lots of possessions is a sign of success? Why?

擁有物品

1. 在你的國家,現今年輕人最想擁有什麼東西?為什麼?
2. 為什麼有些人想擁有很多東西?
3. 你認為擁有很多東西會讓人快樂嗎?為什麼會?/為什麼不會?
4. 你認為電視和電影會激起人的擁有欲嗎?它們為什麼有這種影響?
5. 人們想要擁有新東西,對社會有什麼好處?你為什麼這麼認為?
6. 你覺得未來人們會將擁有很多東西視為成功的象徵嗎?為什麼?

準備期增分祕技

祕技 1　筆記學習法
祕技 2　口語練習心法

附錄1　基礎文法快速複習
附錄2　指標詞的使用
附錄3　考生常問的問題

IELTS 雅思口說
準備期增分祕技

筆記學習法

1. 準備一本專屬的「Idea Book」

快去買一本漂亮的筆記本,我們要開工囉!

想要達到口若懸河的境界,首先需要大量的背景知識,所以在準備 IELTS 口說期間,考生需要大量涉獵不同的口試考古題。科技類、商業行為類、文化類、親子教育類等,每一種主題都要有能力可以討論個三五分鐘。而要能深入討論這些主題,考生還需要準備大量的字彙並確實學會運用,才能順暢地談論你想要表達的內容。

以歸納的方式來準備單字

考生可以準備一本屬於自己的 Idea Book(我稱之為「梗書」)。例如在準備 Restaurant 這個主題時,就可以把相關的單字像下面這樣寫在 Idea Book 上。如此一來,無論是在準備 Part 1、Part 2 或 Part 3 的相關主題時,都可以同時運用上。

restaurant

Tasty Steakhouse	appetiser/main course
T-bone pork chops	ratings
crème brûlée	affordable price
excellent services	10% service charge
presentation of food	customer satisfaction survey

考生也可利用本書「Part 2 口說高分練習題」(p. 84) 的五大常考
主題來歸納單字。例如有關 People 主題可能用到的單字，就全
部整理在一起，稍加分類：

People

physical appearance: muscular, dark-skinned, petite
characteristics: sophisticated, highly-skilled, quiet
personality: a man of few words, confident, adventurous
jobs: blogger, professor, scientist, homemaker, physician
relationships: colleague, high school classmate, mate/friend
others facts: billionaire, fluent German speaker, photographer

建議考生至少準備二十種不同主題的單字，並隨時增加字彙，這
是個提升口說能力的重要祕技！

2. 學習新字要有方法

善用英英字典

想要增加字彙量，在口試中運用更多字彙，最簡單的方式就是參
考英英字典裡的解釋。例如想描述自己國家的 cultural tradition
（傳統文化），就可以參考 Oxford dictionary 對 **tradition** 這個字
解釋：

a belief, **custom** or way of doing something that has existed for a
long time among a particular group of people

若將這個解釋稍微變化一下，就可以變成提到 **tradition** 時很棒
的換句話說：

Tomb-sweeping is a Chinese **custom** that we've been practising for a long time.
掃墓是中國人長久以來的習俗。

善用同義詞辭典

除了英英字典之外，也要勤查同義詞辭典 (thesaurus)，因為同義字、反義字的使用是口試裡加分的關鍵。

例如你想表達自己是個**樂觀**的人，除了可以說：

I'm a **happy** person.

還可以利用同義字、反義字加油添醋：

My friends always say I'm very **positive** and **cheerful**. I agree because I really don't like **pessimistic** thinking. I always try to **look at the bright side** or **find the silver lining** when I'm in a difficult situation.
我朋友總是說我非常正向開朗。我同意，因為我真的不喜歡悲觀的想法。當我面對困難處境時，我總是努力往好處想，找出希望。

準備口試時，將新學到的單字、英英字典的解釋、同反義詞跟一句**背得起來的例句**抄在 Idea Book 中。另外，甚至可以更進一步用這個新字來造句練習。

例如剛學到 authentic 這個字，便可以在 Idea Book 中加入：

authentic /ɔːˈθentɪk/ adj. If something is authentic, it is real, true, or what people say it is

- There's a Greek restaurant in town which serves wonderfully
  prepared authentic dishes.
  （劍橋免費英語詞典上抄來的例句）

- I could never afford an authentic Gucci handbag.
  （自己造的句子）

這個動作因為比較費工，所以整理單字的原則在精不在多，但務必做到**每個字都要實際會使用**。

這些筆記一定要固定拿出來複習，例如把每週的星期天空下來，當作整理、背誦筆記的時間。

3. 學新句型要有方法　平時在閱讀英文文章或看英文影集時，要把 Idea Book 放在手邊，若看到或聽到一些很喜歡的句子，就趕快把這些句子抄下來，並且時常拿出來複習、造句。例如：

範例一

The more people watch television, the more stupid they
become. （從書上抄來的句型）

造句：
- The more fast food you eat, the more unhealthy you become.

- The less meat people eat, the less carbon dioxide they
  produce.

263

It is essential for women to be financially independent.
（從書上抄來的句型）

造句：

● It is important for everyone to have empathy.

● It is impossible for Olivia to find a man she wants to date.

在準備 IELTS 期間，把自己喜歡的句型抄在筆記本上或存在手機裡，隨時拿出來練習。走路時、坐車時、每天睡前花個五分鐘練習這些句子。例如：

● Honestly, I'm not very interested in _____. I don't _____ very often, but there is _____ I like/do called _____.

● This is a great question for me because I've got a lot of ideas about _____.

● One (place/thing) I've wanted to (go/do) for a while now is (Australia/scuba diving).

● In my imagination, (Australia) is always sunny, with (wild animals) and (beaches) not far from where people live.

練習時要想像自己是在跟人說話，試著加入臉部表情、肢體語言及手勢，讓自己看起來輕鬆自然，切忌像讀稿機械人一樣死板。

口語練習心法

1. 創造一個處處聽 得到英文的環境

播放英語廣播節目來當背景音

說話語調呆板，不容易讓人產生興趣，是很多考生的問題。這可能跟台灣人平常的說話方式有關，講中文的時候語調含蓄平淡，突然要在講英文的時候做出語調的高低起伏就變得很困難。

想改善這個問題需要長時間練習，平時可多**利用零碎時間**（準備出門時、通車時、做家事時）**聽英語廣播**，甚至可以跟著句子大聲複誦，模仿英語母語人士抑揚頓挫的說話方式（但也不要像演舞台劇那麼誇張），日積月累就會習慣英文的高低語調。

看英文影集或電影練口說

看影集是練口說的黃金時光，但最好是獨自觀看以免把旁人搞瘋。為求效果，看的時候要有樣學樣地**模仿劇中人物說話的抑揚頓挫與音量**。音量偏小的人剛好可藉此機會把聲音練大，因為不管任何場合，音量小就容易給人缺乏自信的感覺。

影集的選擇上，還是要設定在現代的影集比較好，以免看了半天只學會像 My Lord、My Lady、Your Grace 這種古人的用法。

模仿自己喜歡的演員說話

找到一個自己喜歡的演員，並模仿他的說話方式是個改善口音的方法。看同一個人的演出幾次以後，你對他的聲音就會感到熟悉，可以降低必須一直熟悉新口音的挫折感。

除了看喜愛的演員演出的電影或影集，也可以找找他們接受訪問或上脫口秀節目的影音檔，你會發現即使是同一個人，在不同場合也會有很多不同的說話方式，你也可以藉此熟悉各種不同的語調。

練習把眼睛閉上，只用聽的來複誦

許多人學英文的方式都是傾向「看」英文，而不是「唸出」英文，所以大部分人的英文閱讀能力都強過聽力及口說。例如看到 not at all 這三個字知道是什麼意思，但聽到英語母語人士用連音講 not at all 卻聽不懂。要解決這個問題，建議考生可以試試「**盲聽複誦**」，閉上眼睛不看英文，只用聽的，同時複誦聽到的英文，確實練習過一陣子後，相信你絕對可以打通長了千年老繭的耳朵！

追蹤你喜歡的英語 YouTuber

YouTuber 會受歡迎，是因為他們在特定領域（例如彩妝品、旅遊、評論、搞笑等）有研究，又是善於表達的意見領袖。訂閱你喜歡的英語 YouTuber 頻道，持續收看新推出的影片，除了可以了解自己有興趣主題的相關英文，還可以接觸到一般學習平台學不到的最新流行文化用語。

2. 習慣一分鐘跟兩分鐘有多長

在練習 Part 2 卡片題時，一定要有時間概念。平時就應以碼錶計時，讓自己熟悉用一分鐘畫心智圖，再即席演說一分半到兩分鐘的節奏感。

事實上，若考生真的準備到上癮了，可以經常練習自言自語，針對任何話題發表小演說，用中文或英文都行。從自己熟悉的事物開始，可以描述自己的一天、說說自己最喜歡做的事情、回憶一下童年最常玩的玩具、講個故事（例如小紅帽或司馬光打破水缸）、重點摘要讀過的一本書，或用本書後面附上的模擬試題、網路上找到的最新考題來練習 Q&A。

一開始還沒有辦法連續說話一兩分鐘的考生，可以多看一些知名 YouTuber 頻道，研究一下他們說話的內容，為什麼可以侃侃而談（卻又不無聊 XD）。

Tip
Steve Allen
廣播節目

LBC 廣播有一個 Steve Allen 主持的節目，他挖苦人的功夫了得，隨便一次調侃都可以持續個二十幾分鐘，是個可以邊學英文又娛樂自己的有趣節目。

這些口語練習不受時間地域限制，洗澡時、等車時、排隊時都可以進行。重點是要每天開口說英文，持續練習，這樣你才可以習慣自己說英文的聲音跟嘴型。

3. 加強文法正確性

對照字稿與音檔做跟讀練習

前面第一點提到的練習方式是以改善抑揚頓挫為目的，考生若想改善文法，就需要另外下功夫，在做跟讀練習或看影集時，把重點擺在文法上。剛開始練習時，可看逐字稿或字幕，但最終仍必須進入不看文字的階段。

所謂「把重點擺在文法上」，是指看文章或跟讀時，專注在「主詞到底是要用 he 還是 she？、是 My friend 還是 My friends？」、「對話中動詞是用什麼時態？」、「句子是現在式，但有沒有主動詞一致（如第三人稱動詞加 s）？」、「名詞單複數如何變化？」、「名詞前面有沒有冠詞（a 或 the）？沒有的話名詞是否有加 s 或用複數形？沒有複數形的話該單字應該就是不可數名詞」等文法細節。

文法要改善，第一步就是要**意識到文法的存在**，要在意文法。若一味追求流利度，文法千瘡百孔，分數是不可能太高的，因此準備時期文法練習絕不可少。

多看兒童英文繪本

若覺得自己程度尚淺，可找有附音檔的英文故事書來做跟讀練習（當然不能選英文字太少的）。有可愛的插畫，單字也比較簡單，可以大大降低自修的困難，讓你專注在動詞跟名詞的變化上，也比較有樂趣。若手邊沒有有聲繪本，在 YouTube 上打關鍵字：children's books read aloud，也可以找到很多影片練習。

4. 錄下自己講的英文　考生可以把自己說英文的樣子錄下來反覆觀看，可以跟 TED 等演講做個比較，看看自己有哪些地方需要改善。例如可能會不自覺地一直眨眼睛或一直沒看鏡頭。透過這種方式可有效調整自己的講話方式同時建立自信心。

另外，每週重複聽同一則 BBC 6 Minute English 或 TED 演講多次，摘要重點，寫下自然、完整的句型後，朗讀錄音再放給自己聽，反覆練習，可加強流利度、連貫性與組織能力。

5. 找人練習對話　口試畢竟還是兩個人在互動，跟自己獨自練習不太一樣。正式口試前，建議還是找人實際練習 Q&A。練習的重點是對另一個人說英文，所以對象不一定要是英語母語人士。你可以練習在家人、一群朋友，甚至是會讓你緊張的人面前說英文，訓練自己即便在很緊張的時候，腦袋也不會突然空白一片，依然能夠聲調平穩地講英文。總之，愈恐懼的事情，就愈要去克服它。

口試當天……

1. 練習呼吸　在考場外進行幾組深呼吸練習，降低自己的緊張程度。

2. 練習跟讀　準備一些音檔，或是打開英語廣播頻道，戴上耳機進行跟讀練習，算是暖身動作，開啟腦袋的英文模式。

3. 快速翻閱筆記　利用最後的幾分鐘把自己精心製作的 Idea Book 翻過一遍（千萬不要忘記帶出門），提醒自己有哪些單字跟句型可以使用。

最後，深吸一口氣，帶上微笑，進去大聲說英文吧！

基礎文法快速複習

以下要點是在提示重要的文法及常犯的口語錯誤。大部分考生儘管說英文時偶爾會犯錯，但應該都已了解相關的文法，若是在閱讀以下要點時，還有觀念不清，或不知道錯在哪裡的情況，就要趕緊打開文法書的相關章節複習，並多做練習題。

冠詞的使用

A + 子音開頭的名詞

a holiday

a university

An + 母音開頭的名詞

an animal

an hour

定冠詞的使用

the president

the environment

the 70's

the Great Wall

the best

the Wright Brothers

the U.S.

the number of people

the only child

名詞單複數

可數

a car	many **cars**
a strawberry	some **strawberries**
a child	lots of **children**

不可數

a lot of **information**

some **furniture**

a piece of good **news**

動詞三態 | **規則變化**

chip	chipped	chipped
affect	affected	affected
receive	received	received

不規則變化

bite	bit	bitten
throw	threw	thrown
steal	stole	stolen

介系詞 | **介系詞的搭配用法**

be obsessed **with**

keep contact **with**

look forward **to**

pay attention **to**

an increase **in**

a change **in** lifestyle

be disappointed **in**

be afraid **of**

介系詞後要加名詞或 V-ing

I'm afraid of **making** a fool of myself.

I'm looking forward to **my sister's wedding**.

✕ My sister work in a hospital.

○ My sister **works** in a hospital.

✕ I have to work overtime when I was an accountant.

○ I **had** to work overtime when I was an accountant.

✕ I always went to my favourite café when I have time.

○ I always **go** to my favourite café when I have time.

✕ I've been to Korea last year.

○ I**'ve been** to Korea **twice**. *or* I **went** to Korea **last year**.

✕ There are many people have part-time jobs.

○ Many people **have** part time jobs.

✕ There have many cars in the city.

○ There **are** many cars in the city.

✕ It is important having a few good friends.

○ It is important **to have** a few good friends.

✕ We didn't ate lunch.

○ We didn't **eat** lunch.

✕ If there is no war, people won't suffer.

○ If there **were/was** no war, people **wouldn't** suffer.

p.p. vs. V-ing   ✗ I'm very interesting in English literature.

○ I'm very **interested** in English literature.

✗ Planning for a holiday always makes me exciting.

○ Planning for a holiday always makes me **excited**.

✗ *The Hunger Games* films are very excited.

○ *The Hunger Games* films are very **exciting**.

名詞單複數錯誤   ✗ I need a lot of informations to write this report.

○ I need a lot of **information** to write this report.

（information 不可數）

✗ Many woman don't want child.

○ Many **women** don't want children.

✗ My supervisor gives me many good advices.

○ My supervisor gives me **a lot of** good **advice**.（advice 不可數）

動詞 vs. 名詞   ✗ I contact with my high school friends.

○ I **keep in contact with** my high school friends.

✗ I'll contact with you.

○ I'll **contact** you.

✗ My dad has a great influence me.

○ My dad **influences** me a lot. *or* My dad has a great influence **on** me.

273

比較級　✕ Global temperatures are getting more high.
　　　　○ Global temperatures are getting **higher**.

　　　　✕ My English is becoming more better.
　　　　○ My English is becoming **much** better.

　　　　✕ Smartphone games are much popular than board games.
　　　　○ Smartphone games are **more** popular than board games.

關代子句　✕ I don't know many people like sports.
　　　　○ I don't know many people **who** like sports.

　　　　✕ I went to a restaurant where has a huge aquarium.
　　　　○ I went to a restaurant **which** has a huge aquarium.

指標詞的使用

指標詞是指用以協助語言流利度與連貫性的用語，可能只是一個單字，也可能是一個片語或短句。

例如，當一個人說 for example，聽的人就可以知道他想要舉例說明；當他說 to sum up，聽的人就會知道他要作結論了。不過，指標詞若使用太頻繁，會顯得通篇都是廢話，但也不能完全不用。考生只要觀察本書答題範例當中的粗體字，便可大致了解指標詞適當的出現頻率。

以下依「功能性」分類指標詞。考生可以選擇自己喜歡的指標詞，在 IELTS 準備期時，試著運用到口試練習中。不過要注意，使用時要加入相應的語氣及表情，考生可參考 MP3 中兩位英籍錄音員錄製「答題範例」時，如何流暢自然地使用指標詞。

思考／拖延時間用字

以下這些都是考官問完問題後，你為了爭取多幾秒的思考時間而拿出來墊檔的話，很多都不具任何意義。後面必須接一到三句完整的句子來完成回答，不能就此打住。

Yes/No	Sure	Maybe
Okay	Right	Well
I'm not sure.	Let me see...	Let's see...
What else...	I suppose...	Sometimes
No way!	Kind of.	I mean...
Definitely (not)!	Absolutely!	Certainly!
Perhaps	Anyway	You see...
Hmm/Uh/Er	How can I put it?	I've got no idea.

You know	To me	Of course
I love/hate it.	It's hard to say.	As far as I know...
Not really.	Both, actually.	Either way is fine.
To tell you the truth...		
I've never thought about it.		
I don't really care, but I guess...		
I guess what I'm trying to say is...		
Most people would say _____, but I actually think...		
I don't have a strong opinion but I guess I would say that...		
You know, this is an interesting question because I was just telling my friends the other day that...		

開場 　大部分的考生都會以 I'm going to tell you about... 或 I'm going to describe... 來開頭，以下提供其他說法供考生替換。記住，開場白只要文法正確、清楚明確即可，不需要在第一句就語不驚人死不休。

Basically	After a bit of thought...
I decided to talk about...	I'd like to tell you about...
I'll try my best to describe...	I'm going to try to describe...
Let me tell you about...	One of my _____ is...
I can't remember all the details, but I can think...	
This question made me think of...	
I've been very interested in...	
I was glad to get this topic because...	

The (place I like best in my city) is...
When I saw this topic, I initially/first thought...
This is a(n) great/ideal question for me because...
This is a(n) easy/difficult question for me to answer because...
One (place I've wanted to go for a while now) is...
One (person who I think would be really interesting to meet) is...
The first person/place/thing who/that came to my mind when I saw this topic was...

結束用語 考生若講太久會被考官打斷，所以結束用語不一定用得上。但還是先準備一兩句來作結論比較保險。

Anyway	All in all	Overall
To sum up	In the end	In short
As I said/mentioned earlier...		
I hope I can make my dream come true.		
That's all I want/have to say (about)...		

表達順序用語 在 Part 2 的小演說中，若需要描述一個經驗或一件事的順序，就需要這些字的幫助。

(At) first → Next → Then → Last/Lastly/Finally		
Before → After (that)		Now → Later
Afterwards	Beforehand	In (six months') time
In the future	When I was...	Last summer/year/April

| A long time/Three months/A couple of weeks ago |
| A few days/weeks/months later |
| As a child/student/new parent... |

表達個人意見 作答時先講 I think... 是要讓考官知道你要發表自己的意見了。以下這些用語是 I think 的變化形，以及一些表達意見前的開頭語。

I find...	For me...	I admit...
I'd say...	Honestly	I'm afraid...
Personally	In my view	In my opinion
Not much.	Generally speaking	I'd love to say...

To tell you the truth...	As far as I'm concerned...
I agree/disagree that/with...	I (strongly) believe that...
I'm (strongly) against...	I'm (strongly) in favour of...
I'd definitely recommend...	As you can (probably) tell...
It seems fair/wrong/fine/crazy to me.	

表達個人喜好 除了 I like、I don't like 之外，表達個人喜好還有很多說法。

I (really) enjoy/like/love/hate...	I'm not very keen on...
I'm (not very) interested in...	I'm (not) really into...
I'm (not) a big fan of...	I don't/didn't/wouldn't mind...
I'm not a (book) lover at all.	I'm obsessed with...
I don't care for...	I'm (very/rather) fond of...

補充前句 / 前文用語 　以下這些用語可讓考官知道你想要補充前面的意見或想法。

And	...too	Also
Plus	By the way	In fact
In terms of	As well as	Besides
Likewise	It's not just (that)...	Other than that
In addition (to)	Apart/Aside from	When it comes to...
Come to think of it		Not only... but also
More/Most importantly		Another ... I'd like to add is...
Let me give you (an/a few) example(s).		

表達相反意見用語 　以下這些用語用於表達前後相反的意見。

But	Or	Still
However	Mind you	Actually
Despite	In spite of	Rather than
The reality is...		On the other hand
Although/Even though		

表達因果關係用語 　以下這些用語用於表達原因或因果關係。

So	So (that)	Unless
Since	Because (of)	
The main reason is that...		I guess it's because...
The significance of this is...		I like(d) (Tokyo) because...

Another reason (I like it) is because...
The (great) thing about (Lego) is that...
I think the main reason (I like it) is that...

換句話說用語　　當你覺得需要更進一步的解釋時，可以使用以下這些用語。

I mean...	In other words	After all
So what I'm saying is...		To put it in another way...

表達不肯定用語　　當你覺得不是很肯定，想表示對自己的意見持保留態度時，可以使用下面的用語讓自己的發言不會顯得太偏頗。

I'm not sure...	I heard that...
Some people say...	Generally speaking
Legend says that...	Something like
... or something like that.	Don't quote me on this/that.
From what I can remember...	I believe/think/suppose/guess...
I can't remember exactly but I think...	
I think I'm right in saying (that)...	
Although it may not be true, I imagine...	

更多指標詞參考資料

https://www.youtube.com/watch?v=BECe_ok1Rl8
https://www.youtube.com/watch?v=HaJ01IG-50U&t=59s
http://www4.fe.uc.pt/english/dms.htm

考生常問的問題

Q1：聽不懂考官問的問題時怎麼辦？

各大題情況不一：

Part 1：若聽不懂問題，依考試規定，考生可以請考官重複問題，但考官只能重複問題，不會提供任何進一步的解釋。

Part 2：若看不懂卡片題的題目，依考試規定，考官只能唸題卡上題目，不會提供任何進一步的解釋。

Part 3：若聽不懂題目，可以請考官重複問題或換句話說。考生可以問考官：

Could you repeat the question?

Could you explain the question?

若聽不懂題目裡的某個字，也可以請考官解釋那個字，例如：

What does ＿＿＿＿ mean?

偶爾請考官重複問題或解釋問題，並不會被扣分。但最好的做法，還是做好萬全準備，IELTS 的口試並不會用到非常困難的單字，每一個問題都盡量答好答滿就對了。

Q2：Part 2 題卡上的所有「Wh- 問題」都要回答到嗎？

不需要。那些「Wh- 問題」只是提示用。只要你的答案是有連貫性與邏輯性的，有些問題沒有回答到並不會被扣分。事實上，若考生真的照著那些問題回答，很有可能會講出一個跳躍無連貫性的答案。

可以，但你必須要在一開始就告訴考官更換或調整的理由，而且主題不能差很多。例如題目為：

問題 Describe a time you helped a stranger.
描述一個你幫助陌生人的經驗。

如果你實在想不出幫助過任何陌生人的經驗，又不想憑空掰一個故事，可以在一開始就跟考官說明：

回答 I can't think of a time I helped someone I didn't know, but I recently helped my sister plan her wedding, so I'd like to talk about that instead.
我想不到自己曾幫助過陌生人，但我最近幫助過我妹妹籌備她的婚禮，所以我想說說那件事。

或者是：

回答 I can't think of a time I helped someone I didn't know, but I was actually just helped by a stranger the other day.
我想不到自己曾幫助過陌生人，但其實前幾天有陌生人幫助過我。

接著再開始說你想講的內容，這樣考官就知道你並不是看錯問題，而你的回答也不算離題。

這是一個口試，考生需要多講話才能展現自己的英文程度。若只以單字而不是句子回答，或不知道要說什麼就沉默以對，考官根本無法評分，考生當然得不到好分數。所以平日準備時，就要找些自己完全沒梗的題目進行練習。

在 Part 1 中，若被問到一個從未準備過的題目，例如：

問題 What's your favourite shop?
你最喜歡的店是什麼？

若一時之間腦袋完全空白，也絕對不能呆坐在那裡，一定要開口說點什麼，什麼都好，爭取一點思考的時間，像是：

回答 Hmm ... my favourite shop ... Well ... I don't shop much and ... I'm not usually the person who does the shopping ... so I guess the shop I go to most is ... the convenience store near work! Yeah, I think that would be my favourite shop.
嗯，我最喜歡的店……嗯……我不常買東西，而且……通常負責買東西的不是我……所以我想我最常去的商店是……公司附近的便利商店！對，我想那就是我最喜歡的店。

說著說著，可能就會想起自己較常去的某間商店了。

在 Part 2 中，如果一個對藝術毫無興趣的考生拿到的題卡是：

問題 Describe your favourite piece of art.
描述你最喜歡的一件藝術作品。

或一個完全不運動的人拿到的題卡是：

問題 Describe your favourite sport.
描述你最喜歡的運動。

一定要想辦法先扯個一兩句，像是：

回答 Well, many people like art/sports, and it's certainly a very easy question for them to answer. But, actually ... um ... I'm really not keen on art/sports so I'm going to tell you what my brother/sister/boyfriend/girlfriend likes because he/she's really keen on art/sports.

這個，很多人都喜歡藝術／運動，這對他們來說一定是非常簡單的問題。但其實我……不太熱衷於藝術／運動，所以我想說說我的兄弟姐妹／男女朋友的嗜好，因為他們非常熱衷藝術／運動。

如此就能調整成不致於離題的回答。但答題時仍需要提到與 art 或 sport 有關的單字，所以就算是沒興趣的主題，相關的基本字彙仍然必須具備。

Part 3 的題目比較抽象，也比較長，考生聽不懂的機會大增。如果在考官解釋後還是聽不懂問題，當下能做的，就是盡量做到聽懂一兩個關鍵字，然後針對關鍵字回答。雖然可能答案會因為離題失分，但分數仍然會勝過完全沒說話的考生。例如被問到：

問題 Do you think that tourism brings more advantages than disadvantages for local communities?

你認為旅遊業為地方社區帶來的優點比缺點多嗎？

這個題目在問觀光業對於地方是否利大於弊，若已經請考官解釋或重複提問，但仍然不太確定要回答什麼，或者只聽懂了 tourism 這個字，請你還是鼓起勇氣針對觀光這件事發表一些看法，什麼看法都好，比如：

回答 Tourism is good because there are more jobs when there are many tourists. People have to eat and go from one place to another, so they need restaurant and drivers.

旅遊業很好，因為觀光客多了，工作機會也更多。人們必須吃東西，必須到處移動，所以他們需要餐廳和司機。

即便沒有回答到題目問的「是否利大於弊」也沒關係，因為考官可能會打斷你或提示你：

問題 What about disadvantages?
那缺點呢？

或是：

問題 What about for local communities?
那對當地社區來說呢？

或是：

問題 Do you think local people benefit from tourism?
你認為當地人可以受益於旅遊業嗎？

你還是有機會被引導回問題核心。所以無論如何，不說話絕對是下下策，一定要避免。

Q5：若我的目標是七分以上，要如何才能得到高分？

想得到高分，當然要在 IELTS 口說的四項評分標準上同時下功夫。流利度佳，發音也已具有母語人士的樣子，那就要在單字詞彙以及文法上多下功夫。

單字詞彙
試著使用較少見、較高級的單字，並減少冗贅的說法，答案要精簡到位。例如被問到：

問題 Do you think charities are important?
你認為慈善團體重要嗎？

若回答：

回答 Yes, they are. I think they are important because they can help many people—for example, people who are poor or sick.
是的，我覺得很重要，因為可以幫助到許多人——例如窮人或病人。

這樣的回答幾乎只是把問題重複一次，只有 poor 跟 sick 兩個字才算是新延伸出的回答。考生必須想辦法加入更具體的內容、使用更精確的語言，才有辦法得到七分以上。例如：

回答 Sure. There isn't always a good system there to help people, and charities are actually the organisations that help poor or disabled people in my country.
當然，因為不一定有良好的系統能幫助大家，而慈善團體是國內真正能幫助窮人或失能者的機構。

文法

文法項目要取得高分，並不是要考生運用寫作時才會用到的複雜文法句構，而是要混合使用「簡單句」、「複合句」及「複雜句」等多種句構。這部分請見本書「**高分祕訣：混搭簡單句與高級句**」(p. 23)。

IELTS雅思口說
模擬試題 8 回

PART 1

Advertisements

*Are there many advertisements in your country?

*What kind of advertisements do you like?

*Why do you think there are so many advertisements now?

*Do you enjoy watching advertisements on television?

PART 2

> Describe a trip that taught you something.
>
> You should say:
>   where you went
>   why you went
>   what you learnt
> and explain how this trip has influenced you.

PART 3

Reasons to travel

*Why do people want to take trips?

*What sorts of things do people learn when they travel?

*Some people say that people will travel more frequently in the future. Do you agree or disagree? Why?

Cultural awareness

*Do most people in your country prefer travelling abroad or travelling within the country?

*What problems can arise when people travel to places with different cultures?

*Do you think people become more aware of different cultures if they travel more?

Mock-up test 2

PART 1

Selfies (Photos of oneself)

*Do you like taking photos of yourself?

*How often do you do that?

*What do you do with the photos you take?

*How popular are selfies in your country?

PART 2

Describe a person who has had cosmetic/plastic surgery.

You should say:

who he/she is

what he/she did

how he/she has changed

and explain how you felt about his/her change.

PART 3

Appearance

*Is cosmetic surgery popular in your country?

*What sorts of procedures are commonly done?

*Some people say that good-looking people are treated better than less attractive people. Do you agree or disagree? Why?

Attraction

*Do you think appearance is more important than personality?

*What makes someone attractive?

*Are people more attracted to people who look like them? (Why/Why not?)

PART 1

Snow

*Do you like cold or snowy weather?

*Have you been to a place where you can see snow?

*What activities can people do when it snows?

*Would you want to live in a place where it snows?

PART 2

Describe a useful mobile app or computer app you use frequently.

You should say:

    what this app is

    what it does

    what benefits you get from it

and explain why this app is useful to you.

PART 3

Technology for life

*What kinds of apps are most popular in your country? Why?

*Do you think these apps help people? In what way? Are any of them harmful?

*Why do some people have so many apps on their mobile phone/computer?

Technology for work

*How has technology in the workplace changed?

*What problems can people have when they are too dependent on machines?

*Do you think people are more productive now than they were in the past?

Mock-up test 4

PART 1
Sweets/Desserts

*Do you like sweets/desserts? Why/Why not?

*What types of sweets/desserts do you prefer?

*When do you usually eat sweets/desserts?

*What is your favourite traditional dessert from your country?

PART 2

> Describe a funny situation that made you laugh.
>
> You should say:
>
>   when this situation took place
>
>   what happened
>
>   how you reacted
>
> and explain why you found the situation funny.

PART 3
Conversations

*What do you think people can learn from having conversations?

*What sorts of problems can people encounter when trying to have a conversation?

*Some people say that people now have fewer conversations with strangers than they did in the past. Do you agree or disagree? Why?

Social life

*What are some of the social activities people commonly do in your country?

*Do you think people will socialise in the same ways 100 years from now?

*Is it better to have a big social circle or a small group of close friends?

Mock-up test 5

PART 1
Passwords
*How many sets of passwords do you have to remember?

*Have you ever forgotten a password?

*How often do you change your passwords?

*What do you do to help you remember your passwords?

PART 2

> Describe a change in yourself that you liked.
>
> You should say:
>
> what the change was
>
> what prompted the change
>
> what you needed to do to make the change
>
> and explain why you liked the change.

PART 3
Change in people
*What sorts of changes do people usually try to make in themselves?

*What motivates people to make big changes in their lives?

*What stops people from making changes even when they know they should?

Change in general
*Do you think it is easier for young people to change than it is for elderly people?

*What affects can changes, such as moving to a new city, have on people?

*What change do you think will happen in your life in the future?

Mock-up test 6

PART 1

Celebrities

*Who is your favourite celebrity?

*Would you like to be famous?

*Has anyone you know ever been on TV?

*Have you ever met a famous person?

PART 2

Describe a method for saving money.

You should say:

    what the method is

    where you learnt about this method

    how often you use this method

and explain whether or not you would recommend this method to others.

PART 3

Personal finance

*What are some reasons why people need to save money?

*Is it better to invest your money or save it for a rainy day? Why?

*If you won a lot of money on the lottery, how would you spend it?

Budgets

*Is it necessary to always live according to a budget?

*What happens to people who don't manage their money well?

*Do you think there are any differences between the way men and women budget?

PART 1

Design and Creativity

*Do you like designing or creating new things? Why/Why not?

*What do you like to design/create?

*Do you design or create anything at work or school?

*Would you like to be a designer? What type of designer?

PART 2

Describe a person who is very rich.

You should say:

who he/she is

how he/she became rich

what job he/she does

and explain how you feel about this rich person.

PART 3

Personal success

*Do you think being rich means being successful?

*What can people do to become rich?

*Some people say that rich people have nothing to worry about. Do you agree or disagree? Why?

Social status

*Some people say that rich people don't deserve a high social status. Do you agree or disagree? Why?

*What problems can people have when they are wealthy?

*How easy is it for people to change their social status in your country?

PART 1
Aliens

*Do you believe there is life on other planets?

*Have you read any stories about aliens?

*Do films usually show aliens as being friendly or unfriendly?

*Why do people want to find aliens?

PART 2

Describe a zoo you've been to.

You should say:

where it is

why you went

what you saw there

and explain how you felt about this experience.

PART 3
Animals

*What are some unique animals that are native/indigenous to your country?

*Is it better to let animals live in natural environments rather than putting them in zoos?

*If you could be an animal, what animal would you like to be?

Endangered species

*What are some of the causes of animal extinction?

*What problems do people have when more animals die out?

*What can be done to help save endangered species?

國家圖書館出版品預行編目 (CIP) 資料

IELTS 雅思口說里茲螞蟻英文說話術 / May Lin、Amy Lovestrand 作；許可欣譯 .
-- 初版 . -- 臺北市：眾文圖書 , 2018.06　面；公分
ISBN 978-957-532-514-5（平裝附光碟片）　1. 國際英語語文測試系統 2. 讀本
805.189　　　　　　　　　　　　　　　　　　　　　　　　　　　　　107008961

IE007

IELTS 雅思口說里茲螞蟻英文說話術

定價 420 元
2019 年 5 月　初版 3 刷

作者	May Lin・Amy Lovestrand
譯者	許可欣
責任編輯	黃炯睿・陳思容
總編輯	陳瑠琍
主編	黃炯睿
資深編輯	顏秀竹
編輯	何秉修・黃婉瑩
美術設計	嚴國綸
行銷企劃	李皖萍・王盈智
發行人	黃建和
發行所	眾文圖書股份有限公司
	台北市 10088 羅斯福路三段 100 號 12 樓之 2
網路書店	www.jwbooks.com.tw
電話	02-2311-8168
傳真	02-2311-9683
郵政劃撥	01048805

ISBN 978-957-532-514-5
Printed in Taiwan